"...The dreamy aspe   ⁞ for
both the mystery ꜔   thor
Brunette to bring moments of emotion and abstraction, as well as a
refreshing majority of female characters, to the standard procedural.
But these unusual women aren't to be underestimated. As Granny
Grace says, 'Take every dream seriously.'

A mystery with an unusual twist and quirky settings; an enjoyable
surprise for fans of the genre."

—*Kirkus Reviews*

"A fascinating tale of mystery, romance, and what one woman's
dreams are made of. Brunette will keep you awake far into the night."

—Mary Daheim, bestselling author of the Bed-and-Breakfast and
Emma Lord/Alpine mysteries

"Cathedral McCormick has the killer app for a novice private
investigator: The ability to enter other people's dreams. But there are
real killers in Cat's first case, and learning to manage her gift in a
world of secrets, betrayal and nightmares is only the start of her
troubles. Gripping, sexy and profound, *Cat in the Flock* is an excellent
first novel. Lisa Brunette is an author to enjoy now and watch for the
future."

—Jon Talton, author of the David Mapstone Mysteries, the
Cincinnati Casebooks and the thriller Deadline Man

"To slip into other people's dreams is Cathedral McCormick's
supernatural talent. Under the spiritually attuned mentorship of her
fellow 'dreamslipper' and soon-to-retire Private Investigator
grandmother, Cat begins to apply this talent to solving crimes. What
follows is a drinkable, page-turning thriller that poses questions about
faith, family, sexuality, and secrecy in an authentically rendered
Seattle landscape. Cat in the Flock, a stay-up-all-night-reading debut
novel, sets the tone for an exciting Cat McCormick series by Lisa
Brunette."

—Corrina Wycoff, author of *O Street*

"Lisa Brunette's *Cat in the Flock* is the satisfying launch to a new detective series featuring Cathedral Grace McCormick, your average Jill with a twist — she slips into other people's dreams. Putting these psychically received clues together with her daytime gumshoe misadventures makes for a clever and entertaining murder mystery. A little Sue Grafton and a dose of Janet Evanovich, mixed with the issues of closeted, born-again Christians, Iraq war veterans with PTSD, and rival love interests for 'Cat' Cathedral, is just the right recipe for a promising new series."

—Rev. Eric O'del, Amazing Grace Spiritual Center

A portion of the sales of *Cat in the Flock* supports Jubilee Women's Center, which provides safe and affordable community housing and support services to help women transition out of homelessness and into independent living.

Included in this edition of *Cat in the Flock*:

Book club discussion questions.

The first chapter of the second McCormick Files book, *Pillow Fright*. This excerpt has been set for this edition only and may not reflect the final content of the forthcoming editions.

Cat in the Flock

by Lisa Brunette

Cover Art: Anthony Valterra, Lisa Brunette, and Kathy Samuelson

Author Illustration: Lindsey Look

Author Photography: Allyson Photography

ISBN 13: 978-0-9862377-0-6

Published in the United States of America

Published by Sky Harbor LLC

1752 NW Market St. #321

Seattle WA 98107

skyharborllc@gmail.com

Direct inquiries to the above address

Cat in the Flock

Book One in the McCormick Files

by Lisa Brunette

Sky Harbor LLC

*For the real Amazing Grace, 1934-2011,
and the Red Door Community she helped found.*

Prologue

She was in a child's bed, a Hello Kitty blanket pulled up to her chin. Stuffed animals surrounded her: a little plush frog with googly eyes, a duck with a faux-leather beak. She heard something that sounded like a fire crackling, and a wash of hot air blew her hair back. Fire materialized in the space above her bed, a devilish man emerging from the flames. He was red, with hooved feet, and he carried a pitchfork. He was floating above her, his veined, leathery wings beating with methodic slowness. She gasped, unable to breathe, unable to scream. The phrase "Mommy, help me" formed in the back of her throat, but she was too afraid to voice it. The devil pointed his pitchfork at her. His eyes were dark as ink and bore into hers.

"Ruthie," he said, shaking his head, "I can't let you get away." He raised his pitchfork up and then down, sinking it through the bedspread and right between her legs.

Chapter 1

Cat woke with a start, gasping and sweating, the sounds of the plane's engines in her ears, soon joined by the sound of a little girl crying. Despite her best efforts not to, Cat had fallen asleep on the long flight from St. Louis, and she'd slipped into someone else's dream. Cat sat up, wiping the sweat from her brow. She wondered who "Ruthie" was. That's what the devil had called her in the dream.

Shaking off the image, her senses returning, Cat realized there was a good chance that "Ruthie" was the girl who was crying in the back of the plane. Cat turned around to see if she could spot her. The seat backs were too high. She unfastened her seat belt and stood up as if to stretch. Nothing in the front rows. She turned and looked behind her. The crying seemed to come from the right side of the cabin. Also coming from that direction was a woman's troubled voice: "It's okay. We'll be there soon. Everything will be okay."

Cat followed the sound of the woman's voice, and there was the girl, sobbing into the woman's arms.

Conscious of staring too much, Cat sat back down. She burned with a strange sense of frustration and embarrassment. Her dreamslipping experiences always told her just enough about people to feel as if she were a Peeping Tom, voyeuristically sneaking into the minds of her dreamers. On the other hand, the dreams told her so little about who her dreamers really were. With strangers especially, she lacked the context that would make the dreams make more sense, give her something to hang them on.

It was Cat's greatest hope that her grandmother, Grace, who shared her dreamslipping ability, would be able to help her do something useful with these dreams. That's why she was moving clear across the country from St. Louis to Seattle: to apprentice with Granny Grace, who had for most of her life used dreamslipping to solve crimes as a private investigator. As Cat's dreams had mostly been an awkward inconvenience in her life so

3

far, Cat felt the weight of all that she had to learn. She sighed and settled back into her book just as she heard the girl's crying subside.

Cat saw the woman and girl once again when they landed at Sea-Tac Airport. The child was in that stage that Cat found amusing in little girls, when they begin to express themselves by dressing in outrageous, girly color combinations. She wore pink high-top tennis shoes with purple pants and a clashing yellow top. In her hair was a fuchsia bow with blue polka dots. They walked on ahead of her as if in a hurry. The woman, who was likely the girl's mother, tugged her daughter along after her as the child tried to keep up on skinny little legs. The girl was pulling a tiny pink suitcase on roller wheels with rainbow-colored letters spelling her name, R-U-T-H, across the front.

Ruthie, the devil had said, *I can't let you get away.* Get away? In little-girl speak, that could mean go on a trip, or a move. But Cat couldn't tell by their carry-ons whether they were on a trip or moving across the country, as she was. Cat lost sight of them in the crowded corridor, and she felt a pang of regret. If only she could have helped that girl...

She neared the security entrance and scanned the crowd for her grandmother, who was never hard to spot.

As if the oversized, pink-feathered hat weren't enough to catch the eye, Granny Grace was waving both glove-clad hands at Cat. Her grandmother was dressed as if she herself had been on a trip, in another time period when travel was a rare activity to be done in one's best attire. The hat was pale pink, wide-brimmed, and adorned with glorious pink-and-cream feathers. She wore a smart brown safari dress with a wide pink belt to match the hat. Of course Granny Grace had donned heels—of a sensible height for strolling through an airport on a Sunday afternoon—but heels nonetheless. Cat recognized them as a pair of calfskin Etienne Aigners that Granny Grace had had for years.

"Cathedral Grace McCormick." Granny's voice rang out over the din of roller-bags and shuffling footsteps.

"Amazing Grace," Cat answered as her grandmother swept her into a warm hug. "Amazing" really was the woman's legal first name; she'd had it changed during her last divorce. And "Cathedral" really was Cat's legal name. But she had her *very*

4

Catholic mother to thank for that one. As Granny Grace put it, "The ones who convert are always the most fervent."

Cat inhaled her grandmother's scent: a mixture of the incense Granny Grace burned in her house, Halston perfume, and peppermint Altoids.

Granny Grace appraised Cat with keen eyes. "Still sporting the college-girl look, I see," she said. Cat wore blue Converse high-tops, jeans with a hole in one knee, and a hoodie. Her carry-on was a backpack, and she had an iPod clipped to her hoodie, the earbuds dangling. Her unruly brown hair was in a no-nonsense ponytail.

"Grandma," Cat whined. "It was a five-hour flight." She paused for effect. "With a connection. In Phoenix."

She received a "hmpf" in return, and off they went to track down Cat's checked bags.

Once they'd secured the luggage, Cat was thrilled to see that Granny Grace had decided to pick her up in Siddhartha, named after the Buddha himself. "I've always preferred his first name," explained her grandmother. Siddhartha was a beautiful '67 Mercedes in mint condition. It was pale yellow, with buttercream leather seats and a convertible top that had never once leaked, her grandmother boasted, despite Seattle's persistent rain. It was a completely impractical car for a seventy-seven-year-old retiree to have, but it fit Granny Grace to a tee. She'd even indulged in a vanity plate: GRACEFUL. It was as graceful a car as ever was built. "With me in the car," she quipped, "it's literally full of Grace."

Granny Grace took off the gorgeous hat, secured it in the back seat, dug a scarf out of her purse, and wrapped it around her hair, which had been meticulously coiffed, Cat knew, by a young hippie stylist that Granny Grace favored. She perched a pair of oversized Jackie O. sunglasses on her nose. "Looks like your ponytail is appropriate after all," she said with a smile as she put the car in gear.

Ah, Seattle. It had been a couple years since Cat had been able to fly out for a visit. She loved the sea-salt smell, the calm expanse of Puget Sound, and the fact that no matter what time of year she visited, her eyes rested on lovely evergreen. Back in St. Louis, everything turned brown and died for at least three months out of the year. Here it was early spring and warm enough to have the top down, with a slight chill in the air. It should have been raining, but the sun was peeking out of the clouds as it began to set in the west, creating pearlescent purples and pinks as the light bounced between the water and the clouds. "Oyster light," Granny Grace called it, like the light playing on an oyster shell.

They couldn't really talk on the drive, what with the wind rushing through, but Cat smiled at her grandmother a few times, who smiled back and once took her hand off the gearshift to squeeze Cat's. They drove home on the Viaduct, both of them aware that its days were numbered; not earthquake-safe, the elevated roadway would be demolished as soon as Seattle got around to officially deciding what to do with its waterfront. They drank in the glorious view: Puget Sound to the left, today calm and grey, with the Olympic Mountains visible beneath a high bank of clouds; and downtown Seattle's eclectic architecture to the right. With her eyes, Cat followed the dark spine of the Columbia Tower up to the top and then looked for the Space Needle to appear around a bend. It was the iconic landmark's fiftieth anniversary, so they'd painted the bottom orange again to match how it looked when built.

Granny Grace's old Victorian house sat at the top of Queen Anne Hill, with an incredible view of the Space Needle and the Seattle skyline and impressive sweeps of Elliott Bay. Not terribly large, it wasn't a mansion, and though it had three floors plus an attic, it was actually quite narrow, with smallish rooms, some of which hadn't been outfitted with closets. Granny Grace said that was because the tax codes at the time of construction counted a bedroom as anything with a closet, and they assessed taxes based on the number of bedrooms. The builder had simply left out the closets.

Cat drank in the beveled glass front door, the grand foyer with its old gas chandelier, and the gleaming stairway banister leading to the second floor. It smelled as it always did, a bit musty but clean, the scent of lemons mingling with incense and sage.

Cat unpacked and settled into her room, the Grand Green Griffin. Every room in Granny Grace's house had been decorated in some sort of theme. The kitchen Granny Grace referred to as

6

the Terra Cotta Cocina, based on the Cuban kitchens she remembered from her days in Miami. The bathroom that Cat favored was called the Tempting Turquoise Tub, and it really was both tempting and turquoise. The Grand Green Griffin wasn't grand in size, but being on the first floor, it had tall ceilings, and it was outfitted in shades of green ranging from kelly to sea foam and featured a griffin carved prominently into the fireplace mantel. Many of the bedrooms had fireplaces, as wood fires were the primary source of indoor heat when the house was built in 1883. Here and there throughout the house were paintings done by Cat's Great-Uncle Mick, who channeled his dreamslipping ability into art. They were vibrant works, the paint thickly applied, like frosting on a cupcake. When Cat was younger, she'd test the paint to make sure it was hard, expecting her finger to come away globbed with it.

Just as Cat finished putting away her things, Granny Grace appeared in the doorway in spandex yoga clothes, which showed off her rather well-muscled arms and the faint hint of ab muscles beneath a slight layer of what she unselfconsciously referred to as "old-age padding."

She invited Cat to join her, and once Cat changed clothes, the two of them moved to the Yoga Yolk. Cat had practiced yoga with her grandmother during past summer stays in Seattle but had never pursued it as a regular exercise. But now that she'd moved there for good and was entering into formal training with her grandmother, yoga was part of the deal, along with meditation, breath work... basically, whatever Granny Grace deemed necessary.

Cat followed her grandmother in a series of sun salutations: downward dog, a lunge forward with one leg, and a standing salute to the sun. Then Granny Grace moved into crow pose, crouching forward till her knees touched her upper arms and then lifting her legs so her whole body was balanced on her arms. Cat couldn't do that pose yet, so she sat in a wide-legged squat, watching her grandmother with admiration. Afterward, they sat in the turret window of the pale-yellow-and-white room, sipping tea and sharing fruit. As the sun had set, Granny Grace lit a few candles, preferring them to electric lights.

"So tell me about your dreamslipping," her grandmother prompted.

"I had a dream on the plane," Cat said. "I think it was a little girl's dream." She described to Granny Grace how the devil with his pitchfork said he couldn't let someone named Ruthie get away. Granny Grace listened intently, sitting cross-legged in her chair, a delicate yellow teacup balanced in one hand. Cat felt the heat of frustration return to her face. "I lost them at Sea-Tac," she said.

"Did you find out who they are, or get some way to trace them?" her grandmother asked.

Cat blushed. "No. Should I have? I mean, the dream—it's not proof of anything."

Granny set her cup down. "Dreams never are, Cat. But if you're going to be a PI, you need to start getting details."

Cat silently accepted her grandmother's instruction, and Granny Grace continued. "You could interpret the dream many ways, it's true. It could simply be a young girl's way of puzzling out sexual curiosities. Some kids begin touching themselves at an early age, you know. It's totally natural. Maybe she has a brother and started to notice—"

"There's no brother," said Cat. "I think it's just her and her mother. They traveled alone. I have this feeling they're all alone in the world."

"Well, that could be your intuition, or your imagination. You're fairly imaginative, you know. As I was saying, she could be puzzling out her first sexual awareness, and maybe her mother is devout. Maybe the devil is a symbol from Christianity that has to do with the shame she associates with her body."

"That's what I'd expect you to say."

Granny Grace smiled. "But what if..." She paused. "What if that's not it? What if someone hurt her, and this is a post-traumatic stress disorder dream?"

Cat sat in silence, toying with her cup. "We'll never know," she said.

"We'll never know," echoed her grandmother.

"I do remember the little girl's name," Cat said, brightening. "I saw it on her suitcase. It's Ruth."

8

"Good. To get the rest, you could have easily taken advantage of the setting. You were in an airport. Everyone's got identification close at hand. I bet the mother had her ID tucked just inside her carry-on."

"You're right, Gran," Cat said, remembering something Granny Grace told her long ago. "'Take every dream seriously.'"

"That's it, Cat." Granny Grace beamed at her, her lips still perfectly painted in pearly pink.

Her grandmother had finally framed the copy of *Vanity Fair* with herself on the cover, Cat noticed. It was hanging there in the Yoga Yolk, its silver frame glinting in the candlelight. In it, Granny Grace was wearing a white bathing suit and sitting on an enormous beach ball. The prop had been her idea. "It was my photo shoot, and I wanted to have a ball," she told Cat. Granny Grace was a tall Mae West type, not thin like the waifs who appear regularly on the covers now. But that was 1957, when models were curvier. Standards of beauty had certainly changed.

Cat gestured toward the image. "I'm glad to see you decided to hang that cover," she said, smiling. "I've always admired it. Sometimes I wish I took after you in looks—instead of this dreamslipping curse we share."

Cat had meant this as a joke, but as soon as she said it, she realized it was something her grandmother wouldn't like.

Granny Grace put her teacup down. "Cat McCormick," she said, "don't ever call our gift a curse."

Cat bowed her head. "Sorry."

Granny Grace gave a sigh, long and drawn out. "I wasn't really a model, you know," she said.

Cat looked up in surprise. It was a long-standing family story that her grandmother had once been a model.

"It was a ruse, Cat. I was *under*cover..." She paused, smiling. "But I ended up *on* the cover. Ha!"

"You never told me that! I don't even think Mom knows."

"There's a lot your mother doesn't know," Granny Grace said. "Or understand, even if she does know."

Cat let that one linger in the air without comment. To put it kindly, her mother and grandmother did not always get along. The dreamslipping gift had skipped a generation, and so had the adventurous temperament. Cat's mother, Mercy, was as conservative as Granny Grace was liberal. And she hadn't been too happy about Cat's choice to move to Seattle and take over

Granny Grace's PI business. She'd called the whole scheme a "fantasy." Cat and her mother had done nothing but fight about it up till the moment Cat left for Seattle.

"Tell me about the modeling case," Cat prompted, pointedly changing the subject.

"Thurston was the top modeling agency in the country at the time," Granny Grace explained. "It was an embezzling case, and the police leads had all run dry. One of Thurston's accountants discovered that money had been taken out of the firm and that it had been going on for a long time. But they didn't know how or by whom."

"Were you able to use your dreamslipping to solve the case?" Cat asked. This was the crux of her apprenticeship with Granny Grace, to learn not just how to focus and control her dreamslipping ability, but how to use it in her work as a PI. She'd need to learn to do this well if she were going to take over her grandmother's agency.

"Yes," her grandmother answered. "But not till I went with the other models on location to shoot a swimsuit series in the Florida Keys. We were all in a hotel together—Largo Lodge, I think it was called. And one of the models had a stress dream. She obviously felt guilty about what they'd done."

"'They'?" Cat asked. "You mean a group of models were embezzling?"

"Yep," said Granny Grace. "It was actually not that hard to track down the evidence, once you knew where to look. But the police hadn't looked. They assumed models weren't bright enough for white-collar crime."

Cat smiled. "Are you sure you're ready to retire?" Granny Grace had been trying to do so for only the past twenty years but kept getting drawn back into one case or another.

"Of course," she said. "After I teach you everything I know."

Cat felt lucky to have Granny Grace's help. Not only was her grandmother going to train her in PI techniques and dreamslipping skills, but she had generously offered to let Cat live with her for free as well. Back in St. Louis, Cat had tried unsuccessfully to find a job. With her degree in criminal justice, she thought she had a shot at getting onto a police force, but all of them were cutting back, and none were hiring. Granny Grace's offer had been a godsend.

"I can't thank you enough, Gran," she said.

"Oh, you can thank me by carrying on my torch. Who else is going to keep the agency going? Over the years, I've had many assistants, Cat, but none of them have had your gift."

Before they turned in for the night, Granny Grace put her hands on Cat's shoulders. "You're going to do well, Cat," she said. "I always knew this was your calling."

Despite the soft, familiar feel of her bed in the Grand Green Griffin, Cat struggled to fall asleep, doubt creeping up on her. What if her mother was right? Maybe "fantasy" was the most accurate word to describe what she was trying to do here. People said Granny Grace was a legend, but no one had ever called Cat anything like that. Cat was the type who tended to blend into the background. Her grandmother left awfully big shoes to fill—and designer ones, at that.

Chapter 2

C at was sitting in full lotus, with both legs crossed, a foot resting on top of either thigh. It was a position she had never been able to do; she knew right away she was dreamslipping in her grandmother's dream. All around her on the floor were bills Granny Grace couldn't pay: the heating bill, another in an exorbitant amount for her cell phone, a medical bill, and others, along with receipts for the money she continued to give to charity. But Cat could feel that she shared her grandmother's thoughts and attitudes in the dream, as if her and her grandmother's minds were fused, so despite the bills, she felt at peace. In front of her was a Buddha statue, and in his palm were coins. He winked and said, "Bless the bills, my Grace. Bless them."

Then the paper bills on the ground around her morphed into hundreds of butterflies—orange and black monarchs and viceroys, pale yellow swallowtails, iridescent blue sulphurs, and delicate cabbage whites. They flew up and covered the Buddha statue, where they sat flexing their wings in the sun. She watched them there, a feeling of peace flooding through her. Then the butterflies rose into the air as if they were one being, circled around her for a time, and then flew off into a ray of sunlight.

Cat woke early, still on St. Louis time and worried about her grandmother's financial situation, despite the odd feeling of peace the dream gave her. Was the dream accurate? Was Granny Grace having financial trouble? She tiptoed down the hall to her grandmother's study. She knew she shouldn't snoop, but the quiet in the house told her Granny Grace was still asleep, and she would have to do a bit of detective work on this one, as her grandmother wouldn't tell her the truth even if she asked. Granny Grace had an overdeveloped sense of pride; she carried herself well and was never one to accept help but was always helping others. Cat certainly had no intention of sponging off her grandmother forever, but if she were having financial trouble, there was no way Cat was going to accept her help in getting the PI firm started, no matter what cryptic, New Agey messages Granny Grace got from the Buddha.

Cat was seated at a rolltop desk, absorbed in the saga of her grandmother's financial life and didn't hear the septuagenarian enter the room behind her.

"I thought you came here to train as a PI, not serve as my personal bookkeeper," Granny Grace said.

Cat turned with a start. "Gran, why didn't you tell me about this?" She held up the cell phone bill, which included calls all over the world, with a balance upwards of five hundred dollars, most of which were past due amounts carried over.

"My cell phone habits are none of your concern, granddaughter," said Granny Grace, ripping the phone bill out of Cat's hands. "Besides, I'm in negotiations with them right now to get that lowered. They're going to fold it under a special 'international friends and family' plan."

"Grandmother," Cat said sternly. "You're giving money away, and at the same time, your bills are piling up." Cat pulled out the statement from her financial advisor. "And judging by this, your investment accounts took a huge hit."

Granny Grace ripped that statement out of her hand, too. "This is none of your business, Cat. And you should know better than to use a dream this way. You've got a lot to learn."

Cat took a step back, realizing how far over the line she had crossed. "You're right," she said. "I'm sorry. Let me make you breakfast, and we can calm down and talk."

She toasted sourdough bread and put out preserves, butter, a bowl of fruit, and a pot of tea. Her hunger satiated and her grandmother cooled down and seated across from her, Cat had to ask, "What exactly does 'SPOETS' stand for? You gave them a couple hundred last year."

"Specialist Pogoists of East Tacoma," Granny Grace quipped.

"Grandmother," Cat groaned. "Be serious."

"Sound Patternists of Elementary Tea Services."

Cat giggled, and Granny Grace smiled. "They're a group of citizens devoted to the study of the largest earthworm in North America," she said.

Cat stared at her. "Earthworm?"

"That's right," she replied. "It's the Society for the Protection of Earthworm Triticales Somas."

"Triticales somas?"

"Yeah. *T. somas.* That's the Latin name. I'll have you know it's several feet long and almost as wide. It lives entirely underground on the Washington Palouse."

"I didn't know you had a soft spot for earthworms."

"Only this one. It's special. Not to say the ones you use in your garden aren't special as well, but this one is unique."

"But Granny Grace, why didn't you tell me you were having trouble?"

"I'm not. Weren't you there, in the dream, Cat? I could feel your presence. So you know that bills are to be blessed."

Cat wouldn't be put off so easily. She pressed her grandmother further. "But why do you give so much away when you're not in a position to do that? You gave another small amount to a group that studies a rare type of moss that only grows on the eastern side of the Olympic Mountains. And the Dykes with Bikes? Do they really need your help? I think there's even a Bisexual Basket-Weaving Bar Mitzvah group in the mix."

"Oh, I only wish. If there's one thing a bar mitzvah could use, it's more bisexuals weaving baskets." Granny Grace crossed her arms and leaned forward on the table. "Look, Cat. I'm seventy-seven years old. This karmic approach to money has held me in good stead for many years. You get back what you put out in life. It works. You wait and see."

"Okay, but listen," Cat said. "You told me I could stay here for free and that I wouldn't have to work while I trained for the PI exam. But I don't think that's practical. I can't do that. I'm going to get a job."

"You'll be putting everything off that way," Granny Grace countered.

"There's no way I can let you support me," Cat said. "I'll keep training with you and working toward my goal, but I'm going to pay my own way." She nodded her head affirmatively, as if to seal the deal.

"Well, if you insist..." her grandmother replied.

"I insist," Cat said.

There was a long silence while they sipped their tea before Granny Grace changed the subject in a tone that meant she was resuming Cat's training there and then.

"You broke the first rule of dreamslipping this morning," she said. "Don't ever use the information gleaned from a dream to invade the privacy of someone you love."

"But isn't dreamslipping by its very nature already an invasion of privacy?"

"Yes, it is," Granny Grace said, a shadow of sadness flickering across her face. "Why do you think I live alone? That's why you can't ever use what you learn like that again. I know you were doing it with concern in your heart, but you crossed a line."

"I'm sorry," Cat said.

Granny Grace reached over and squeezed her chin. "Don't be sorry, Cat. Just remember the rule."

"I will."

"Good. By the way, don't chide yourself for invading the privacy of your dreamers. That's a waste of time. This thing is involuntary—it's not like you can turn it off. Believe me, I've tried. That's why I call it dreamslipping. We can't help slipping into other people's dreams."

Cat sighed, feeling pressure inside her chest release. "Thank you for telling me that," she said.

"Our first appointment today is with a meditation guru," said Granny Grace, clapping her hands together. "Your training has begun."

The guru—Guru Dave was his name—held meditation classes on the top floor of a record store, so in addition to the singing bowls he employed, there were the ever-present strains of whatever music the clerks downstairs happened to be playing. For Cat's first class, it was polka music, which the hipsters must have been playing ironically. So when the guru asked her to empty her mind of everything and to cultivate nothingness, she couldn't help but picture a bunch of men in lederhosen and women dressed as Heidi hefting huge beer steins into the air.

When Guru Dave spoke, he drew out his syllables so that it took him twice as long as everyone else to say the same thing, but the effect on the listener was trancelike. "Let gooooooooo of attaaaaaaaachment," he intoned. "Reeeeeleeeeease your eeeeeeegooooo."

The only thing Cat felt herself let go of was the contraction in her lower abs, the "root lock," as Guru Dave called it, which she was supposed to hold, it seemed, for an eternity.

At the end of class, which consisted of sitting cross-legged (Granny Grace was in full lotus, of course) till her lower back hurt and her brain was screaming insults at Guru Dave, he asked what insights she had to share with the rest of the class.

"The rhythm of life is in everything," Cat said. "Even beer."

Guru Dave thought this was profound, and Cat inadvertently became his star pupil. But nothing got past Granny Grace. After class, she teased Cat. "You've been to one too many Oktoberfests."

"I could use a little bit of the rhythm of life after that class," Cat said. "This tea isn't quite cutting it." They both burst out laughing.

That first couple of weeks in Seattle were a whirlwind for Cat. She accompanied Granny Grace to more meditation classes, and while nothing broke through her skepticism about them, she did find herself enjoying both the time to sit and think, as well as the strains of music from the store downstairs, which ran the gamut from classic rock to folk to R & B. They practiced yoga twice daily—an energetic round in the morning at a studio near the house and a slower style called yin that Granny Grace led in the Yoga Yolk each evening to wind down.

Her grandmother also took her shopping, and over protests that they didn't have the money, she helped Cat create a wardrobe "more befitting a PI." Granny Grace had a knack for how to find deals at consignment shops, cobbling together a selection of well-made pieces with less expensive accessories, so that the overall look was sophisticated and fun.

There were more direct lessons in dreamslipping as well, but Granny Grace took her time. Instead of showing Cat how to do "fancy tricks," as Granny Grace called them, they were taking an inventory of Cat's dream life up till now, which for the most part meant excavating through some awkward revelations Cat had had about her various boyfriends and how the dreamslipping had interfered with her ability to have what she called "normal" relationships with them. For example, she'd dated an emotionally unavailable soccer player for far too long, mainly because he wasn't an active dreamer, and there were no issues to confront. Prior to that, she'd dated a psych student whose own dreams bordered on disturbing, and he was only too willing to spend hours analyzing them, to the point where Cat felt *she* should be charging *him* for her therapy services.

"You can use the information in dreams to solve a mystery or catch a crook," Granny Grace said, "but healing someone like that— that's a different kind of work."

"Yeah, and I'm not cut out to be a psychotherapist," said Cat.

"It's really hard to know things about people that you can't talk about with them," said Granny Grace, as if she were thinking about her own past. But then she shook it off, changing the subject, and Cat didn't want to press her.

Cat also immediately set about looking for a job, with dismal results. She tried to find something as close to her chosen profession as possible. She sent out more than fifty résumés, interviewed with six recruiters, and heard nothing in return. She couldn't even get a part-time job at a supermarket, as the hiring manager there said she was overqualified and would be gone at the first opportunity. She sent résumés into the ether, and she imagined them evaporating into ones and zeroes in some large central database where bored clerks sat typing all day.

What finally got her a job were her grandmother's connections.

Granny Grace took Cat to a fundraiser for one of her favorite charities, City Goats, which promoted goats as an alternative method for removing noxious weeds from vacant lots, as well as a more environmentally friendly way to trim back grass lawns. The fundraiser was at a hotel on the Seattle waterfront. Dale Chihuly glass sculptures tastefully referenced the shapes of goats everywhere you looked, from the horned chandelier above the ballroom to the bearded chin sinks in the bathroom.

Granny Grace was busy networking for future PI clients; Cat could hear the melody of her laughter across the room. Cat took a breather from the talk to stand at the window facing the Sound. She watched as two green-and-white ferries, their lights reflected on the water, passed each other on their ways to and from Bainbridge Island. She remembered her first ferry ride in Seattle, when she and her parents came to visit when she was six. She thought Puget Sound was a river like the Mississippi, but it startled her for being so blue. The Mississippi was muddy, like coffee with lots of cream.

"We hear you're starting up Grace's PI firm again," said a voice that brought her back into the room. It was Simon Fletcher, one of her grandmother's best friends. Following close behind him as usual was his partner, Dave Bander. The two were never separated; they seemed to function in every respect as a unit. They both wore immaculate tuxedoes that looked tailor-made for them as opposed to rented, and both men's hair was close cropped and spiked slightly with gel.

But it's not as if they were truly twins. Dave worked for a nonprofit with a creative, accepting environment, and, particularly at fancy events like these, he wore makeup—a little "manscara," as he called it, and sometimes "guyliner." Simon, an architect, had a Roman nose, stylish frames perched gallantly upon it, as if he'd personally designed the sweeping features of his own face.

"Hello, Simon!" Cat said, giving him a hug. "Word does get around. Yes, I'm hoping to take over Granny Grace's firm. But she's training me first."

"I bet she is," said Dave, who gave her a kiss on the cheek. "There's no better teacher than Amazing Grace."

"What did she ever teach you?" Cat asked.

"Didn't your grandmother ever tell you how we met?" asked Simon.

"No, she didn't."

"Well, Dave here went to her for spiritual guidance. He was forty-two, unhappily married—to a woman, let me add—and working as a corporate lawyer for a chemical company. After a couple sessions with your grandmother, he filed for divorce and quit his job. I met him two years later at one of Grace's legendary cocktail parties."

"My grandmother, the matchmaker. And now you're helping those in need," Cat said, finishing the story. Dave was a lawyer who represented women pressing charges against abusive men.

Dave put his hand in Simon's. "But most importantly, now I'm happy." The two smiled at each other.

"I didn't know Granny Grace counseled people," she said.

"It was part of what she did as a volunteer for a meditation center," Dave explained.

"Yes, that was back when Dave was dabbling in New Age spiritualism, trying to find himself," said Simon, a teasing hint to his tone.

"Don't mock it," Dave said. "It led me to you, didn't it?"

"True," he admitted. Then, turning to Cat, he asked, "Has your grandmother taken you to her meditation class?"

Cat laughed. "You mean, have I sat in the presence of Guru Dave? Yes, I have. And my spirit has transcended the physical sphere and is entirely without ego attachment."

Simon snickered. "Oh, God. It's all over once the chanting begins."

"At least I don't have to shave my head," Cat said. "Guru Dave thinks shaving hides what the divine has created."

"I once had my chakras realigned," Dave said. "My heart chakra slipped down to my butt." The two men roared with laughter.

"Now, how are you *really* doing?" Simon asked once the laughter died down.

"Honestly speaking," Cat admitted, "I'm having the hardest time finding a job. I can't even get work as a barista. Of course, it would help if I'd ever made something besides my mom's drip coffee."

"It's rough out there these days," said Simon, and Dave nodded in agreement.

"We've halted construction on one of our condo projects," he continued. "The irony is, we have to pay to have a security guard on the premises."

"Say," Simon faced Dave, looking as if a lightbulb had popped up over his head. "Maybe she could be our booth guard."

"Yeah, yeah," agreed Dave. "The guy they've got out there now just sleeps all day. Cat would be great!"

They turned to her. "We know it's beneath you, sweetie," Dave ventured, "but think about it. We'd love to have you as our rent-a-cop!"

As they moved to greet some friends of theirs, Dave, the bigger jokester of the two, squeezed her arm. "Hey, Cat, did you see the satyr in the bathroom? Crazy what that Chihuly can do with glass, isn't it?"

Simon pulled him away, making tsk-tsk noises. "Dave, I think that's only in the men's room." Then turning to Cat, he winked and said, "We'll call you about the guard gig."

And that was that. Cat had her first full-time job. At first she thought it wouldn't be so bad. She imagined she would be like the security guards at the hospital where she'd been a candy striper: sit in an office all day, maybe even watch a little TV, walk around the building every hour, piece of cake.

But when she showed up for her first day—make that first *night,* since she'd been given the highly despised 11 p.m. to 7 a.m. shift—she met Tony, the security company's general manager. Tony only came up to Cat's shoulder in height, and he had a row of broken, crooked, yellowing teeth. He smelled of cigarettes and mothballs.

"I'm here to guard the building," Cat said by way of introduction. Conscious of favoritism, she didn't mention Simon and Dave.

"You're not guarding a building," Tony barked at her.

"I'm not? Well then, what am I guarding?"

"A construction site."

"Well, yes, I know they're not done building it. Am I guarding the equipment?"

"No equipment," he replied. "The contractors cleared that out already."

"Um, I don't understand," said Cat. "What *is* there?"

"About three floors of an eight-story *condom* project," Tony said. He leered at Cat to see if she had heard his mispronunciation.

She decided to ignore for a moment his attempt at wit, and the fact that this constituted sexual harassment. "I know that, but what am I protecting? Are they afraid the copper pipes will get stolen?" She knew copper was sometimes stolen out of abandoned buildings and sold for scrap.

"Yeah, that's part of it, smart girl. The other part is liability. Someone gets hurt there, they sue your fairy friends." He made a little flying Tinker Bell motion with his hands when he said the bit about Simon and Dave.

So Tony already knew her ties to the owners. This was not going in a good direction, and Cat hesitated to ask the next question—after all, this was Seattle, and it had been raining for the last three days.

"Is there a roof?"

"Only in part of the building, but that don't matter none to you. You'll stay outside the condo in the hut."

Tony hadn't lied about the booth, and she thought maybe his word for it, "hut," was more accurate. Cat spent her first week sitting in a four-by-four hut with one tiny window. She had a radio that ran on batteries, her flashlight, and a clipboard of papers on which she was supposed to record her rounds. The bathroom was a port-a-john about ten feet away.

To make the job even duller, Tony had carefully instructed her about how this security thing worked: "You make your rounds every hour on the hour. You take ten minutes to make the rounds, no more, no less. The rest of the time you stay in the hut."

"Won't that make it kind of easy for someone to avoid security?"

Tony looked at her with contempt. "Listen, smart girl, here's how it works. We contract with the client to provide security. In the contract we specify exactly what we will do, and we do exactly that. If a representative from the company comes by to check on you at five minutes after the hour, and you are in the hut, you are fired. On the other hand, if he comes by at fifteen minutes after the hour, and you are not in the hut, you are fired. Do I make myself clear?"

"So what if someone steals something at half past the hour?"

Tony had a surprising ability to convey disdain with his expressions. "It's an empty building. And you'll spot the thieves before they ever get around to ripping out any copper, trust me."

The only bright spot for Cat was that Granny Grace let her drive Siddhartha to work, since by bus it would have meant three transfers and more than an hour-long trip to the Eastside. Granny Grace had taken Cat out in the old Mercedes for an instructional test run. The car handled beautifully; it was the smoothest ride she'd ever driven. On Cat's first day of work, Granny Grace had been on hand to bid her bon voyage.

Cat sat in the driver's seat while her grandmother assessed her from outside. "The only thing missing is your attitude," she observed. "You look like someone borrowing a Mercedes for the day. You need to drive it like you own it."

"Now how am I supposed to look like that when I'm wearing a rent-a-cop uniform?" Cat asked.

"Put these on," Granny Grace ordered, handing her a pair of her Jackie O. shades.

"Gran, it's dark and rainy outside."

"So what? Now stick your chin out."

"There. That's my granddaughter." Granny Grace smiled her approval. "Don't let the birds poop on Siddhartha," she added, patting the car's fender as Cat started it up. "He's used to the garage."

Chapter 3

Cat was standing in front of the building she was supposed to be guarding. The bit of yard leading up to it had been stripped of vegetation, and weeks of Seattle rain had turned it to mud, her feet sinking a bit as she walked. A dusting of snow had fallen, making the entire area seem new and pleasant instead of derelict. It smelled fresh and clean, like the first snowfall of winter back home. She looked down at her feet and saw a pair of expensive leather boots instead of the cheap Velcro-fastened shoes the security agency issued her. She was in someone else's dream.

She walked up to the condo building and paused. Something was definitely wrong here. The building as she knew it was only partially built—construction had halted abruptly at floor three, though there were eight in Simon's architectural plans. But it looked now as if it had been finished. And now she could get inside. She wasn't supposed to go inside—she was meant to stay in her guard hut out front unless making rounds outside the building—but the door was wide open.

The inside of the building consisted of grey concrete and looked vaguely utilitarian, like a school or hospital. She walked slowly, disoriented, nothing seeming familiar to her. Suddenly, down an empty corridor, she heard a faint squeaking, honking noise. It was a gosling, covered in mottled fuzz. It squeaked and honked frantically, as if afraid and missing its mother. Cat felt a rush of protective instinct then, as if she were its mother, and then a terrific fear mixed with anger hurled around inside her chest. She felt herself straining to push her feelings out through her body. She looked down at her arms. Sharp pinpricks of pain ran up and down the length of them as feathers burst through the fabric of her clothing. She felt her chin and nose grow and harden into a beak. She opened her mouth to let out a cry, and it came out as a loud hiss. Instinctively, she wrapped her wings around the gosling.

Then a man carrying a rifle and wearing a hunting cap appeared around the corner. Cat hoisted the gosling onto her back, ran outside, and spread her wings. Just as he reached the doorway to the building, she was airborne. He fired a few shots in the air, which zinged past her. Cat could see Canada in the distance, represented by a multicolored map, the border between it and the United States showing as a red line. That was her destination. She pumped her wings harder, the gosling on her back crying in squeaks muted by the wind. If only she could get there...

Cat woke up sweating. The clock in her guard booth showed 2:13 a.m.

She had always wondered why these digital clocks seemed only to come in one color, devilish red. She'd fallen asleep on the job, which could be a firing offense—if anyone ever bothered to check on her. Cat knew by the feel of things that she'd been dreamslipping.

There was a real problem with this particular dream, though. She knew from experience that she had to be physically close to the person dreaming. Maybe a couple hundred feet but not much more could separate her from the person whose dream she entered. Cat stepped outside the hut. The condo building was close enough, but it was vacant and locked up tight. The streets were lined with parked cars. If someone were asleep in one of them, they might be close enough. Sweeping her gaze down the row of cars, she saw nothing out of the ordinary, only what looked like upper-middle-class Seattleites' vehicles, a few Volvos, lots of Priuses, all of them empty.

Cat walked around the booth and looked to the other side. Nothing but an empty space where the condo would have lovely landscaping, were it completed. Cat looked back at the incomplete condo—unlike in her dream, it was its proper three-story height. It was well within her range. Someone was sleeping nearby, and the most likely place was inside the structure.

Cat felt torn about whether or not to investigate this dream further. She had been working for only five days, and she needed the job. Should she investigate and risk getting fired? She reasoned that it was her duty to protect the site.

There was indeed a roof on only part of the building, so they'd placed a tarp on the other side, and she could hear the rattle and snap of the blue plastic as it shifted in the wind. It was supposed to be an empty building. It was not time for her rounds, and if the "representative of the company" that Tony mentioned came by and found her hut empty, she'd be out of a job. But then, in her five days (nights, really) on the job, she had yet to see anything more than raccoons knocking over trashcans. They had looked at her with an expression that seemed to say, "Hey lady, where's our food?" But even they didn't come back the next night.

As Cat walked up to the front of the building, a flock of geese flew overhead, reminding her of her dream.

Just as in the dream, she had to step carefully to avoid the worst of the mud, but there was no snow on the ground. The front door was locked as usual. Nothing had been tampered with. Cat walked around to the back of the building to check out the rear entrance. There was a padlock on a loose chain dangling from the handles on the doors. She touched it to find that the lock was only resting in place, as if someone wanted to make it look as if it were locked, but it hadn't been secured. She unhooked it from the chain, unwrapped the chain from the handles, opened the door, and stepped inside.

The air smelled slightly musty, as if mold were just beginning to grow, but the sawdust smell was still strong enough to cover it up. It was not even slightly warmer inside the building. Cat rubbed her arms with her hands and shivered. It might even be colder in here than outside, she thought to herself. She flipped on her flashlight, and the faint glow showed bare walls that had nothing more than drywall covering studs. The floor was just plywood. Then she heard it: a noise coming from upstairs.

Cat's heart began to thump in her chest, making her chide herself for not being the brave PI that Granny Grace was. She could search this building from one end to the other, which would take a while, or she could try to use some logic. She asked herself, if I were going to sleep here, where would I sleep? Whoever was trespassing would know there was a security guard who made regular rounds. Cat began to make her way upstairs. There were boards and tarps lining the stairwell, but there was a clear path in the center. She crouched down to look at the steps. She could see her own fresh footprints in the dust but could not make out if there were others besides hers.

The rooms on the outside would be too cold, even on the first floor. The interior rooms would be the warmest and driest, especially on the second floor, on the side that had a roof. Cat turned the corner in the stairwell and stopped abruptly. The door to the second floor was open just a crack.

She switched off her flashlight and cautiously approached the door, gently pushing it open. There was a sharp clatter. Cat turned on her light quickly and saw an empty paint can rolling on the plywood floor. She flashed her light in that direction. Nothing.

The condo units did not have doors, so Cat quickly ducked into the nearest one on her left. Bare studs like bones allowed her to see almost from one end of the unit to the other. The bathroom was the room furthest from the cold building exterior, and it was also the only room in the unit that had drywall. Her father had worked in construction, so she knew at least something about the way buildings were put together. She made her way through the maze of wall studs, piles of two-by-fours, and holes in the flooring where some valuable amenity was going to be installed, until she reached the bathroom door. There was no knob, just an empty hole cut into the door where the knob would be fitted. Cat gently put her fingers into the hole and then swiftly yanked open the door. The room was empty.

A series of muffled thumps reached her from the hallway. Footsteps. She sped back through the labyrinth of studs, nearly stepping in the hole in the floor. Cat jogged down the hallway to the opposite stairs on the far side of the building, playing her flashlight up and down. Someone had just raced out of one of the rooms and taken the back stairs. She was sure of it; there was dust in the air.

When she reached the stairs, she stopped long enough to listen. There was a sharp bang. Cat was certain it was the downstairs door banging open against the wall. She jumped the first flight and landed with a loud thud on the turnaround, despite trying to move quietly. The door was open at the bottom, but jumping would likely mean stumbling out the door into an unknown situation. Cat took the stairs as quietly and quickly as she could. She landed at the base softly and carefully headed through the door.

"Just what do you think you're doing?" It was a man's voice.

She spun around in the direction of the voice. He was taller than Cat, and he wore a starched white shirt and a loud tie with angular red-and-yellow stripes, a black jacket over it with the name M&O Security emblazoned in red on the front, the zipper slicing right through the middle of the ampersand in M&O so that his jacket seemed to shout "MO" at her. Having grown up in St. Louis, "MO" meant Missouri to her, the Show-Me State.

"M-making my rounds," she said, at once aware that not only was whoever she'd been stalking getting away, but that her job was now on the line. This must be the "representative of the company" that Tony had told her about. For all intents and purposes, this man was her boss, though M&O didn't assign mere security guards with set supervisors. Any of these "representatives" could fire her.

"Not in here, you're not," Mr. M&O Security declared. "Didn't Tony tell you under no circumstances should you enter the building?"

"The back door wasn't secure," explained Cat. "I had to check it out."

"Yeah, I noticed that," the man mused. "So, you didn't break in here?"

"No," she said. "Didn't you see? The lock wasn't broken. It just wasn't clicked into the padlock all the way when I found it. I heard something, and I came to investigate."

"Investigate, huh?" he replied. "What did you hear?"

She tried to think fast. Crying would be too alarming. "Scuffling around," she said. "You know, like thieves casing the joint." As the phrase came out of her mouth, she inwardly rolled her eyes at herself. Thieves? Casing the joint? Really?

The man chuckled. Actually chuckled. His laugh was the type of laugh for which the word "chuckled" had been coined.

"Okay, Nancy Drew," he said. "I get that you've got a pretty dull job out here, sitting on your ass for eight hours doing nothing. It's easy to hear things, concoct some mystery to 'investigate.'" He used air quotes as he said "investigate."

"And you got in here somehow without breaking the lock. Maybe one of us didn't shut the lock all the way. As for the people you heard, it was probably a bunch of meth heads looking for a place to squat. You ever get into a tussle with a tweaker?"

He waved his clipboard at her as he said it, and a beam of light bounced off the metal clip and illuminated a strange shape behind him, something she'd missed before. It had a face.

"No," she admitted. "Not exactly." She'd read about methamphetamine addicts in her senior synthesis class, and there had been some role-playing sessions in class as they debated current drug statutes, but as with a long list of real-world things, her knowledge was strictly textbook.

"Well, it's not a pleasant experience," he warned. He took his own flashlight and shined it at a spot on his temple where she could see a starburst-shaped scar. "See that? It's from a broken beer bottle, hurled at me by a tweaker."

"Wow," she said, stalling for time. "That had to hurt." Cat shifted her posture and leaned to the side to get a better look at the face behind him, though she made it look as if she were leaning in to admire his scar. The face was smaller than an adult's, and it looked askew, as if it were lying at a strange angle. It was a doll, she realized.

"Almost lost an eye," said Mr. M&O.

"What happened to the tweaker?"

"Oh, you don't want to know that," he said. "I was the least of that guy's worries. He used to sleep in one of the old library buildings where he'd spend all night rearranging the books they'd left that had been damaged by rain. Those tweakers are like that. Obsessive-compulsive. Had his own goddamn Dewey decimal system all set up in there. He didn't throw the bottle at me because I was arresting him or anything. He threw it because I was messing up his books."

Cat seized the opportunity to try to gain his trust, since she and Mr. M&O were on storytelling terms, to ask something she'd been wondering all week. "It does get really dull out here all night," she said. "Would it be all right if I brought a book or something?"

"A book?!" he exclaimed rhetorically. "Whaddya wanna read for?"

27

Cat turned the question over in her mind. Then she turned it over again. Nope, she thought, there was no way to answer that question that made any sense at all.

Mr. M&O must have felt Cat's confusion, as something seemed to soften in his voice, though she couldn't see his face. "I thought you were going to ask if you could have friends in the hut. The answer to that would be no. But a book... Do you think you could pay attention okay to the building if you had your nose in a book?" he asked. It was a genuine question, only halfway rhetorical this time.

"Oh, yes," explained Cat. "I'm an ace at multitasking. I wrote my graduation thesis in one night while babysitting triplets."

"Is that so," he said. In the wan light Cat could feel him warm to her. "C'mon, bookworm. Let's get you back to the guard booth. Yeah, you can bring a book. It might help you stay awake. But the next time you hear something, you call us on the radio. Don't go messing around with tweakers all by yourself. What would you do, hit 'em with your flashlight?" He chuckled.

"I hadn't thought that far ahead," Cat said, and there was truth in her words. "I majored in criminal justice, so I guess I thought I knew what to do. But I'll call you for help next time," she promised, playing up to him a bit. As soon as his back was turned to open the door, she crouched down, scooped up the doll, and stuffed it into the pocket of her jacket.

Outside, Mr. M&O secured the padlock on the chain around the handles. "Maybe one of the construction crew left this open," he speculated. "They're always coming back for stuff they left behind."

Once he climbed into his red company van and left, she fished out the doll and took a look at it. It was a Raggedy Ann doll, like a newer version of the one she had as a child, but well worn. Raggedy Ann's dress was stained with what looked like chocolate ice cream. Some of her red yarn hair had been pulled out at the roots, and her freckles were sun-faded.

Chapter 4

C at stepped onto the platform with her ticket in one white-gloved hand. The deckhands had secured the moorings, and at last she could board the riverboat. It was a grand steamboat with a paddle wheel the height of a six-story building. She smoothed down the front of her dress, shifting her corset deftly with one hand so that the other passengers wouldn't notice her adjustment.

"All aboard, St. Louis," said the lead deckhand, who reached out to assist Cat as she stepped up. But his arm suddenly turned to feathers, and Cat couldn't get a firm grip. She slipped and fell backward, and instead of the platform rising up to meet her bottom, she plunged into the cold waters of the Mississippi River.

"Stupid girl," the deckhand yelled, screwing up his face and shaking a finger at her. "I've got half a mind to let you drown." She recognized him then. It was Tony from M&O Security. Cat felt a strong tug as the current started to pull her away from the boat, away from shore. She looked out toward the opposite bank, but it wasn't there; the water turned blue before her eyes and unfolded itself for miles. She could see the Olympic mountain range in the distance. The pull was so strong. She could just let go and allow it to carry her away...

"Cathedral!" Someone was yelling her name from shore. She turned. A tall, silver-haired woman with a frilly parasol was waving at her. Granny Grace! Her grandmother reached out with the parasol, which magically extended itself far out into the waters right within Cat's reach. She grabbed on and let herself be pulled to shore. When she reached her grandmother, the woman smiled and said, "Cat, I slipped into your dream."

Cat woke, startled. "Granny Grace?" she called. "Granny Grace!" No answer. She launched herself out of bed and ran in sock feet up the stairs to the third floor, to her grandmother's room, the Sumptuous Scarlett O'Hara. The room was bathed in red, from the rose-red walls to the velvet bedspread. Granny was napping on a chaise lounge in the corner. Cat gently nudged her awake.

"Oh, is that you, Cat?" Granny rubbed her eyes and sat up on the chaise lounge.

"It's me."

"What's the matter, Cat? You look upset." She moved over on the chaise, clearing a space, and motioned for Cat to sit down. Cat remained standing.

"Grandmother," she said, drawing out her syllables. "Were you—do you know how—oh, balls," she cursed. "Were you walking around and talking to me *in my dream*?"

Granny Grace smiled. "Maybe. I don't know. Why don't you describe it to me, and I'll tell you if I was there."

"This isn't funny," Cat frowned. She didn't like being toyed with by anyone, not even her grandmother.

"Oh, you're upset. Sit down, Cat. It's all right."

Cat sat down but continued to glare at her. "You talked to me, didn't you? You said, 'Cat, I've slipped into your dream.' Plus, I could see you. You weren't inside my head. I could see you."

"Well, yes. I suppose I did that. By the way, why didn't you tell me you were homesick?"

"Homesick? What are you talking about?"

"Oh, all that nostalgic St. Louis riverboat nonsense. I half expected Huck Finn himself to make an appearance."

"I'm not homesick. And answer my question. How did you do that?"

"I think you are. It's okay, you know, if you are." Granny Grace put her arm around Cat, who wouldn't allow herself to be distracted, although she had to admit a feeling of homesick longing was welling up inside her just now.

"How. Did. You. Do. That?" she repeated.

"Do what?" Granny Grace took the rubber band out of her hair, smoothed the errant strands back, and secured it again.

"Step outside of me. Show up in my dream. Rescue me. Talk to me. Take your pick, Gran. I want to know how you did all of it."

Her grandmother smiled with self-satisfaction. "Well, then you'll have to come back to my meditation class, won't you?"

Cat groaned. She'd been putting off the class easily all week because of her new job. "Don't tell me I have to sit for hours saying nothing but *om* in order to learn how to do that stuff."

"It would help, Cat. Your mind is too westernized. Meditation would get you to still the chatter. It's like a bunch of monkeys in there, isn't it?"

"I'm about to howl like one." Cat was feeling grumpy, put out, and frustrated. She crossed her arms over her chest.

"Don't pout, Cat. It's not very becoming."

Cat sat in silence.

"Here, let me teach you something." Granny Grace took her hand, placed her palm facing hers so they were palm-to-palm. "Do you feel where we meet? There's you, and there's me. We are connected, but we will always be separate. No matter how hard I press," she explained, pushing into Cat's palm with her own, "we'll always be separate. Our minds are the same way. When you dreamslip, you're stuck to the dreamer's consciousness, but you never lose yours. You're both there, just like our palms."

"So when you're dreamslipping next time, Cat, focus on the place where your minds meet, and move them apart. Once there is space between your minds," she emphasized, moving her palm away from Cat's, "You can walk about freely." She waved her hand in the air.

"Okay, I don't know what any of that means, but I will try it." Cat yawned.

"You're still tired, aren't you?"

"Yeah, I can't get used to this sleeping-all-day thing."

"Why don't you go rest for a bit longer, and I'll bring you some food."

"You don't have to do that," Cat protested. But it did sound tempting.

A couple hours later, Cat woke after a stretch of thankfully dreamless sleep to find Granny Grace in her doorway with a tray of food and an announcement.

"Our presence has been requested at the Fletcher-Bander residence," she said, plopping down on the edge of the bed and placing the tray of food on Cat's lap. The movement upset the Raggedy Ann doll, which had been lying next to Cat on the bed. It fell to the far side of the bed, and Cat ignored it. She didn't feel like talking about the doll and the condo dream with Granny Grace just yet. Her grandmother had made poached eggs, Cat's favorite, with extra-crispy bacon and one of her homemade blue cornmeal biscuits. Cat's mouth watered greedily at the sight of the fig preserves, also homemade.

She sat up in bed and feasted on her grandmother's food.

"Simon and Dave really know how to throw a party. It's a good thing we got you that cocktail dress," said Granny Grace. "I can't let you wear what you wore to the City Goats party." Cat had attended wearing jeans with clogs and, her nod to the formality of the evening, a men's black velvet dinner jacket. "You looked like a kindergarten teacher," she muttered.

The cocktail dress that Cat had bought while out with Granny Grace was red and formfitting, with spaghetti straps. She put that on with a pair of black heels. Granny Grace thought the look was incomplete, so she went to her room and came back with a strand of black pearls.

"I've been saving these for you," she said. Cat's heart melted. "Just look at yourself," Granny Grace said, turning her to face a mirror. The pearls accented her slender neck, brought out the deep, mysterious quality of her dark eyes. Cat couldn't believe how sophisticated she looked. Granny Grace put her arms around Cat, both of them gazing into the mirror. Cat saw that she had her grandmother's heart-shaped chin, and though her grandmother was much fairer, they both had the same bow-shaped lips.

"Your old friend Lee is going to be there, by the way," Granny Grace said, and hearing his name made Cat's heart jump. It'd been three years since she'd seen him last. The problem was, well, it was complicated. She and Lee Stone went back a long way.

The Stone family used to live in Granny Grace's neighborhood, but Lee's parents had recently retired to Arizona. Lee had been Cat's first kiss, when she was fourteen and he sixteen, over one of the summers she had stayed with her grandmother.

He'd been drinking a grape soda of all things, and to this day she couldn't drink anything grape-flavored without the memory of that kiss washing over her. She was standing on the landing step of her grandmother's house, Lee a few steps down to match her height. She could feel his heat, his nearness; the air around them changed, and her heart fluttered. Then his mouth was on hers, sending threads of electricity down through her body. He broke away from her and smiled. She teetered on the step, and he caught her.

"Easy, girl," he said. "It's a long way down when you fall from up here." She couldn't have agreed more.

But she'd always had to go back to St. Louis at the end of the summer. Lee said she was too smart for him, that she'd go on to college but he wouldn't. When she was still in high school, he enlisted in the military. Once his parents began spending their winters in Arizona, they might have drifted apart except that Granny Grace was really good at staying in touch with everyone. Her grandmother must have made sure Dave and Simon invited the whole Stone family to the party, and Cat wouldn't put it past her to have done this for Cat's benefit, knowing that Lee would accept the invitation as well.

Simon Fletcher and Dave Bander lived in one of those modern, sustainably built houses very popular among the progressive, wealthy set in Seattle. Simon, a well-respected architect whose credits included a video-game company's headquarters and an alternative shopping mall in Vancouver, BC, had designed it himself. The roof of their house was made of plants. Cat had never seen anything like it before.

"It's a mixture of sedums and fescue," he'd told her at the City Goats fundraiser, saying it as if he expected her to recognize the plant names. Presumably, most Seattleites would have.

As Cat and her grandmother looked for a place to park Siddhartha on the crowded street, Cat remembered Simon's description of the house, though she'd never been there before. Every detail had been thought of in the ecologically friendly, sustainable sense, from the tile floors, reclaimed when an old school was demolished, to the system Simon had designed to capture rain and funnel it into their balcony water garden.

Such a house did not have an obvious main entrance, apparently. Even though Granny Grace had been many times a guest at the Fletcher-Bander home, they had to poke around a bit to find it. There were swales to absorb runoff instead of a front yard. The hanging gardens of Babylon had nothing on these two.

"It's the lovely Cathedral Grace," Simon intoned as he swung open the front door (a section of reclaimed marine pier). Cat didn't mind his use of her full name. He was an architect, after all; he studied cathedrals for a living. His voice had a musicality that made the name sing. He and Dave were both members of the Seattle Men's Choir.

"We're so glad you could make it." Dave swept down the stairs (reclaimed bowling alley planks) and motioned for his two newest arrivals to join the party near the fireplace, which was powered by biofuel. The only downside (or maybe this was an upside?) to the fireplace was that it smelled faintly of french fries, as the fuel came mainly from used oil from restaurant fryers.

Dave and Simon settled down beside Cat and Grace on a modern couch that wrapped in a perfect crescent so that all four of them could sit on it and still carry on a conversation. There were clusters of people in various levels of Seattle evening attire spread throughout the open-plan living space, wearing everything from jeans and Birkenstocks to cocktail dresses like the ones Granny Grace insisted they wear. It was her grandmother's persistent complaint that Seattleites dressed entirely too casually for almost every occasion.

Tonight, in less formal attire, Simon and Dave were a study in contrasts. Dave wore Seattle active wear, which meant expensive casual clothes from REI that would give him ease of movement, breathability, and water repellancy, should he suddenly feel the need to venture out into the wilds for a hike or trail run. On his feet were shoes that Cat felt didn't actually qualify as shoes. They fit like gloves, with full separations for all ten toes, and only a pad for the sole. Simon, always the more tailored dresser, wore khakis and a button-down shirt.

"So tell us, Cat," Simon inquired, "how's the security guard gig going?"

"It's great," she answered brightly. "I've got lots of time to read." She winked.

"Oh, good," piped up Dave. "We were afraid you'd be bored."

33

"Cat's never bored," said Grace. "She has an active mind. Besides, she has to pass her PI exam."

"That's right," said Cat. She continued, "And actually, there has been a bit of excitement at the condo." She told them about hearing noises, going to investigate, and finding the doll. She eliminated the part about the dreamslipping, of course.

Grace listened intently. "Did this just happen last night? You haven't told *me* about it."

"Yes, and no. I hadn't had the chance."

"Well, M&O hasn't said anything to us about it," said Simon. "Have they called you, Dave?"

"No."

Cat thought to herself that maybe Mr. M&O hadn't reported the incident. But why? Maybe he was protecting her from Tony's wrath. She *had* gone off protocol by wandering around inside the condo building, and he seemed to like her.

"Well, this is no good," frowned Simon. "It sounds like something's going on there."

"I agree," said Dave. "I don't like it at all."

At that point, none other than the mayor of Seattle himself drifted over. He was a reformed hippie who had shaved his beard but still rode a bike to work every day, just to make a point. He commended Grace on her work with City Goats, reaching down to kiss her hand with reverence. Granny Grace introduced Cat to him, and the three of them exchanged polite pleasantries until the mayor said, "Amazing Grace, may I speak with you in private? I've got a personal matter I'd like to discuss with you."

The two of them drifted off to Simon's home office, leaving Cat to navigate the crowd alone. Simon and Dave had resumed their hosting duties in the kitchen and bar.

Cat felt a hand, gentle, on the small of her back. She spun around to see Lee Stone, in full military regalia. "Sergeant Stone," as his troops called him. Cat took in his incredibly impressive physique, which had to be well beyond even the military's requirements for elite Rangers.

"How's my girl?" he asked.

She simultaneously bristled and warmed to the "my girl" reference. "As well as can be expected, sir," she said, giving a mock salute.

"At ease," he said, laughing. "I see you're just as snappy on your feet as you used to be."

"Only when I'm surprised by a soldier in dress uniform," she said. It was all she could do to resist flinging herself into his strong arms. His parents were in attendance, too, she now noticed. She smiled at them across the room—two excessively tan retirees.

"So you're here to stay now," he said, leaning closer to her.

Cat had been single since she and Grant, the fussy soccer player studying electrical engineering, broke up in her junior year of college. She had been enduring one heck of a dry spell. Tempted as she was by a couple of bar meet-ups that could easily have turned into one-night stands, she just hadn't had the energy for the emotional fallout she knew she'd experience from those. Cat was the kind of woman who always got attached. And not in the creepy, let's-get-married-after-one-date way. She just never had the stamina for casual sex. It was a heady, emotionally intense experience for her, especially with the inevitable, added intimacy of being privy to her partners' dreams.

She still remembered slipping into one of Lee's dreams years ago, back when they were both still in high school, he a senior and Cat a sophomore. He'd been in discussions with army recruiters about his future while most of his classmates were busy researching colleges.

In the dream, he wore a parachute and was flying by transport jet to a destination where he and the rest of the crew would be air-dropped. Sitting in the jet with him were his father, dressed in the army uniform he'd worn in Vietnam, and his grandfather, wearing his World War II-era uniform. Both men had been enlistees, just like Lee. Cat remembered Lee's fear about deciding to choose a military career for himself, especially since he would likely see combat.

His father was leaning against the wall of the transport, smoking a joint.

"I've seen things I wish I could forget," he said, smoke slipping from his mouth and nose. "But I doubt I ever will. If they gave me the choice now, I don't know if I'd go." He took another drag on his joint, and this time, peace signs and doves flew out of his nose and mouth. "I might tell Uncle Sam to fig off," he said, and Lee couldn't help but laugh in the dream at his father's signature way of cussing, how innocent it seemed in that moment. The doves and peace signs disappeared in the air with a popping noise, as if they were fat bubbles.

Then the girl in the famous black-and-white photo, an iconic image of Vietnam, the girl whose clothes had been burned off by napalm, appeared out of nowhere, screaming. She ran right into his father, both of them disappearing into each other as if they were an old film strip melting on a reel.

His grandfather spoke up at last, as if he'd been silently observing and waiting for the right moment to talk. "Your dad didn't get a very honorable war," he said. "According to the history books, anyway. But that's got nothing to do with it. There's atrocity and honor in every war, there is."

At that, his grandfather began a marching drill that lasted for several powerful minutes. He stopped, stood at attention for a few seconds, and relaxed. He tossed his rifle at Lee and said, "Step in, Private."

Lee caught the rifle easily and fell in step with his grandfather. He missed a couple of moves, and the old man gently corrected him. After several rounds, he had the pattern down. They marched together until his grandfather turned on his heel and said he had to go now. He stood facing Lee and briefly squeezed the sides of his grandson's arms, a brusque stand-in for an actual hug. Pointing a finger at Lee's heart, he said, "You've got everything you need in here."

At that, he turned, grabbed a parachute, and jumped.

In the dream, Lee's fear dissipated, and taking its place was a powerful sense of responsibility, which seemed like it was two responsibilities rolled into one. The first was to live up to the men in his family, who were both decorated war heroes. The second was to protect something large and sprawling but worth protecting, and that was freedom; it was to Lee everything that made him a human being, the right to make one's own choices and way in the world without the threat of force.

Cat remembered waking up from that dream overwhelmed by a passion to serve, to protect humanity. She'd never felt anything like that in another person's dream, and it was probably the thing that had both drawn her to Lee and also made him seem so elusive.

You're here to stay now. The comment was loaded. It was half question, half admission of interest. When he wasn't on a tour of duty, Lee lived an hour away, near what was now called Joint Base Lewis-McChord, or simply "JBLM," a fusing of the Fort Lewis army post with the old McChord Air Force Base.

He knew Dave and Simon, but he was clearly here to see her.

"Yes," she answered, trying not to breathe too heavily, but her heart was racing. She actually felt swoony.

"I'm glad," he said. "Cat, it's good to see you."

Her voice caught in her throat, so she smiled at him.

Something in his face showed her smile affected him. "Can I get you a drink?" he asked. Lee went to the bar and made her a gin and tonic himself, as he didn't want to disturb the hosts, who clearly had their hands full. Even though it was more of a hot-weather drink for her, something she drank during the sweltering St. Louis summers, it grounded her a bit with familiarity. She loved the tanginess of the limes and tonic.

The party was in full swing by this point, and there was nowhere to sit. They stood in a doorway near the bar, but that turned out to be a stage entrance. A couple of actors burst through the doorway between them, one wearing a matador costume, the other presumably the bull, as he held his index fingers above his head. Their routine went on a good fifteen minutes and involved several rounds of audience participation. Lee was pulled in once as replacement bull. He played along admirably.

Once the impromptu play was finished, someone turned the music up. It was Adele singing "Rolling in the Deep." Cat and Lee tried to talk, but he had trouble hearing her above the din. He kept leaning in toward her with his right ear, and she noticed that on his left he wore a hearing aid. After a few frustrating attempts at conversation, Lee scanned the perimeter of the room, spotted a set of glass doors leading outside, grabbed her hand, and pulled her toward them.

"There," he said, closing the door behind them. "It's quiet out here."

The night was clear enough to see a full moon and stars between patches of grey clouds. Down below, the outdoor lights in the Fletcher-Bander garden illuminated the outlines of ferns and early summer flowers.

It was a little nippy on the balcony, and seeing her shiver, Lee took off his uniform jacket and slipped it over her shoulders. His arms were around her as he did this.

"Is it too cold for you?"

"No, Lee," she replied, looking up at him. "I think *you're* making me shiver."

"Oh," he said, swallowing hard. For a tense moment, he looked down at her as if he were in pain.

She reached up and touched his ear, the one with the hearing aid. He closed his eyes for a moment, savoring her touch.

"What happened here?" she asked.

"Iraq," he said. "I got a little too close."

She waited for him to elaborate, but he didn't. He'd always been a man of few words. In that respect, she knew the military life probably suited him.

She couldn't take her hand away, not just yet. There were patterns of white scars running from his ear to the sides of his face that she hadn't noticed before. She let her hand slide down the side of his cheek to his jaw. He reached up and took her hand, his eyes opening. He moved her hand to his mouth and kissed it.

The motion made her catch her breath. She felt her body sway toward him. One of his arms slipped around her waist, and with his other hand he cupped her cheek, drawing her in for a kiss.

She felt something burst open inside her, and she couldn't help it; she wrapped her arms around him as if she'd never again let go.

"Cat," he said, holding her tightly.

They broke apart and looked at each other. A wicked smile turned up the corner of Lee's mouth, and they both erupted in laughter.

"Damn, girl," Lee said. "It's been too long."

"Since you've had any, or since you've seen me?" Cat teased.

"Well, both, if you must know the truth."

"It's the same for me," she confessed.

His face turned serious again. He pulled her close, pushed her gently against the balcony railing, and leaned into her. She could feel his excitement, tense, needy.

"I want you," he whispered. "Tonight."

Something in her heart detonated, sending cascades of warmth down through her belly and between her legs. She wanted him, too.

She was gasping for air. "How?" she asked, laughing a bit, trying to recover. "I'm at Granny Grace's. You live down there in militaryland."

"Come home with me," he said. "I'll drive you back."

Could she abandon Granny Grace at the party for a tryst with Sergeant Stone? She turned it over in her mind. She hadn't been with this man since high school... But she still remembered the feel of him, how he fell asleep with his arms around her, holding her all night. And in the morning, they'd made love again. It was better with Lee than it had been with her most recent boyfriend, fussy Grant, who seemed to have more passion *and* stamina on the soccer field than he had in bed. She also had to admit to a certain curiosity about Lee. She wanted to see the world he inhabited; she wanted to move in his space, watch how he lived.

"Let's go back in and mingle a bit," said Cat. "Then we'll see how the evening should end." She smiled teasingly at him and then slipped through the door and away.

Cat found Granny Grace ensconced in the living room talking to several well-known writers, those she recognized as part of Seattle's literati. But her grandmother was the one telling stories, regaling the writers with tales of her PI escapades.

"Little did the killer know that I was hiding behind the potted palm," she was saying as Cat walked up. "I recorded his confession word for word." The gathering exclaimed.

"Well, hello, dear," Granny Grace greeted her as she saw Cat. "I thought you'd vanished under the full moon."

"I was talking with an old friend," mumbled Cat, blushing as the literati stared at her.

"I bet," said Granny Grace, winking. "This is my granddaughter," she explained to her audience, "Cat McCormick. She's tough as nails, and she's taking over Grace Detective Agency."

The crowd oohed and ahhed at that, and Cat flushed further with embarrassment, feeling anything but tough as nails. Here her grandmother was, networking on her behalf while she was out on the balcony canoodling with an old flame.

Cat spent the next thirty minutes explaining her background and her plans to a group of overly interested writers. On the one hand, she could imagine them making mental notes about her for a character sketch. On the other hand, you couldn't throw a rock in Seattle and not hit a writer, there were so many of them, and they all knew each other. She figured the time was well spent getting into their network.

After that, she and Granny Grace made a concerted effort to work the room.

Cat's grandmother introduced her to the head of a fishing industry association. He was celebrating a victory that night, as his group had just received an award for designing a system that saved endangered seabirds, both murrelets and terns, from getting tangled in their longline equipment.

"Fishermen, praised for our environmentalism," he told Granny Grace. He was at least a decade her junior but clearly charmed by the woman and eager to impress her. "We longliners are green," he declared, one hand pulling the tip of his white beard, the other clasping a sweaty drink. The ice cubes tinkled against the glass as he gestured. He leaned in toward her grandmother as he spoke, touching her arm occasionally. She smiled and egged him on, congratulating him for proving that industry could regulate itself.

"I've always been a fan of enlightened self-interest," Granny Grace remarked.

"Self-interest?!" The man reacted as if hurt. "My dear woman, this one was truly for the birds."

She laughed at his play on words, tilting her head back and smiling widely. Granny Grace fingered the pearls at her neck, a gesture that Cat realized was a tad flirtatious. Her senses sharpened, and she began to perceive a tension between the two. Romance? Why not? That meant it was time for Cat to make a graceful exit.

She scanned the room, hoping Lee hadn't given up on her. There he was, leaning against the bar, in deep conversation with Dave. She sauntered over toward them.

"It's all about the fore-foot strike," Dave was saying. He was talking about his strange toe shoes. Lee seemed skeptical, but Dave was doing his best to convince him.

"Think about it," Dave urged. "Human beings were born to walk barefoot. It's the unnatural shoe forms that are ruining our knees."

"You might be right," Lee conceded. "But if I were walking through a dusty alley in Fallujah, I'd rather be wearing combat boots."

"Touché, sergeant," said Dave, holding up his glass in salute. "Touché."

Lee spotted Cat and turned, his face lighting up. But Dave intervened. "Cat, there you are. Listen, Simon and I have a proposition for you."

"Hey, I'm the one who's supposed to be propositioning her," Lee protested as Dave swooped in, taking Cat under one arm.

"Watch out for G.I. Joe," Dave warned with a laugh. "He'll ship out and break your heart. But enough of that now. We know you're already sort of working for us, indirectly," he said, "but we'd like to hire you."

Just then Simon appeared over Dave's shoulder and chimed in. "Yes, Cat. We want you to act as a PI there at the condo."

Cat was confused, but the idea of her first real PI assignment excited her. "Is this about the break-in?" she asked. "The doll?"

"Yes," Simon said. "We think you're right—it could be nothing, but what if there's something going on? Granny Grace has a hunch about it."

Ah, so Granny Grace's mark was all over this one, thought Cat. Well, she had a hunch, too, and she was planning to continue her investigation anyway. Why not get paid for it?

The two men steered Cat into their office, where Simon took out a checkbook, filled out a check, ripped it out, and handed it to Cat.

"Consider yourself on retainer," he said. Cat's eyes seemed to be playing tricks on her. It was made out for five thousand dollars.

"I can't take this," she said.

"You don't want the case?" Dave put his hands on his hips defiantly.

"I want the case," Cat replied. "But that's too much."

"Why? Because we're friends?" Simon asked. "You should charge us what you'd charge anyone. We don't need a favor. You're in business."

Cat didn't know what to say. She thought about her salary—if it could be called that—at M&O. It was twelve dollars an hour. Doing the math didn't help slice it any better—she made less than twenty-five thousand a year, and that was before taxes. If she couldn't live with Granny Grace, she'd really be in trouble, as the cheapest rent she'd seen in Seattle was a studio apartment for eight hundred and fifty bucks, and utilities were extra. Add another six hundred a month in expenses and student loan payments, and she wouldn't be able to make ends meet.

"You both have been so generous already," Cat noted.

"Pshaw," countered Dave. "We've got an overqualified security guard at our condo. You're a bargain for what M&O is paying you. And now we're taking advantage of your rock-bottom PI fees because you've just launched your practice."

Simon murmured agreement. "Besides, Cat, if there are people running around inside our condo building, we need to find out why. Especially if a child is involved."

"I'd be honored to have you as my first clients," said Cat. "But I'm not yet licensed, bonded, and insured."

"Well, this will help you get that started, right? Consider it a warm-up case," Dave affirmed. "Do we have a deal?" he asked, holding out his hand for a shake, Simon following suit. She shook their hands, and the three of them returned to the party. Lee was still waiting for her over by the bar, and the crowd had thinned.

"So what's the verdict?" he asked. "Has the lady decided how the evening should end?"

Cat looked him square in the eyes and, brimming with a newfound confidence, announced, "The lady has decided this night should *never* end."

An hour later, Cat was standing in the picture window of Lee's condo, the lights of downtown Tacoma flickering below her. He lived in a brand-new building built into the side of the hill that sloped up from the Thea Foss Waterway and Puget Sound. The condo was smallish and located in an iffy neighborhood, but it had an incredible view; she could see the cool ice-blue glow of the twin sculptures flanking the walkway to the Museum of Glass, as well as its signature metal cone, outlined against the dark sky.

She'd decided to keep the knowledge of her first real PI job to herself, and she wanted Granny Grace to be the first person she told anyway, so she said nothing to Lee. Besides, it was code not to discuss her clients or their cases with anyone, she already knew.

Cat felt Lee slip his arm around her waist and nestle his face into her neck. It made her weak-kneed, and he deftly removed the drink from her hand and took her in his arms. They kissed passionately,

41

expressively, his eyes full of wonder, she thought, that the two of them could find themselves together like this again after so long.

His place was modern and sleek, very male. She could tell he wasn't there very much, that this was his landing pad when he wasn't on a mission. It was spotless; Lee had always been Spartan in his tastes. Another reason the military life probably suited him, she surmised. It was a far cry from the eclectic clutter of Granny Grace's house.

What little artwork there was had to do with his work. His *life*, she thought, for this was far more than work. Above the gas fireplace was a spectacular oil painting of his Ranger battalion on a mission in Iraq. On the mantel were medals, a framed patch. She felt her breath catch as she took in the evidence of who her Lee had become.

"Does it bother you?" he asked. "What I do for a living?"

She put on a brave face. "Not at all. It's not that different from what I do. Or rather, what I'm trying to do. We're both sort of in law enforcement. You're just more... elite." It was a reference to his service in the Rangers, of which she admittedly knew next to nothing, except that they were the cream of the crop.

He chuckled. "Law enforcement. Right." He sighed, looking at her with an expression of utter longing mixed with something else: responsibility, pain. "I think I better show you something."

He walked over to his laptop, a silver MacBook Air perched on the granite countertop. They sat on his barstools, and he played a video for her.

"This is one of my missions," he said. "One that aborted. This is classified, so I'm going to show you, but if anyone asks, you never saw it." She looked to see if he was putting her on, but he was dead serious.

It was grainy aerial footage of several Rangers sneaking into a compound from different entrances.

"See those guys?" he asked, pointing to a group of hooded Iraqis on a high wall, unguarded. It was clear the approaching Rangers hadn't counted on them being there.

"We get the call to withdraw," he continued. On-screen, the Rangers backtracked as quickly as they could.

"Wait for it..." he said. For a couple of tense seconds, the Rangers cleared, and the Iraqis held position.

"Now." Cat watched as an airstrike from above, seeming to come from the same aerial position from which the video was being shot, obliterated the entire compound.

Cat was still holding her breath. She let it out slowly, watching the debris on the screen settle.

"Those people I just saw," she murmured. "They're gone."

"Yes," he said. "They were the enemy."

She sat there, her desire for Lee mingling with anxiety and the sinking realization of just how much she'd taken on by agreeing to go with him tonight.

"This is what I do with my life, Cat," he explained, his hands reaching for hers, which were poised on her knees as she sat on the barstool. He stood, letting go of her hands again.

"What do you want?" she whispered.

He smiled, his hand reaching up to caress her face. "Right now, I just want to do this," he replied. "Later, I will want to do more. And after that, Kitty Cat, I have no idea."

It was his old nickname for her. *Kitty Cat, please come back.* He used to say that at the end of the summer, when she told him good-bye. For a moment she teetered on the edge of a decision, to go or stay. This was her Lee, the one she used to run around Seattle Center with, playing in the bowl fountain, each of them trying to time a run through the bowl so as not to get doused with water in the next spray. She remembered the feel of his hand in hers the summer she was sixteen, how they both knew he was joining the army in the fall and it would be their last summer together. It seemed he held her hand constantly, clutched it tightly, as if he didn't want to ever let go.

He was still her Lee, no matter what life had thrown at him. She would stay.

He opened a bottle of red wine, poured two glasses, turned on the gas fireplace, and motioned for her to sit—between his legs. He then proceeded to give her a deep massage. As if some kind of expert, he worked out a kink in her right shoulder that had been bothering her for weeks. The top of her cocktail dress was in his way, and he said, "Let's take this off." She let him unzip the top, but left her strapless bra on. He unclasped it, letting it fall to the floor. Cat felt the warmth of the fire on her breasts, his hands on her back, and then his hands delicately tracing her nipples.

"So beautiful," he said, breathing heavily. She could feel him hard against her back. "You're stunning, Cat. You always were."

Cat had always felt she'd been shortchanged in the bosom department. She grew to an A cup at sixteen and never grew any larger. But she'd learned in college that plenty of men liked small breasts. "A mouthful," said one. "Pert and perfect," claimed another.

She was so turned on she felt woozy. His hands on her breasts grew more insistent, pinching her nipples till she cried out. "Let's go to the bedroom," Lee offered, and she answered, "Yes."

His condo was two stories, his bedroom on the second floor. Her cocktail dress was still unzipped, but she held it around her. He took her hands and motioned for her to let go of the dress.

"Leave this here," he said. "I want to watch you walk up." He smacked her butt lightly as she moved in front of him. She was wearing nothing but a black thong bikini now, and she walked up those stairs and right into that man's life.

Chapter 5

C at was in a grocery store. She could smell the rotisserie chicken wafting over from the deli, and in front of her was a giant display of olives, with a sign hawking "two for one." But something was wrong. There was a gun in her hands, a military semi-automatic. Lee would probably carry a gun like that, she thought, and then she realized she *was* Lee. Those were his feet she was looking at, his size eleven combat boots. They were covered in dust.

There were other people in the store: moms and dads with kids sitting in carts, young single hipsters carrying grocery baskets, elderly women with their coupon books out in front of them. Cat felt a need to protect them all, to not let the evil in the world touch them. But it was as if they couldn't see her. They went about their shopping, oblivious to her mission.

She knew the insurgents were there, hiding. She turned a corner cautiously, heading down the frozen food aisle. There was one of them, the enemy, behind a shopping cart where a little girl in a yellow sundress played cat's cradle with yarn between her hands. Her mother had gone to the next aisle to pick up something she'd forgotten.

It's just like a hajji to use a kid for a shield, said a voice in Cat's head. It was Lee's. Hearing his voice jarred her. She thought of what Granny Grace said about meditating on the places where she and Lee were connected and trying to see space between them. She tried it, but all she could get was the feeling of being stuck inside Lee's body.

Lee withdrew to another aisle. S/he caught a glimpse of herself/himself in the reflection on a glass door. There was his strong jaw, his slightly off-kilter nose. *Peel away from that,* she thought, trying to see herself as Cat, and he as Lee, to sort of "pop" herself out of him. It didn't work. She doubled back, and there was the man he called a hajji, lobbing a grenade at her. It exploded over her left shoulder. She could feel the debris hitting the side of her head in a million shards of pain. Her left ear felt wet from her own blood. And then the sound in her ear went dead, giving her head a lopsided feel. She blacked out, falling to the ground. Before she hit the floor, she woke up.

Next to her was Lee, crying out and flailing. "No!" he yelled. "He's getting away!"

She shook him till he woke. His eyes were full of fear, pain, and anger, as if he were still in the dream. Some dreams were so real, she knew, they were hard to leave behind.

"Lee," she said. "It's okay. You're home. I'm here." She wrapped her arms around him and stroked his back, murmuring, "It's okay, it's okay." He moaned.

He finally regained his composure and sat up with a start, reaching for his left ear. His hearing aid was on the nightstand beside him. He had surreptitiously taken it off before getting into bed with her last night. He pulled his hand away from his ear as if expecting to see blood. Then he rubbed his ear as if it ached. He took a deep breath, shook his head, and said, "I'm sorry about all that."

"You don't have to apologize," she responded, sitting up and stroking his chest. "It's totally understandable."

"What's understandable?" he asked, stilling her hand as if her touch were suddenly too much for him. "Having a nightmare?"

"Uh... nothing," she mumbled, taking her hand away. This was certainly no time to reveal her dreamslipping talent, if there ever was a time. "Yeah, having a nightmare. Everyone gets them."

"You mean everyone who's been to war," he shot back. "Look, it was just a silly dream. I thought I was on a roller coaster and fell off."

"Uh-huh. Sure."

"I don't believe in all that shellshock BS," he insisted. "That's for weak-minded guys who never should have signed up in the first place." He was angry and shaking a bit.

"Okay, Lee," she said, reaching out to him. "Okay."

A few hours later, she was back at Granny Grace's. Lee had held her hand the whole drive home, but they spoke little. When he dropped her off, he got out of the car to say a proper good-bye before she hiked up the set of steep steps to Granny Grace's front door. He took her in his arms for a warm hug and sweet kiss. Then he took her hands.

"I'm going to Virginia for a training session," he said. "I'll be gone for a couple weeks." Cat felt her heart bottom out, which surprised her, since she would likewise be preoccupied for the next couple weeks for sure with her new case. He continued, "But I want to see you when I get back."

"I'd like that, too," she agreed, squeezing his hands.

She went directly to the Grand Green Griffin in walk-of-shame style, even though at twenty-two she was entirely too old to feel as if she needed to be ashamed of sleeping with someone. She knew Granny Grace would be tactful and respectful, as she always had been. Her grandmother was much more liberal about Cat's sex life than her own mother had been. When Cat lost her virginity at sixteen, her mother's knee-jerk response was, "Well, you give it away pretty easily." The comment had cut Cat to the core.

Cat traded her bedraggled cocktail dress for yoga pants and a hoodie and lay down on her four-poster bed. She ran over the evening, savoring every detail. Lee had been... amazing. He was gentle when she needed him to be and take-charge when she needed that, too. Their sex had been suffused with passion, long moments staring into each other's eyes, and for her, more climaxes than she could count on one hand.

Granny Grace appeared in her doorway inquiring about breakfast, but Cat told her she wasn't hungry. Lee had cooked for her, scrambled eggs and toast. And now she had the day off, and she looked forward to doing absolutely nothing.

Granny Grace walked over to her dresser and set the unwanted tray of food on top of it.

"I'm glad to hear that your doughboy made you breakfast," she remarked with a wry smile. "It's the least he could do."

Cat snorted at the word "doughboy."

"I'm not here to pry," Granny Grace said. "I had my own fun last night."

"Mr. All-for-the-Birds?"

"The same."

"So how much fun did you have?"

"Let's just say that the longliners have good equipment."

Cat laughed at her grandmother's characteristic brazenness. "Granny Grace! He's not still here, is he?"

"Oh, God, no," she replied. "Men are like strays. Invite them in and feed them, and they never leave."

"You're terrible!" Cat joked, lobbing a pillow at her.

"Pot calling the kettle black!" her grandmother retorted. "Or are you and Sergeant Swift planning nuptials?"

Granny Grace bent down to pick up the pillow and noticed something else on the floor, saving Cat from a complicated reply about how she didn't see Lee as a one-night stand but couldn't think of herself as a military wife either.

"What's this?" her grandmother asked. It was the doll that Cat had found in the condo. "Is this the doll you mentioned at the party last night?"

Cat sat up. "Yeah. It must have fallen off the bed."

Her grandmother had the doll in her hands, its dress flipped up over its head as a result of getting kicked around on the floor. "Oh!" she exclaimed, her face suddenly alarmed. She sat down on the edge of the bed and held out the doll to Cat. "Have you seen this?"

Someone had taken a ballpoint pen and scribbled so hard between the doll's legs that the pen had actually ripped through the cotton.

47

"No," she said. They both sat there looking at it for a minute.

"That's not good," Cat said.

"No, it's probably not," agreed Granny Grace. "But... we need more information."

"And I'm going to get it," Cat affirmed. "I'm officially on the case. Did Dave and Simon tell you? They're my first clients."

"Those devils!" Granny Grace replied. "They didn't even mention it." She grinned ear to ear. Then she turned serious. "We'll have to move more quickly on our plans than we thought. I'll have to formally reopen my practice. You'll have to be my employee."

This was something they had talked about before Cat had taken the job as security guard. In Washington State, Cat needed three years of experience to get her license or pass a test that she wasn't quite ready for and for which there was no manual. Passing it required knowledge of city, state, and federal laws and codes, the study of which had put her to sleep on the airplane.

"With the amount Simon and Dave gave you and your own savings, can you get bonded?"

Cat had already thought all of this through and was ready with the answer. "I have just enough, Granny Grace. It'll wipe out my savings, but it's just enough."

"You don't have to do this, Cat," she said. "We can wait. There's no rush."

"I'm ready, Granny. I don't want to wait. This is what I saved the money for, and with the five thousand match from Dave and Simon, it's all coming together. I want to do this."

Her grandmother smiled again ear to ear. "Now tell me everything that's happened in that condo building."

Cat told her about the break-in, the noises she heard, the doll. She also recounted the strange gosling dream.

"There's something going on there," observed her grandmother. "It's not tweakers. It's not just kids playing around. There's something going on."

Her grandmother's reaction echoed her own gut instinct on the matter. But here she was with a day off, and for now she wanted to lie around and do nothing.

"I'm glad you're already in your yoga clothes," Granny Grace said suddenly, brightening. "It's time for class."

"Noooooo," Cat groaned. "Can't I just hang out today?"

"You tell me, Cat. How was it over at Lee's? Did you dream with him? How'd that go?"

"I couldn't separate my mind from his," she confessed.

"Well, that might have something to do with not being able to separate yourself from his body, but maybe it's time to still the monkey chatter, eh?"

Cat could hardly argue.

Her grandmother was a star student and insisted on setting up in the front of the studio, a tall-ceilinged room painted orange, with skylights. "The energy is more powerful here," she said. "Plus, I have an unobstructed view of my *drishti*." She liked to stare at the center of a mural with a spiral in the middle and symbols for each of the world's major religions on the periphery—a cross for Christianity, a crescent for Islam, a Star of David for Judaism, a wheel for Buddhism, a yin-yang for Taoism, and the Hindu word for *om*.

This teacher was less woo-woo than some of the others, sparing them the talk about universal oneness that made Cat want to roll her eyes. But instead of getting right into the yoga, she started the class with meditation, and Cat had to fight the urge to leave. "Think of a time when you were a child and you felt completely at peace," the instructor intoned. Cat immediately thought of the pool in the apartment complex where her family lived when she was only four. She had a Styrofoam floatie that her mother would strap to her back, and she'd paddle around the pool all day long.

She took deep *ujjayi* breaths, as she'd been taught, and she felt much more at peace than she had in previous classes. She forgot about her back and hips, the discomfort of sitting cross-legged. She experienced the details of the pool with such clarity that it startled her: the smell of chlorine, the hum of the pool filter, a long-handled pool net, rusty around the rim. She felt her little girl's body, tiny and sharp under the water. She looked at her tanned hands, the little white half circles in her nails. Her fingers were pruned.

She lay back in the pool and let her spirit float up, out of her own body, toward the sun... And then she felt fear. She was falling. Her eyes jerked open. Her breathing quickened. She was sweating.

"Are you okay?" It was the teacher, crouched down beside her mat, whispering.

Cat nodded, going back to her breath. A long, slow breath in, her tongue relaxed, a reedy sound in the back of her throat. And then a long, slow breath out, through her nose.

She focused on the religious harmony mural in front of her. Because of the angle of the sun coming through the skylight above, the gold paint on the cross glinted in the light. Cat thought in that moment something that surprised her.

She missed going to church.

She had attended church with her family all her life. She'd gone to a Catholic university in the city where she grew up, and she'd often gone to mass with the students there; there was a very popular midnight mass on Sundays for students returning to campus for the week. She didn't consider herself anywhere near as devout as her mother, who could be found at the cathedral several days each week, involved in one activity or another, but Cat had found comfort there. She thought she could give it up, at least for the time being, since Granny Grace found little solace in Western religion, but maybe she couldn't. Maybe Cat needed it.

After class, they were having tea and rice-flour muffins at a little shop Granny Grace liked to frequent.

"So how was that?" her grandmother asked her. "I heard you get a little emotional."

She told her about the pool memory and of floating up and then falling.

"Ah, yes," said her grandmother. "Your ego finally surrendered."

"I think something's missing in my practice," Cat countered.

"Oh?" said Granny Grace. "Well, I was hoping to try tai chi next week."

"No. That's not what I need." Cat realized that sounded too harsh. "What I mean is, yeah, I'm happy to try tai chi, but I think we're missing the obvious."

Granny Grace looked at her quizzically.

"I'm Catholic, Granny Grace," Cat said. "In case you hadn't noticed."

"Well, but that's just your mother's doing. Now that you're an adult, you can follow your own path—"

Cat interrupted her. "Exactly. Now that I'm an adult, I can follow my own path. Not my mother's. But not yours, either."

Her grandmother looked taken aback. There was a long silence in which she regarded the tea leaves floating at the bottom of the pot in front of them.

"Do you still want my help?" Granny Grace asked, raising her hard eyes to meet Cat's.

Cat sighed and took her grandmother's hand. "Of course I do. I need your help more than ever now. But I need to bring some of my old life along on the journey."

Her grandmother's eyes softened. She squeezed Cat's hand. "You'll have to do all the integration on your own," she said. "The pope and I parted ways a long time ago. I have no intention of going back."

"I get that. I do."

Granny Grace smiled. "I'll do anything I can to help you. Will you keep up with the yoga and meditation?"

"Yes," Cat agreed. "But I also need to find a church."

"Wait a minute," Granny Grace said. "Why didn't I think about it before? Simon's still clinging to his Catholicism." She stopped, looking a bit guilty. "Let me rephrase that. *Simon continues to worship as a Catholic.* He attends a very liberal-minded church on Capitol Hill. You should try it. They're known for their music. That's how he got started in the Seattle Men's Choir."

As it was Saturday, Granny Grace immediately got Simon on the phone, and arrangements were made for Cat to accompany him to church on Sunday.

That morning, Lee sent her a text message: *Kitty Cat, I'll be back.* He was on his way to Virginia.

The cathedral where Simon worshipped was a beautiful Romanesque stone building with a rotunda, the exterior covered in green tile that brightened when it rained. Cat felt a rush of giddy homesickness as they walked through the entrance. There was the familiar hush as the haphazard noises from the street were replaced by reverent silence. Her heels clipped on the marble floor. She smelled incense, someone's perfume. It was White Shoulders, her mother's usual fragrance. Mercy would be proud of her attending mass, Cat thought, though she wasn't doing this for her benefit. Cat dipped her fingers into the holy water font and crossed herself with it. Simon did the same. Together they walked in and took a seat near the front.

"This church is very committed to public service," he whispered to her, gesturing toward a photo gallery on the side wall. "Those are pictures of the ministry's work helping to repatriate Hmong refugees. They also have a renowned program helping street kids here in Seattle." When Cat asked, Simon explained that the Hmong people had fled Laos during the civil war.

To Cat's surprise, a woman gave not only the two liturgical readings, which would be common enough, but also the gospel. For the homily, she was joined by the priest, and the two of them delivered it together, taking turns in a sort of dramatic reading style. It was the priest, however, who performed the Eucharist. The woman spoke well; it was obvious that she had put a great deal of thought into both what she would say about the biblical readings and how she would deliver them. She spoke of Jesus' death as a "cosmic event." This was God's dramatic act to fight evil in the world—a sacrifice, not a violent battle. Cat had never thought of God's sacrifice of Jesus as part of a cosmic battle between good and evil. She wondered then if Granny Grace believed in the existence of evil in the world. Most likely not; none of the meditation or yoga teachers had ever mentioned evil. Their work seemed to center on how to de-stress and counter one's ego, not how to respond to acts of pure, unmitigated evil committed by human beings.

Cat remembered a nightmare she had had, her own this time, the night of September 11, 2001. Jesus appeared before her, a man wearing blue jeans. He was waving a terry-cloth towel above his head printed with the American flag.

"Evil is alive and living in the hearts of men," he warned. She'd awakened, her heart filled with pain and fear. Her face was wet; she'd been crying. It was a heady dream for an eleven-year-old to have, and it stayed with her.

After the first reading, there was a psalm for the congregation to recite. This verse reverberated through Cat, as it captured exactly how she felt: "Give me back the joy of your salvation, and a willing spirit sustain in me."

The music *was* good: a local singer-songwriter performing with her band. She sang a hymn called "Spirit Blowing Through Creation," her voice husky. By the end of the performance, she had the congregation on their feet clapping and singing along with her. When Cat turned to give the sign of peace to Simon, he ignored her outstretched hand and gave her a sweet bear hug instead.

Chapter 6

Cat felt wet. Her clothing was damp and clinging to her body. For a split second she thought she was a little girl again, waking from having wet the bed. She opened her eyes to find herself in an adult man's body, lying in a puddle of water. The ground around her was soggy and had been torn up. Puddles of mud and damp earth surrounded her. She was completely alone, no signs of life anywhere. All she could see in any direction was the muddy, torn-up earth and then a thick, wet fog in the distance.

She stood and looked at herself. She was so covered in mud she could barely make out that she was wearing a man's suit. In her hand was a little doll, an angel with a harp, likewise covered in mud. Its blond hair was streaked with grime, the halo a tarnished gold wire. She stared at her hands: they were delicate, not calloused from hard labor, but they were a man's hands, the fingernails bitten to the quick. Fear crept up in her, fear that she'd get hypothermia out here in her bare feet, and fear that she didn't know where she was or where to go. But was this her fear, or the dreamer's? She tried separating her own emotions from his, tuning in deeply. She began to feel the loopy edges of her own fear: unfamiliarity, aloneness, cold. Out beyond that were the jagged edges of his. It felt like shards of glass, his fear; it was cold and irrational, and it spun inside a terrible hatred of all this dirt and squalor.

He was in control; she was just along for the ride. The two of them, the man and Cat riding sidesaddle to his consciousness, peered into the horizon and made out the tip of a roof in the distance, showing through the fog.

They walked in that direction, the muddy ground sucking at their feet and making them unsteady as they walked. There was a sudden movement out of the corner of their eye, and they turned quickly to see the tail of a snake disappearing into a hole in the ground. So there was life out here, Cat thought. But it was her own thought, not his.

And it wasn't just one life. It was many. There were more holes, more snakes. Hundreds of them, all around them. One darted toward their ankle to strike, and they jumped just in time to avoid it.

The building loomed into view. It was a rough shack, like ones she'd seen on farms back home. They raced to the door, pulled it open, jumped inside, and slammed the door shut with both hands.

Dust fell from the ceiling and onto their head. Still pressing against the door as if the snakes outside could burst through, they peered side to side in the dimly lit room. Light came in only from one smudged window and the cracks between the rough-hewn boards that made up the walls. A thick layer of grime lay over everything. There was a bed on one side, a mass of rumpled yellow sheets piled in the middle of a soiled mattress. On the other side was what passed for a kitchen—a tiny sink overflowing with dirty dishes. Bugs crawled across the pans, plates, and the filthy drain board.

They let go of the door, satisfied that it would not swing open on its own, and turned around. What Cat saw made her react with surprise, but her dreamer had seen it before; she could feel the contented recognition in him. This is what he'd come here for. This would make everything okay again. It was a glossy white cabinet with a tall spire at the top, in the style of an old-fashioned rural church. The roof of the shack slanted upward to double the height on that side to make room for the spire.

She didn't know what to make of it. It was a beautiful, elaborate cabinet showing fine craftsmanship, completely out of place in this shack. The cabinet was locked, but the man had the key in his pocket. He pulled it out, inserted it into the lock, turned, and opened both doors.

Behind it were dozens of wooden cubbyholes, each about two feet wide by two feet tall and housing a porcelain doll dressed as an angel.

Cat could feel the heat of a red wall of fire and need inside him raging toward the dolls in the cabinet. There was a strong feeling of ownership and also responsibility. It was up to him to deliver them from evil. It was up to him to make sure they didn't sin. He was their keeper; he would make them obey the will of the Lord. The temptations were so raw. The dark, powerful sins of the flesh could tear a little girl to pieces inside until she let evil overcome her, making her hungry, making her spread her legs and let her juices flow, beckoning men with her ripe, red—

Cat recoiled against the force of the man's roiling emotions, knocking herself back. She hit the door behind her, hard. And there was the man in front of her; she could see his lean back in the muddy suit. She'd done it. She was out of him. He stood there gazing at his angels. He seemed unaware of Cat's presence.

"My pretty little angels," the man said in a voice with a lovely cadence that sounded familiar to her. "So perfect," he intoned, his voice reverent. "So clean."

He looked at the muddy angel in his hand, sighed, and walked over to the sink overflowing with dishes.

"Auntie never cleans this place," he muttered. "She's hardly ever here. Always out with her men." One by one, he took the dishes and threw them to the floor, where they shattered, the bugs scattering under the floorboards. Once the sink was empty, he washed the mud from the angel. Then he walked her to the white cabinet and set her into place. He stood there with his arms crossed, admiring his work. Then suddenly he stopped, pointing to two cubbyholes near the top left. They were empty.

"Those two are missing," he cried, his voice growing angry and hard. "Sherrie and the girl. They're supposed to be here." For the first time he turned and looked at Cat directly, but his eyes didn't seem to register that he saw her. She must be invisible to him, she realized. His face looked familiar to her, as if she'd seen him before, but his eyes were black, like onyx stones. His was the emptiest gaze Cat had ever seen. She expected him to come unhinged, to be angry to the point of losing control, but he did not; in fact, he seemed to shrink into himself like a quasar, the focus pulled in more tightly. With an even, heavy tone, he announced, "I need to get them back."

Cat woke, this time fully aware that she had been dreaming and with the presence of mind to know what she needed to do. It wasn't time for her rounds, but she left the hut anyway, taking her backpack and her flashlight with her.

She'd been waiting for this moment for days.

Cat walked to the back of the building and took the bolt cutters out of her backpack. In a matter of seconds, she'd cut the newly secured padlock and was inside the building. She allowed her eyes some time to adjust to the light, keeping her flashlight doused. She knew exactly where to go—to the second floor. She walked quietly up the stairs, feeling her way as she went.

She crept softly, listening until she heard breathing. There was definitely someone in here. Her dreamer!

She stepped slowly, her hand on the flashlight.

The room was darker than the hallway had been. Someone had papered the window, blocking out light from the streetlights, the moon, and the stars. She could make out a very large figure covered in blankets on a makeshift bed, plywood under a cheap mattress, and piles of clothes and other belongings strewn throughout the room.

The element of surprise would be to her advantage this time. There was no way she was going to let her trespasser get away. She crept up to the bed. Her sleeper had his back to her and the blankets up over his head. Cat took a deep, calming breath and then reached out for the top of the blanket.

She pulled the blanket down, shining the flashlight on her sleeper, and saw not one head, but two. A woman and a little girl. Cat remembered a name in rainbow-colored letters on a pink roller bag: R-U-T-H. It was the girl from the plane, the one who'd dreamed of a devil with a pitchfork.

Cat startled them both awake, the woman reacting first in horror and then surprise, as if she expected to be caught, but not by Cat. The girl opened her mouth as if to scream, but the mother instinctively clamped her hand over her mouth. "Shh!" she hissed. "It's okay. Don't yell."

"Who are you? What are you doing here?" Cat demanded.

The woman sat up on the makeshift bed, gathering the blanket around her for warmth. Her attention was on the girl. "Sh, sh," she said, rocking the girl in her arms, her hand still clamped around her mouth. "It's okay. No screaming. It's okay." The girl slowly quieted down, but big tears flowed from her shut eyes. Cat felt bad.

"I'm sorry," she said. "I didn't mean to upset her. But you're—" Cat struggled to define the exact offense these two innocuous people could possibly be charged with committing. "Trespassing," she settled on, though the word rang out in the dim room as a hollow accusation.

"Don't turn us in," the woman said. "Please. We're homeless."

Cat looked around the room. They didn't have much, but there was a space heater and a cell phone plugged into a plateless wall socket. The builders had wired the building for electricity before the project was halted, though no light fixtures had yet been installed. If they were homeless, they were either really good at scavenging, or someone was helping them. A cell phone would need a billing address. Cat scanned the pairs of shoes lined up on one side of the wall. The woman's were brand-new, high-end hiking shoes, and their neatly folded clothes looked well made and new as well. Plus, she knew these were the people she saw on the plane. She needed no confirmation, for the girl's dark, sad look was burned into her memory, and there was the pink roller bag with R-U-T-H in rainbow lettering across the front.

"I saw you on the plane," Cat said. "From St. Louis."

The woman's eyes widened a moment in fear and then narrowed. "No, you didn't," she said. "It must be a mistake. I'm from Seattle. I'm homeless... My husband left us, and I lost my job. I found this building and knew I could stay here for a while. Please... don't tell anyone we're here."

"We need to get you out of here. We need to get you better... accommodations." Cat couldn't believe she'd just used the word "accommodations," as if this were a resort.

"No," the woman refused. "The shelters are full up. There's nowhere for us to go. We're safer here. We have food." She gestured toward a stack of canned beans and vegetables on a wooden construction spool in the corner, acting as a kitchen table. There was a backpacking stove and several bottles of fuel. The woman was certainly prepared.

Cat sat back on her heels and sighed. "If they find you, I could lose my job," she said.

"I won't mention you. You didn't know we were here."

There was something earnest in the woman's face, not to mention desperate, that made Cat decide to help her even though she knew the woman was lying.

"Okay," Cat agreed. "But I want to try to help you. Maybe a church—"

"No!" the woman cried out violently. "Not a church. I won't go to a church."

"Sorry," Cat apologized, wary. This woman was obviously in some dire emotional situation. Cat would have to tread lightly to not set her off.

The girl spoke up then. "The church people are weird. But I like the singing. I like baby Jesus."

"Sh..." the mother said, attempting to rock her to sleep. "She needs her rest," the woman explained to Cat.

"This is no place for a kid," Cat remarked. "I can't leave you here."

"We won't be here that long," the woman said. "We're waiting for my sister. She's taking us to Canada. Please..."

Her words prickled Cat's memory banks. The gosling. A mother goose. Canadian geese, heading north. She'd slipped into this woman's dream.

But the angel dreamer—that was someone else, and he was still nearby, possibly still asleep. She needed to find him.

"All right," Cat said, sighing. "I'll let you stay here the rest of tonight, but we have to come up with a better solution than this."

The woman narrowed her eyes at her. "You don't understand. This is the best solution for us. We're so close."

The girl had already fallen back to sleep in her mother's arms. Cat replied, "I'll check on you in the morning." Then, unsure that it was the right thing to do, she left them there, in their makeshift bed.

She walked down the stairs, out of the condo building, and back out to the street. She scanned the nearby buildings. The neighborhood was zoned for mixed-use, but most of what was here wasn't livable space but office buildings, shops, and restaurants. The city had been actively trying to mix the use in the neighborhood, encouraging more residential units so more people could live and work in close proximity. But the initiative had been halted by the real estate market collapse, the Fletcher-Bander project being just one example. There were a few other stalled projects. Behind the condo was an enormous pit in the ground where a builder had begun digging a sub-level parking garage. On either side of the condo site were half-empty commercial real estate buildings with retail spaces at street level, "for lease" signs in their windows.

So a sleeper would be too far down the street for Cat to be able to slip into his dream, or in an apartment building too close to a hundred other dreamers—unless, like she'd thought before, he were in a car.

She scanned up and down the rows of parked cars. Again, nothing stood out to her. Slowly, she walked past them, looking carefully for anything out of the ordinary. There was a Texas plate on a brand-new red Prius that caused her a split-second of excitement, but the car was utterly empty, and clean, too: nothing but a Starbucks coffee cup in the drink holder to show it had been recently driven.

There were more than the average neighborhood's share of Priuses, a few Hondas, and a couple of the newer domestic cars. Then she noticed him: a figure sitting in a white sedan, asleep in the front seat, as if he'd been waiting for someone and dozed off. She couldn't quite make out what he looked like, but it was a man. She glanced at her cell phone to check the time. It was 4:05 am. What was he doing out here?

She debated what to do. It wasn't exactly her jurisdiction. He wasn't on the condo property, and she had no reason to call the cops on him, as it wasn't against the law to sit in a car. But the fact that he was sleeping in a car in this area at this time of night was suspicious. She wanted to at least get a better look at the guy, see if he was the one in the dream. She crept toward the car, quietly, hoping he'd remain asleep.

The car looked nondescript, like a rental, but maybe he was just the type not to put any bumper stickers or other identifiers on his vehicle. Rental agencies didn't mark cars as theirs in order to deter theft on tourists, so rentals tended to blend in, making it harder for law enforcement to identify them. The telltale sign of a rental is a bar code sticker either on the driver's side door or the windshield. If she had an in with the agency, she could ask them to run the bar code to tell her the name of the renter. If she were a cop, she could run the plates, but that wasn't an option, obviously. Granny Grace had friends on the force, but Cat couldn't take the time to get that going and risk losing her dreamer. She moved quietly around to the driver's side, taking care not to let her shadow, cast by the streetlight behind her, fall across his face.

And what a face it was. She didn't have to see his eyes to know this was her dreamer. He was unshaven, as if he'd been on the road a while and neglecting the razor. There were lines running down from the sides of his nose to his jaw line. His chin had a cleft, too deep to be considered a dimple. His eyebrows had been trimmed professionally in the past, she could tell, but they were beginning to grow strays again. He had sandy brown hair, slicked back with gel. On the seat next to him were a laptop computer, a cell phone, and his wristwatch, a gold metal band.

Cat looked down at her M&O-issued attire: a white shirt with M&O Security emblazoned in red on a patch over her right pocket. It would have to do. She took the flashlight off her utility belt and tapped his window with it.

The man startled awake and squinted in the beam of the flashlight. He rolled his window down.

"Yes? Can I help you?" he asked.

"I'm with a security firm patrolling these buildings," said Cat. "Mind telling me what you're doing out here at this time of night?"

"As a matter of fact, I do mind," he replied, peering up at her. His eyes were blue-grey, not black as they'd been in the dream. He was wearing a sport coat, a gold cross pinned to the lapel. "It's a free country. And I don't have to explain myself to a rent-a-cop."

Cat faltered. He did have a point. But she pressed on.

"I'm supposed to report any suspicious behavior to management," she declared. "And you're looking pretty suspicious. Unless you've got a good reason for sleeping out here in your car at this time of night, I'll have to report you."

The man appeared to regain his composure, and Cat got the impression she was watching him put on a mask as his demeanor suddenly changed.

"I'm sorry I snapped at you, miss. You woke me up, and I was a little crabby. I hadn't meant to fall asleep. I was waiting for a friend who lives in the apartment building down the street, and I guess he's taking his sweet time. We were going to get an early breakfast and then hit the links at the country club. It opens at five thirty. We like to get started when the sun comes up."

She knew his story was a lie, as the apartment building he waved to was barely occupied, with huge orange signs out front begging for tenants, and there were plenty of empty spots closer to it where he could have chosen to park.

"It's okay," Cat told him. "I'm no angel when someone wakes me up, either." The deep wrinkle on the left side of the man's face twitched when Cat said "angel."

"Sorry to bother you," she finished, stepping back.

"No matter," the man said, rolling up his window. He started his car and pulled out of the space. He paused at the apartment building, as if making a show of contacting his errant golf buddy, and then drove away.

Cat had the license plate: TGH 756. She went back to the guard booth and called Granny Grace. "Sorry to call you so early, Gran," she apologized. "I need one of your old friends at the Seattle PD to run a plate."

"Ha!" Granny Grace exclaimed. "Grace Detective Agency is back in business!"

"Can you get someone to run it right away?" Cat asked. "I was in this guy's dream, and he was in a car outside the condo building. There's a woman and a girl sleeping in the condo, Gran. I had to leave them there—"

"Excuse me? What are you talking about?"

"They won't budge. They say they're homeless, but I saw the girl on the plane to St. Louis, I know I did. She was the one in the dream."

"Wait. Slow down, Cat," Granny Grace said.

"We don't have much time, Gran. Get someone to run that plate. I've got to find out who that guy in the car was. I think he's after the girl. Gran, what if he's why she scribbled on that Raggedy Ann doll?!"

"Oh, God, Cat." Granny Grace was silent for a beat.

"My shift doesn't end for a couple of hours. I'll keep watch on them while you have someone run the plate."

Cat reassured Granny Grace that the girl and her mother had heat, blankets, food, and water. She also gave her the details of her interaction with the man in the car. Then she hung up the phone and sighed deeply.

She toyed briefly with the idea of bringing Mr. M&O into her confidence about their hidden condo inhabitants. His real name was Greg Swenson, she'd found out after their first encounter, and he seemed like a decent guy. But she didn't know him well enough, didn't know if she could trust him. He would most likely tell Tony, who would turn the mother and daughter out, or worse, turn them over to the police for breaking and entering. She couldn't let that happen. Besides, this was officially her first case, and she wanted to solve it herself.

Cat went back to her guard booth.

Two hours later, her phone rang. "I've got a lead on our car sleeper," said Granny Grace. "The car is registered to Dobson Rental. So unless he likes to rent cars for his morning golf trips, you're right, Cat, he's definitely lying."

"Thanks, Gran," Cat said. "My shift's about over, and I think I better head to Dobson. But first I'm going to talk to the woman and girl one more time and see if I can get them to move."

"Good idea," replied Granny Grace. "You probably spooked your stalker, though. He won't be back anytime soon."

"Let's hope not," Cat said. She hung up, grabbed her flashlight, and went back to the condo.

Inside, the girl was asleep in her mother's arms, but her mother was wide awake. Cat found her sitting up in the makeshift bed, a desperate look on her face.

"What do you want?" she whispered at Cat.

"I just want to talk," Cat said, keeping her voice low so as not to wake the girl. She motioned to the hallway. The woman gingerly moved her daughter off her lap and tucked her into bed without waking her.

"Please," the woman pleaded with Cat. "I asked you to leave us alone."

"Is someone after you?" Cat asked.

The woman didn't even flinch. "No. Of course not. Why would you say that?"

"Because I found some guy in his car out there on the street. It seemed like he was looking for someone."

This time the woman's face registered a shiver of alarm. "My ex," she hissed. "He's dangerous. Did you tell him we're here?"

"No, of course not," Cat responded. "Tell me who he is. I'll protect you."

The woman scoffed. "Protect me? If anything, you're going to put me and my daughter in danger. So I suggest you forget we're here and go on about your business."

Cat was at a loss for what to say to convince this woman to leave.

"I'll call my sister," the woman said. "She'll help me. Please, leave us alone. We don't need you meddling."

Cat tried to reason with the woman a few more rounds, but she wouldn't budge. She refused to leave the condo, and Cat couldn't get her to give any more information about her ex-husband.

It would soon be time for Cat's shift change, so reluctantly she left the woman behind and headed back to the guard booth. She put a call in over the radio to say she'd found the lock on the condo building busted. Greg Swenson intercepted her call.

"Broken, you say?" He sounded concerned and angrier than he had in the past. Gone were the Nancy Drew jokes. "You didn't try to inspect the building by yourself again, did you?"

She swallowed hard and decided to lie, abiding by the mother's wishes to keep their presence a secret. "Of course not," she said. "I know how to follow orders."

"That's good. I'm on my way over there now to sub for your replacement, who's called in sick once again. I'll check it out myself."

After they signed off, Cat found the number for Dobson Rental on her smart phone and called. It was too early; the office was still closed. She would probably have better results if she went there in person. However, she couldn't show up at the rental agency wearing her M&O uniform. She'd use her new PI credentials to get the rental company to tell her who that man was.

Greg got to the guard booth lickety-split, and Cat felt somewhat relieved that it would be him in the booth and fixing the lock, instead of the usual lackey, a woman who showed up with a box of donuts and fuzzy pink headphones that looked like earmuffs—when she did show up, that is.

Still, it was hard for Cat to leave the condo site. She had to fight her instincts to head up there, grab Ruthie and her mother, and take them to Granny Grace's, where they'd be safer. But would they? Her logic told her she needed to find out more before acting. Besides, that woman was clearly not going to trust Cat.

She arrived home to find Granny Grace in the kitchen with the longliner, who had clearly spent the night. So much for men being like stray cats, she thought. She only had time for polite pleasantries before heading to her room to change. Cat dressed hurriedly, glad that Granny Grace had been such a good influence on her wardrobe. She chose the most intimidating look she could muster.

Her grandmother rapped on the door just then, and Cat let her in long enough to brief her on more of the morning's events.

"Remember to approach them with confidence," Granny Grace instructed. "If you believe you're entitled to X and demand X, you'll get it."

As soon as it opened at 8 a.m., Cat walked into the office of Dobson Rental wearing a smart pants suit, her hair pulled back in a bun. She presented her PI license to the guy behind the counter, who thoughtfully tugged at his lip ring as he contemplated the implications of giving Cat what she asked for—information on who rented one of their cars.

"Never seen one of these before," he said. "Better check with the boss-o." He went behind the wall behind the counter, disappearing for a full five minutes. Then out came a gentleman whose white Dobson Rental shirt stretched over sizeable man breasts. Lip Ring followed him, appearing for all intents and purposes like the boy who went and got his father to deal with the grown-ups for him.

"Ma'am, I'm happy to give you information," said the boss. "That is, if my customer is being investigated for a crime, and the police are involved. Is that the case?"

"Not exactly," said Cat. "But he was questioned outside an abandoned building where there had been a recent break-in. He was sitting in your rental vehicle but led questioners to believe it was his personal vehicle." Cat didn't feel it was necessary to say who did the questioning, and implying that the rental vehicle could potentially have been used in a crime might give the manager reason enough to reveal the name.

He stared at Cat for a full minute as if turning the problem over in his mind and then sighed. "All right. I'll give you his name, driver's license number, and home address. But I can't give you anything else. His payment information is off limits."

"Of course," Cat said, keeping her calm demeanor. But inside, she was shouting, "Uh-huh! That's how we do this thing! I'm a PI now, so suck it!"

After a few minutes, the boss came back out with a file folder full of printouts from their computer system.

"It's funny," he told her. "Someone else just called asking about this same car. He really must be up to something."

Cat wasn't sure what to make of that. Maybe he'd got into something else while using the rental car? At any rate, she had her dreamer's name, Jim Plantation, and his address, which was... wait a second. He lived in southern Illinois, near her hometown, St. Louis. The hair on the back of her neck stood up. Could this be *the* Jim Plantation? Jim Plantation of Plantation Christian Revival Church was powerful, wealthy, and well respected, having run one of the largest, most successful evangelical churches in the Midwest. Not at all the kind of man you'd expect to be caught in a lie on a Seattle street in the middle of the night.

She thanked the two men at Dobson Rental and bolted out of their office.

Cat drove Siddhartha as fast as she could back to the condo site. She pulled around back instead of going past the guard booth in front, where she knew Greg would be. He hadn't yet replaced the lock. With a sinking feeling in her gut, she said a silent prayer that her actions hadn't placed the girl and her mother in danger. Even with Greg in the booth, it felt to Cat now that she'd left them all too vulnerable.

Cat ran inside, took the steps two at a time, and burst into their room.

It was empty. No shoes, no pink roller bag, no makeshift bed. She'd been too late. Jim Plantation had recovered his missing angels. Cat had practically turned them over to him.

Scanning the length of the room, she stepped on something: a child's hair barrette, pink and glittery. She picked it up and stuffed it into her pocket.

Searching up and down for signs of anything—Jim Plantation's rental car, the mother and girl—she went back out to the street. There was nothing. Greg appeared in the doorway to the booth.

"What are you doing back here, and so dressed up? Job interview?" he asked, but he wasn't smiling.

"Did you see anything?!" she yelled. "Did you see anyone head into the condo building?"

"Nope," said Greg. "This place has been deader than a doornail. I was getting ready to fix that lock, just to give myself something to do."

"They're gone," Cat cried, realizing as she spoke that she was spiraling out of control. "There were people in that building, Greg. And now they're gone!"

"Cat, what are you talking about?"

"They're gone, Greg! He took them! You let him take them!"

He stepped toward her. She shoved him away, beating against his broad chest, knowing what she was doing was all wrong. But she couldn't stop. It felt too close in the booth, and she was so angry at herself, and she directed all that anger at Greg, beating on his chest with her fists. He was staring her down with an intensity that intimidated her, but he kept his arms at his sides, maintained his calm.

"Cat," he said. "Stop."

She put her arms down.

He spoke again, his voice measured. "Tell me the truth. Did you bust the lock on the building?"

Something inside her broke under his gaze, and she admitted, "Yes."

He looked away from her. After a few tense seconds, he returned his gaze to her and said, "You're fired."

Stunned, Cat backed out of the booth. She turned around and ran away from him, back to her car. She had to get away from him, get away from that place. She drove in a blur of tears and panic but managed to get home in one piece.

As soon as she parked Siddhartha in the garage, she slumped over the steering wheel, feeling defeated before she'd even begun. Her first PI case, and she not only blew it, but she possibly put a little girl in danger. And to top it off, she'd been fired from her lowly job as a rent-a-cop.

After a while, she felt a hand on her shoulder. Granny Grace.

"I didn't hear you come in," Cat said.

"You were sobbing too loudly."

"It's all a mess, Granny Grace. Maybe I'm not cut out for this."

"Come, dear. Let's go inside, have some tea, and you can tell me what's happened."

Cat let Granny Grace lead her inside. They sat at the thick wooden table with bench seats in the Terra Cotta Cocina. She sat in silence, collecting herself, while Granny Grace heated the kettle and then poured it over tea in an antique Chinese pot. She set two matching red ceramic teacups down on the table.

"Now, what did you find out at Dobson Rental?"

Cat told Granny Grace everything. Her grandmother listened intently, asking questions all the way. When Cat further explained that the mother and the girl were the same people she saw on the plane, Granny Grace exclaimed, "Serendipity! Or is it fate? Either way, it's a heck of a coincidence, Cat. Seattle's just one gigantic small town—our six degrees of separation are only three. But that's really something. One might think you were meant to take this case."

"Just so I could fuck it up?!" Cat wailed.

"You haven't gotten to that part yet," Granny said calmly. "Tell me what happened."

She told her the rest. Granny Grace heard her out, lips pursing when Cat described leaving the mother and girl behind in the condo building and her mouth shifting to an outright frown when she described returning to find them gone.

"What do I do next, Granny?" she asked.

"Well, what do you think you should do?"

Cat traced the wood grain in the tabletop with her fingernail. She saw herself on a plane heading home.

"Fly to St. Louis," she said.

"You're going to throw in the towel already?"

"No. I need to track them down. I think he's taking them back to St. Louis, back home."

"Are you sure this isn't just a way to retreat back to your own home?"

"I'm sure. Think about it," Cat speculated. "He's a respectable member of the community, a celebrity, even. He's got enough of a hold on his wife and kid that they had to go into hiding to get away from him. So, back in his possession, they'll be made to play along. That's how it works. He's in control."

65

Granny Grace's face broke into a look of pride. "You're right, Cat. As much as I hate to see you leave, I think you're right. However, you're still working for Simon and Dave. It'll be their decision for you to continue the case."

Cat didn't want to waste any time. She set up a meeting with her clients for that afternoon. Both men were alarmed to hear that a woman and girl had been hiding out in their half-finished building. They made Cat tell them all the details to make sure the girl was okay, that the two weren't cold or hungry. She assured them that they had been fine.

"Maybe we should just call the police in Illinois," Simon suggested.

"What would you tell them?" asked Cat. "There's no proof of anything. You know how the domestic abuse dynamics work. If you can even persuade the police to go over to Plantation's house, he'll deny everything, and so will the girl's mother. She's clearly terrified of him, and he has all the power. Let me go back there. I'll find them and help them get somewhere safe first before involving the police."

"She's right," agreed Dave, whose work with domestic abuse cases gave him insight. "Cat's got a better chance of helping them if she goes there herself."

"I'll stay with my parents," Cat told them. "I don't need anything more from you guys. Your retainer was enough."

"It's not a money issue," explained Dave. "In fact, I bet Simon will agree with me when I say we have no problem paying for your flight and expenses while there. It's your safety we're concerned about. This case just escalated into something else."

Granny Grace was about to speak, but Cat interrupted her. "But this is the something else I'm meant to do," she insisted.

There was a long silence as the four of them looked at Cat. They seemed to be regarding her with new eyes.

"Well, it's settled then," Simon said. "You're going to St. Louis."

Chapter 7

C at was wearing an orange sari and dancing in a Bollywood number around an extravagantly dressed woman on an elephant-shaped dais. Along for the ride in this dream, Cat did not possess these kinds of dance moves herself, so she stayed fused with the dreamer and enjoyed the spectacle.

A man in a gold Nehru jacket passed out orange-and-purple-swirled lollipops that were also sparklers. Cat danced with the lollipop, sparks flying in the air around her as she moved, creating orange and purple tracers in the air. Then she licked the lollipop, and an incredible taste, like oranges and grapes and honey melded into one, swirled across her tongue. When she began to sing, sparks flew out of her mouth.

Then a bad guy in black clothes and an evil monkey face jumped into the middle of the dance floor, smoke pouring out of his eyes. The smoke overtook Cat, and she woke up, coughing.

She'd fallen asleep on the long flight to St. Louis, and she had no idea whose crazy dream she'd been in this time. There were too many people coughing around her, and a quick glance in all directions told her nothing about who might have dreamed a Bollywood opera.

Sometimes dreams were like that. Just strange trips of the mind.

It'd been only three months since she'd left St. Louis, but she felt years older. In that short amount of time, she'd made the transition from college girl to young adult. She'd got herself licensed as a PI. She'd had a tryst with an old flame, she'd taken up yoga and meditation, and she'd found her own church. Even the way she dressed had changed. Gone were the hoodie and jeans. She was wearing leggings, quality leather boots, a tunic with a knit scarf around her neck, and gold hoop earrings. Her hair was still in a ponytail, but it was neater and secured with a stylish clip.

Her mother met her at the airport this time, wearing a necklace that had been a Christmas gift from Cat, a silver strand with an angel charm. That she was wearing the necklace signaled to Cat a gesture of peace, as they'd fought bitterly before Cat left for Seattle and hadn't really spoken since.

Whether the wearing of the angel necklace was a conscious ploy to signal a truce to her daughter or a subconscious tell that she missed her, Mercy did seem genuinely happy to see Cat. There were tears in her mother's eyes when she hugged her.

"You look so different," her mother commented. "Cosmopolitan."

Cat felt oddly guilty for straying so far from the girl her mother had said good-bye to, especially since Mercy hadn't approved of Cat's decision to move to Seattle and take over Granny Grace's PI business.

"I guess," Cat said awkwardly. "These clothes are new."

"Well, you look nice," her mother remarked. "Taller, even."

"Thanks," Cat replied. "It's probably just the boots." She turned her ankle to show the low heels.

They walked in silence to the baggage claim. "So how's your grandmother? Still acting as if she's twenty-nine?"

"Eighteen, more like it," Cat joked, just to show she was on her mother's side for now in the perpetual Cold War between Mercy and Granny Grace.

Her mother smiled at that. "Dragging you to her New Age pagan classes, is she?"

"There's a little of that," Cat admitted. "But I've found a good church, a Catholic one."

Her mother brightened further. "You don't say? Well, I'm very happy to hear that, Cat. Very, very happy."

The ride home with her mother was many shades different from the dramatic convertible ride she'd taken with Granny Grace in early May. It was her mother's car, and not Granny Grace's, that would seem to belong to the older of the two. The silver-grey Chevy Impala was a four-door sedan, very sedate. Her mother's careful reserve broke down once they were in the car, though.

"So why haven't you called?" she asked accusatorily. "It's been three months."

Cat sighed. "I don't know, Mom. Maybe it was the last thing you said to me. 'This PI thing is a fantasy' isn't exactly a swell send-off."

"You know I didn't mean it." Her mother drove cautiously and carefully, obeying the speed limits and the traffic lights, not cavalierly, the way Granny Grace did. Her hands on the steering wheel were manicured but bore clear polish.

Cat said nothing. The truth was, her mother *had* meant it.

"I just don't want you to do anything dangerous. Or stupid. Not that you're stupid. But your grandmother—"

"I'm not Granny Grace, Mom."

"I know. But she lacks strong values. She certainly wasn't always the best mother for me. I know you tend to idolize her, but you didn't get dragged all over the country like I did, always chasing some crazy case she was working on. A different school every year, always having to leave my friends, no stability... And she's been a bad influence on you in the past."

Her mother was referring to the summer Cat tried marijuana for the first time. "Are you going to drag that old saw out of the shed now? Jeez, Mom. That was a million years ago. I don't regret the experience, and all Granny Grace did was tell me the truth. She lets me decide for myself."

"And I don't?"

Cat was steaming mad but trying desperately to keep their argument from spiraling out of control. No matter what she did, she always seemed to push her mother's buttons, and vice versa.

"Not then you didn't, Mom. I was sixteen, but I was still your baby. I get it."

"She had no right."

Cat softened her tone. "All she did was answer my questions. I'm the one who decided to give it a try."

Cat remembered the house party she'd gone to with her friends in Seattle, the skunky smell of the pot, like her grandmother's incense. But it had burned her throat, made her eyes itch. And hours later she raided Granny Grace's cupboard, frustratingly trying to quell her munchies with rice cakes slathered in soy nut butter. Granny Grace had heard her rummaging around and come to investigate, quickly guessing what state Cat was in. And respecting Mercy's wishes, she'd had to fink on Cat that summer, which meant Cat had to start her junior year in high school on restriction.

It was her mother's turn to sit in silence, and Cat let her. She was noticing St. Louis pass by outside the window. The city was far older and arguably much more architecturally interesting than Seattle, where it seemed as if nothing—outside of Granny Grace's rare Victorian—had been built before the 1960s. She was glad her parents had remained in the city proper rather than moving out to the suburbs like a lot of other people.

They drove a while in silence, her mother navigating the inner and outer highway loops to get them from the airport out in the suburbs into the heart of the city. Cat caught her first glimpse of the Gateway Arch, reflecting the sun in flashes of bright light as they moved toward it. Apologies to the Space Needle, she thought, but the arch was the most elegant of all public monuments.

"So what are you doing back here, Cat?" her mother suddenly asked. "It's a bit soon for a visit, especially since you haven't even called."

"I was homesick," she answered. It was true, if she wanted to be honest with herself, just not the whole truth.

Her mother glanced at her suspiciously. "You were homesick. Right. I mean, sure, I believe that, but unless you swung some kind of job out there I don't know about, there's more to this visit than that, Cat. We're not the kind of people who can afford to fly half-way across the country to cure a passing bout of homesickness."

"Okay. Fine. I'm investigating a case. I can't tell you more than that."

"Oh, really. Well, why did you move out to Seattle if you were going to end up investigating a case back here in St. Louis?"

It was a good question, actually. She had to give her mother credit for that. But there was no answer for it, and it was meant rhetorically anyway. Cat felt the question lingering in the air. They were headed down their own street, signaled by the sound of the car tires wobbling over World's Fair-era cobblestones spared all these years from asphalt. Her mother parallel-parked like the expert she was, and they went inside.

Her father was much more welcoming, without any of the attitude and guilt-tripping, and Cat wondered why *he* hadn't picked her up at the airport. Maybe he wanted them to hash out that stuff alone beforehand. Retired now, her father had commandeered the dining room table for his model car hobby. He was working on a '79 Camaro this time, black with white racing stripes. Cat admired his handiwork.

"Dad, you can't see a trace of glue here. And how'd you get the steering wheel to spin?"

"Ball bearings," he responded, his eyes smiling at her above his bifocals. "I can't wait to see how they survive the explosion."

"Explosion?"

Her mother appeared in the doorway to the kitchen. "From the firecrackers," she explained. "He waits till the Fourth of July, loads them all up with firecrackers, and blows them to smithereens. It's a total waste, if you ask me. Show her all the other cars you've got out in the garage, Joe. There was a '57 Chevy, my favorite, bubble-gum pink, too, and he destroyed the poor thing on the Fourth."

"C'mon, daughter. If you can't stand the heat, get out of the kitchen." He grabbed his cane on the way out. His life as a construction worker had taken a toll on his body, and he'd had a hip replacement the year before. He took several walks a day to keep fit.

"So what brings you back to St. Louis so soon?" he asked. "I can't imagine it's the weather." He took a handkerchief out of his pocket as he said this and wiped his already perspiring brow. It was like an oven out in the yard with the sun beating down. Cat took off her scarf and was relieved when they entered the cool darkness of the garage.

"You, Dad." She squeezed his arm affectionately.

"Oh, I'm not above flattery," he said. "Especially from pretty girls. But I know a liar when I see one."

She laughed at his frankness. Her daddy always had been a straight shooter.

He flipped the overhead light on to reveal a row of classic model cars: a '76 Corvette, a GTO, a Rambler, and a Trans Am. They had all been built with the same meticulous attention to detail.

"So you're blowing all of these up."

"That's right."

"Why? They're so perfect. Why not keep them?"

"I can't take 'em with me when I die," he explained.

"You're only sixty-five, Dad."

"Well, you see..." he began, putting on his best Granny Grace imitation, "I've chosen the path to Buddhist enlightenment. I eschew the material world. I seek nothingness..." He paused, took a matchbook from his pocket, and used it to light a stray firecracker lying on his workbench. He held it between his thumb and index finger for a few seconds before releasing it in time for the burst.

"Aw, I just like to blow stuff up." He grinned like a little boy.

Cat laughed. Her father picked up the GTO and scratched at imaginary flaws in the bodywork. "Are you going to tell me what you're doing out here, Cathedral Choir?" He liked to play with her name like that. It made her feel at home, so she plunged in.

"I'm investigating a case," she revealed.

"Back here? Why?"

"I know it sounds strange, but this case has a St. Louis connection," she said. "I'm following a mother and child who tried to run away. They're from St. Louis, but the mother and her girl were in Seattle. The father showed up there. And then... I-I lost them. I think he brought them back here..." She trailed off.

"Oh," her father said. "I see. I think. How do you know the mother doesn't just want to punish her husband? Could be one of those custody battles."

"Because, Daddy. I've been inside his head. I know."

Her father was silent. He didn't deny her dream ability outright the way her mother did, but he didn't approve of it, either.

"I've said it before, and I'll say it again—" he began, but Cat broke in.

"'Dreams are not a legitimate law enforcement tool,'" she recited. "I know what you think, Daddy. But Granny Grace, she's teaching me a lot."

"I'll bet she is," he said. Then again: "I'll bet she is. You know that woman once got the mayor of New York to put her up at the

Waldorf? This was back before you were born. Ed Koch, he was the one. Probably one of the numerous men scattered across hither and yon whose hearts she broke."

Cat smiled at the image of Granny Grace living it up at the Waldorf while she was supposed to be investigating a case.

"I know you can't talk about it," her father continued, "But if an old beat-up hard hat can be of any assistance, you let me know."

He moved to turn off the garage light so they could go back inside the house. "I will," Cat promised.

"One more thing, Cathedral Bell," her father added, leading her out the garage door. "You be careful. If this guy chased his wife and kid all the way out to Seattle, who knows what he's willing to do."

Cat nodded. "I will, Daddy."

Chapter 8

She was standing outside in her mother's garden. At her feet, or her mother's feet, to be more accurate, the ground was dug up as if she were readying to plant something new. Cat became aware of her mother's consciousness. Her mother yearned for something to grow here in this ground, something she couldn't have, something denied her. Cat felt for the edge where she ended and her mother began. It was a jagged light along the seam of Cat's mind. If she concentrated on it, she could pull away, and separate...

There. She was out. In front of Cat, her mother stooped down to the ground. She pulled the angel charm from her necklace and buried it. Then she sat back on her heels to watch it grow.

It was some time before a tendril shot up, but then it grew quickly, sprouting and then growing into full size. It was a plant, but it was also an angel. Its face glowed fiery red and then cooled to reveal... Cat's face. It was Cat. Her mother had grown her.

Then she pulled another angel off her necklace and buried it, too. She sat back to watch it, but nothing grew. Her mother crawled over to the place where she'd buried it and dug it up. She cried, clutching it in her arms as if it were a dead baby.

Cat went to her mother to comfort her, but when she tried to put her arms around her, it was like grabbing at the air. Cat's arms went right through her. Her mother didn't seem to see her. Cat remained an invisible observer in her mother's dream. And again, her mother took an angel charm off her necklace, buried it, and waited for it to grow. Only in Cat's case did the angel charm grow into a child, but she kept repeating her actions nonetheless.

Cat woke up. She was in her parents' guest bedroom, staring at a crochet owl hanging on the opposite wall. Its eyes bored into her as if to say, *Do you see now why your mother is bitter?* Oh, wise owl, Cat thought, please go away.

She had always hated dreamslipping in her parents' dreams. It felt more like a violation of privacy with them than it did with anyone else, and afterward she always felt a bit awkward with them. In junior high and high school, when her dreamslipping ability arrived with the onset of puberty, she mostly didn't understand their dreams. They seemed to be about a world Cat didn't know, an adult world of anxiety, loss, and fears she could only guess at. To spare herself their dreams as much as to gain her independence, she'd opted to live in the dorms in college, even though she was going to school right there in St. Louis, and then she'd moved into an apartment her junior year.

But this dream she recognized. Her mother had had variations of it before. Cat felt the dream as a heavy weight. Her mother and father had not been able to have any children after Cat, and this dream proved that her mother, at least, had never fully made peace with that.

Cat rolled over, went back to sleep, and was thankfully spared from her parents' dreams for the rest of the night.

She was awakened by the smell of bacon. It was a rare treat for her back in Seattle, what with Granny Grace's inclination toward vegetarianism, selective though it was. As long as it was free-range, grass-fed, unionized, free of antibiotics, and raised in a cruelty-free manner, she'd partake.

Cat wandered down to find her father making bacon and eggs. "Sleep well?" he asked, and she lied and said yes even though the truth was she'd tossed and turned after her mother's dream. He motioned for her to sit down at the table and dropped a plate in front of her.

"Dad?" she asked. "How's Mom doing? She keeping busy?"

"Oh, she's got her church lady activities," he replied as he dropped a couple more strips of bacon into the frying pan. "They tried to recruit me, but me and God, we only need one meeting a week," he said.

"I worry about her empty-nest syndrome," Cat said.

"Yeah, well, since you moved out pretty much right after high school, she had to deal with that years ago."

Cat felt an old, bittersweet feeling return. She knew on some level her dad knew *why* she'd moved out so early even though she went to school in the same city and could have saved money by living at home. But they'd never discussed it directly.

"I'm sorry," Cat muttered, and her father shot her a sympathetic look.

"Oh, it was good for her," he said, sitting down with his own plate. "She's fine, you know. The church work really does make her happy. She's a bit of a legend at St. Elizabeth's. They adore her. If she seems otherwise right now, it's probably just your unexpected visit stirring her up."

Cat sighed. "I'm sorry about that, too."

He put his hand on hers across the table. "We know you're pursuing your dream—ha, in this case, literally." He stuffed a bacon strip in his mouth and smiled. "Besides, we're both flattered that you got so homesick."

He made up a plate of bacon and eggs for her mother, taking care to add a grouping of fresh fruit. It was set down at the table at the moment Mercy appeared in the doorway, as if rehearsed.

"Good morning, my dears," she greeted them. Cat looked at her mother's face, already made up tastefully. She did look good, after all. No dark circles under her clear blue eyes. She'd always taken care of her skin and aged gracefully. She was a beautiful woman, part Granny Grace and part... some man whose identity was a mystery. Mercy had never known her real father, and Cat had never had a grandfather on that side of the family.

This morning, her mother didn't seem sad. She seemed to have fully recovered from the prickly attitude she'd had yesterday upon Cat's arrival, and she chatted both of them up about the work her parish was doing to plant gardens in poor neighborhoods to give people healthier, more economical food choices. Cat thought of Granny Grace's work with City Goats. Despite their differences, the apple hadn't fallen far from the tree.

After breakfast, Cat returned to her room and pulled out her laptop. She needed to get to work tracking Jim down as quickly as possible. She needed to find the woman and the girl.

She combed through articles on the Plantation Revival Church, most of which were laudatory. It had grown from a congregation of only twelve founders to serving thousands in just a few years. Whereas other churches struggled with the graying of their congregations, the Plantation church attracted many younger followers, in part because Jim Plantation had embraced social media and seemed to be a natural at building a brand, both his own personal one and the church's as a whole.

He was very outspoken against abortion, his church lobbying against it at both the state and federal levels, though any ties to clinic bombings had been roundly refuted. The Plantation ministry also specialized in a "reintegration program" for people who had experienced attractions to those of the same sex or had acted upon them—they helped people "cleanse" themselves of these "manifestations of the devil" and then worked with them to "fully reclaim Jesus" in their hearts and minds. The church's drug rehab program was also renowned, such that local university academics had studied its efficacy and found that a focus on the person's spiritual life helped replace the need for drugs, or as one skeptic cynically put it, "It works because they replace one opiate, actual drugs, with another, religion."

The church also had a celebrated youth ministry, with an active "Teen Scripture Squad" and "Baby Bible Brigade." Cat stared on-screen at a full-color photo of pretty, wholesome-looking girls in an article on the youth program. There was Jim, in the middle of them, his arms outstretched to embrace the girls on either side, a wide grin lighting up his face. Could the man in that photo be capable of hurting those girls? Were they his "angels"?

Then she found another article, more recent, and the only negative piece of news on the church she'd been able to locate: the assistant director had recently committed suicide. His name was Larry Price, he'd been with the church since its foundation, and he was only fifty-seven when they found his body in his office on church grounds. It had been ruled an apparent suicide with no pending investigation.

The suicide raised some questions, as Sherrie's escape happened in the aftermath of that. There could be a connection, but Cat wasn't going to find out looking through news articles. She debated what to do. She couldn't just show up at the church and start asking questions. They'd clamp down so tight she'd never see Sherrie and Ruthie again. Neither could she assume that they would be able to leave with Cat if she did find them there. They'd clearly been in hiding in the condo building, and Jim had some kind of hold on Sherrie, or she'd just file for divorce like everyone else. Cat would need to slip into the church unnoticed and investigate from the inside.

She bounded downstairs to find her mother packing up a bag for her day's work in her church's gardening program. She had on a rather elegant sun hat, and for a moment, Cat caught a resemblance to Granny Grace in her mother's side profile: the aquiline nose, the high cheekbones.

"Mom, before you take off, I need your advice."

"Oh?" her mother said, pausing to stow a pair of pale yellow gardening gloves in her bag. "Is it for your investigation?" Her mother's face showed she felt flattered to be asked.

"Yes. Say I want to join a Christian fundamentalist church. How do I do that? You know, and make them believe I'm for real."

"A fundamentalist church? Which one?"

"I can't tell you."

"Well, I don't know. Hmm... I'd say you should try to be yourself as much as possible. Regulars can spot a faker a mile away. You'll already be faking interest in their beliefs, so you better keep as close to the truth otherwise."

Cat smiled, tiptoed over to her mother and kissed her on the cheek. "Mom, you're a genius."

Her mother grabbed her shoulders. "Cat, promise me you'll be careful."

She took her mother's hands in hers, shifted them off her shoulders, and said, "I promise."

A few hours later, Cat headed across the river into Illinois, where the Plantation Church headquarters was. She'd secured a rental car and stuck a sticker in the window for her alma mater, St. Elizabeth's High School, so at a glance it would look like she owned it. She took one of her goofy college graduation gifts, a teddy bear wearing a cap and gown, and perched it in the rear deck so it could be seen through the car window.

The Plantation Church was in the middle of cornfields, and it was much more than a church. The complex, she had read, boasted a main church set up like a concert venue, with stadium seating and mega screens, and two other, smaller worship halls. There was a state-of-the-art gymnasium with an Olympic-sized swimming pool. Notably absent from the roster of physical exercise offered in Jesus' Gym was yoga, as Jim preached it could lead a person's soul too close to Satan, and he outright forbid his congregation from practicing it. Cat could just hear Granny Grace chortling at that one. There was also a parade ground for outdoor revivals and a dormitory to house students attending the youth camps. She hoped to be staying in one of them as soon as this evening.

As she turned onto Plantation Drive, she saw the last of the ubiquitous animated billboards advertising the church. It showed a couple riding a donkey right through a pair of golden gates into heaven. "It doesn't matter what you ride in on, as long as your destination is heaven," read the caption.

A mile or so past the billboard, Cat drove into a parking lot so large that it put the one at the megamall off the highway to shame. She wondered if the lot was ever full; it was only about twenty-five percent occupied now, but then again, it was mid-week, a Wednesday.

She parked the car, glanced down at her clothes, and took a deep breath. Cat was dressed as herself circa 2008, the year she graduated high school. And that's the role she'd be playing till she got what she needed from this place. She was glad her mother hadn't tossed her high school T-shirt and sweatpants, St. Elizabeth's H.S. emblazoned across her chest and butt. She'd checked it out in the mirror before she left, and without makeup and with her hair in a ponytail, she judged herself young-looking enough to pass.

She grabbed her old high school backpack out of the back seat and hoisted it onto her shoulder.

Cat walked through the front doors and glanced into the main church hall. It was quiet, with a few worshippers sitting in chairs and reading the Bible. She could see out of the corner of her eye a woman at a reception desk in the foyer watching her. Good. Playing hesitant and lost, but curious, Cat ducked into the gift shop. A religious shop was no big deal to her; she'd been in many a Catholic supply store. But this one was noticeably light on iconography and heavy on literal messaging. She flipped through a rack of T-shirts that said "It's Adam and Eve, not Adam and Steve" and "Champion for Christ" before turning back toward the church hall. The woman at the intake desk was still there and still watching her, but Cat avoided eye contact with her. Instead, Cat wandered into the church hall, choosing a seat about midway down. She sat there for a very long time in silence. Then the woman from the desk suddenly appeared at the end of her aisle. Cat glanced at her and nodded that it was all right to approach. The woman sat down next to her.

"Hello. I'm Anita Briggs." She offered Cat a milky white hand to shake. She was a pale-skinned redhead with a prominent hooked nose. "What brings you to our ministry?"

"I don't know," answered Cat. She'd recalled some techniques from a few acting classes she'd taken in college and was drawing on them now, becoming the character she needed to be. "I was driving down the highway, and I saw a sign for this church. I already have a church, so I'm not really sure why I'm here. I mean, my parents have a church, and I've always gone to theirs. We're Catholic."

"I see that," Anita observed, motioning to the high school name in white-on-red letters printed across Cat's chest.

"I just—" Cat feigned struggling for the words. "I just feel so lost. I graduated this spring, and I don't know what I'm supposed to do with my life. I don't know what matters. God hasn't—" Cat hesitated, looking at the woman imploringly.

"God hasn't what?" Anita placed her hand delicately on Cat's. Cat allowed herself to feel the woman's touch as warm and real. She let it bring tears to her eyes.

"He hasn't... spoken to me in a long time. I guess that sounds weird." She let tears spill down her cheeks.

"No, it doesn't," Anita sympathized. "I can't promise you that He'll speak to you here, but you can try to listen. You came here for a reason. Maybe that was God's way of asking you to tune in."

"Yeah," Cat said. "Maybe."

"We have services on Wednesdays and Sundays," Anita continued, "plus a study group on Mondays and a social every Friday."

"Oh," Cat said, making her voice sound resigned. "Well, I'm supposed to go away to college next week. It's a month before school starts, but my parents signed me up for this 'freshman experience' program."

"Sounds like you're not too excited about it."

"No, not really." Cat tried her best to look forlorn, hoping Anita would take the bait.

"Would you like to meet some of the congregation?" Anita asked, leaning in closer to Cat. "There are some girls your age here."

"Oh, sure," Cat assented. "I don't have anything else to do today. I'd love to."

Anita led Cat to an antechamber where a gaggle of girls were cutting shapes out of felt and gluing them to banners. "Be a soldier for Christ," read one. On another: "Make friends, love thy enemy."

"They're making banners for the main hall," explained Anita.

"Hi, I'm Hope," said a sweet-faced girl with blue eyes and black hair. She was wearing a St. Louis Cardinals jersey that said "P.J. Simms." Cat had recognized the name on the back when they'd entered; he was the heartthrob on the team, the one a lot of girls crushed on these days.

"I'll leave you girls to chat," said Anita as she exited the room.

Hope introduced Cat to the others and fetched her a root beer out of a refrigerator in the back of the room. Cat wanted to ask them a million questions but knew to play it cool.

"What's it like to go to a Catholic school?" they asked Cat, crowding around her. She was taken aback but shrugged off the question.

"It's no big deal," she said. "Just like regular school, except you talk about God for some of the classes. We didn't have to wear uniforms. They stopped doing that in the nineties." The girls were transfixed, so she continued. "The nuns wore regular clothes, not habits. Nobody hit me with a ruler or anything." The girls laughed.

"My foster dad says all priests are basically pervs," announced a girl in the back. Wendy was her name. She chewed gum noisily, pulling it out of her mouth in a long string, her fingernails painted with glittery orange polish. She regarded Cat with suspicion. "Were you ever molested?"

Cat bristled at the question but understood its source all the same. It was something she'd encountered from time to time, and it was one of the reasons she was reserved in Seattle about her Catholic upbringing. She realized Wendy had given her an opening.

"No, but my dad says evangelicals are pervs, too. They just know how to hide it better." The girls giggled nervously. "Were *you* ever molested?"

Wendy smiled as if recognizing one of her own and preparing for a saucy retort. "No, but sometimes I wish Jim would molest me. He's hot, and his sermons get me all worked up inside." She ran her hands along the sides of her body as she said the bit about the sermon. The girls were laughing hysterically now.

"Really?" Cat gasped. "Have you ever tried to get with him?"

Wendy rolled her eyes. "That man is *pure*. He's like a direct descendent of Moses."

The rest of the girls concurred. "Yeah," said a blonde named Tina. "I'm used to getting lots of attention from guys, and Jim's never once flirted with me."

Hope spoke up angrily then. "And he would *not* approve of this conversation."

"She's got that right," said Wendy. "Jim makes us scrub our makeup off, and he's against cleavage." More laughter.

"So we're all Jim's little angels?"

Cat's question quieted the room. Even Wendy looked suddenly pious.

"Yeah," intoned Hope. "He sees the angel in all of us. He sees us as blessed and pure. He sees us as the best we can possibly be."

Tina nodded. "I've never felt so good as I feel here."

"Amen," said Hope. "Amen," repeated the others.

Cat joined them in making banners, learning more about their families and backgrounds. Hope had been raised in the faith; her father was an English teacher at a private evangelical elementary school, and she aspired to follow in his footsteps. She loved and studied Shakespeare, had already read all of his plays, and had performed in the usual, popular ones. Wendy had grown up in foster care, her last, most permanent family all committed evangelicals. Tina's family was born-again; they had lived a godless life, she said, until her parents decided to try Jim's church.

Anita came back to retrieve Cat but hung on the sidelines, attending to a banner of her own and observing Cat for a while. After some time, she offered to walk Cat out.

"Listen, Cat, I have a feeling about you," said Anita. "These girls are all participating in a precollege program to serve the ministry before they head off to school. It's usually reserved for well-established members of the flock, but we could make an exception. You seem to fit in here, and after all, you came here, searching, and if we think you can find God here..." She paused, waiting for Cat's reaction. It was the offer Cat had been hoping for. She'd read about the precollege program in her research and figured it was her best shot at getting inside.

"I-I don't know," Cat replied, affecting a hesitant tone. "I'd have to think it over. Talk to my parents."

"Of course," Anita replied with a friendly smile. "Take your time. Talk to them. Call me—or tell them to call me—if you have any questions."

"I will," she promised. "I'm really interested in coming back here."

"That's great," Anita said, squeezing her hands together as if in prayer. "You'll have a wonderful time here and learn a lot about yourself and about God. If you decide to convert, and I'm not saying we expect you to, we'd embrace you as our own."

Chapter 9

C at was in a supermarket, holding a gun. She smelled rotisserie chicken and glanced at a display of two-for-one jars of olives. People passed by her, rolling their carts, oblivious to her mission. She wouldn't let them see her, wouldn't let the evil in the world touch them in any way. It was important that they go on about their business, their lives safe.

There was her enemy, hiding behind a girl in a yellow sundress playing cat's cradle, sitting alone in her cart. Her mother had gone to another aisle to fetch a forgotten item.

It's just like a hajji to use a kid for a shield, said a voice in Cat's head.

She recognized the voice. It was Lee's. She withdrew to another aisle.

Then she separated her mind from Lee's long enough to wonder how she could be walking in his dream—his recurring nightmare, as it turned out—if he was training in Virginia, while she was in St. Louis. The only dreamslipping Cat had ever engaged in was with dreamers sleeping in close proximity to her. That seemed to have been the rule, and Granny Grace had never told her any differently.

She didn't have time to ponder it further. She, or Lee, had doubled back by then, and the man Lee called a hajji lobbed a grenade at her. Again, it detonated over her left shoulder. Pieces of it hit her head in a million points of pain. Her left ear went dead; she felt blood dripping down the side of her face. She blacked out.

She woke gasping, the feeling so real that her hand instinctually felt for her left ear. Finding it dry and her hearing intact, Cat let out a breath and tried to think over what had happened. There were only two possibilities. One, Lee was lying to her about his training session in Virginia and was in fact here at the Plantation Church, somewhere in the dorms or near enough for her to be able to access his dreams. Two, somehow she was able to pick up Lee's dream halfway across the country.

She sat up in bed and grabbed her laptop, trying not to let her bunk creak too loudly. Wendy was sleeping in the bottom bunk, and Hope, Tina, and several other girls were nearby. How was it that she hadn't picked up one of their dreams instead? This had never happened to her before.

She logged onto Facebook. She'd deactivated her account in order to go undercover in the church so that no one would "friend" her through that site and see anything that contradicted her cover story. She set it live again just long enough to pull up Lee's page. He had "checked in" to several spots in Virginia that weekend: a crab shack, a flight museum, and a horse farm. She googled "Virginia" and "military installations." According to his check-ins, he was in Virginia Beach. Was there an army post there? Yes. Fort Story. She also looked up the distance between Virginia Beach and St. Louis. It was close to 800 miles.

Puzzled, she reached for her cell phone. It was 4 a.m. in the Midwest and only 5 a.m. in Virginia, but she knew Lee rose early. She sent him a text: *Good morning, Sgt. Stone. How did you sleep?* About five minutes later came his reply: *Hello, Kitty Cat. Funny you should ask. Bad dreams. Gotta go. Kisses.*

Cat felt the hair on the back of her neck stand up.

Could his dream be so strong that it got into her head from so many miles away? That didn't make sense. Between here and there, thousands, maybe even millions of people were having nightmares. She hadn't even told Lee that she had gone to St. Louis, so it wasn't as if he could project his dream to her or even think of her in St. Louis as he fell asleep either. Another possibility startled Cat: that she and Lee had a connection that could span the distance.

She felt her heart hurt. Actually hurt.

Unable to sleep, she shrugged off the Lee problem and decided to get up and poke around. She dressed in a pair of loose jeans and the "Champion for Christ" sweatshirt Anita had given her as a gift. Hope had briefed Cat on the dress code, which specifically outlawed her high school sweatpants, not because they were from a Catholic high school but because they had writing across the butt, which would attract the male gaze, presumably. Cat wandered through the dormitory—there was a nice common space filled with brand-new couches and a flat-screen TV—and into the main church hall, which was always open. The altar wasn't ornate by Catholic church standards, but it was impressive, with an enormous metal cross affixed to an angled section of wood behind the podium, all of it backlit by about a hundred or so lights.

She thought about Jim Plantation's dream, the one with the snakes, the disgusting shack, and the cabinet full of angels. Snakes were a pretty obvious metaphor for the devil. And there were so many of them—temptations everywhere. The horrible shack, a den of iniquity. He'd mentioned something about his aunt never being there, and about her being with men. Maybe Jim had been raised by her, and she was too busy to really care for him. Who knows what the comment about men could signify—either a loose lifestyle or an illegal profession borne of necessity? Cat didn't want to judge the aunt, but she did feel some compassion for a child raised in that shack, whether it was a real place or just how Jim thought of his childhood home. The church cabinet full of angels definitely represented a life of deliverance and order in the midst of all that chaos.

"Trying to tune in?" A voice from behind startled her. She turned. It was Anita Briggs, walking up the aisle toward her.

"You're up early," Cat said.

"It's good for the soul," Anita replied. "When the sun comes up in the morning, that's when I feel closest to God."

Cat realized then that Anita reminded her a little of Granny Grace. A less attractive, less cosmopolitan version, but this woman carried herself with the same depth and wisdom. Cat felt a bit of regret as she realized that Anita truly wanted to save her, not for the growth of the congregation, but for Cat's own good.

"Will Jim be giving the sermon this morning?" Cat inquired. She'd arrived in time for the Friday social, helped the Teen Scripture Squad finish the banners on Saturday, and was eager to continue her investigation of Jim. She'd turned up very little on Saturday, and it felt as if her case were growing cold.

Anita blanched at her question, however. "Oh, Jim. No. There's been... some sadness in our church. A tragedy. Jim and his family are taking some time to recover from the loss privately. He's on leave."

Cat felt the bottom drop out of her stomach. Jim wasn't even here? How could this be? Now what was she going to do?

"Sadness?" she asked gently, though she was certain that Jim had simply used his assistant director's death as a convenient cover story for leaving his church duties behind while he stalked his wife and child in Seattle.

"One of our church administrators... passed recently. He was one of the founders. It was a tremendous loss for our entire congregation." Anita stared up at the cross as if thinking of something she couldn't discuss.

"Oh," Cat replied. "I'm so, so sorry."

Anita shook it off and offered Cat a wan smile. "All part of God's plan. We don't have to understand it to accept it."

They stood in silence for a moment, looking up at the cross. Then Cat asked, "Who's going to give the sermon?"

Anita smiled weakly. "That would be the Reverend Chambers," she said. "He's been with the church as long as Larry and Jim have. He used to host services in his home when we were just a small gathering of hopefuls." She paused, as if remembering some long-ago time. "Come, help me get the coffee brewing and set out the cornbread and fruit. We won't get the same crowd what with Jim gone, but they'll still want snacks after services."

Anita was right about the crowd. Admittedly, Cat had nothing to compare it to, but Wendy and the other girls had regaled her with stories of packed pews, everyone on their feet and singing. It was a decent crowd for a church service these days, she thought, but there was a dampened sort of feeling when Rev. Chambers took the podium. He was a good speaker, but he lacked the enigmatic quality she'd seen in Jim's recorded sermons, which she'd watched online.

Rev. Chambers talked about the power of prayer and the people he'd seen healed by it. "Some are healed physically, some emotionally, and some spiritually," he said. "Jesus' spirit breathes through us all, healing in all ways."

To Cat's surprise, he addressed Jim's absence head-on: "Our captain has left the helm, and I understand you could feel bereft. We can only trust in God's light to bring our leader back to the fold."

After the service, Cat mingled with the congregation members, trying to tease out information without arousing suspicion. She'd so far discovered that Jim had been gone for close to three months. People were speculating, spurred on by Rev. Chambers' speech, that he had abandoned his flock. She definitely got the sense that his period of grief should have ended a respectful amount of time ago, and since nobody had seen hide nor hair of him—it was expected that he and his family would continue to worship, even if he were taking a break from the altar—people were becoming worried, resentful, and in some cases, even alarmed. "Jim's congregation needs him," muttered one woman to another, who nodded and closed her eyes as if to hold back tears. "And Jim needs us," the woman replied.

Cat tried to make this odd rift left by Jim's absence work for her, with some success. She found out that Jim and the assistant director, whose name was Larry Price, had been best friends since their boyhoods in southern Missouri. Rev. Chambers himself told her this as he polished off his second helping of cornbread. He was a distinguished older gentleman who carried a black cane with a silver tip shaped like an eagle. She held his coffee cup for him as he wiped his hands and beard with a napkin.

"The two were like brothers, except they got along better than most brothers," he told her. "There wasn't a decision that Jim made that he didn't discuss with Larry first."

"Why would he kill himself?" Cat whispered. "I'm sorry to ask. I just... I just joined the church, and the suicide thing has me spooked."

"I can't answer that, miss," he said. "Why does anyone? It's not for me to judge, that's for the Lord, but personally, I think it's a sign of moral and spiritual weakness."

"Did Mr. Price seem... weak?" Cat asked.

The man paused, looked up at the ceiling, fingering his cane. "Yes. In some ways he did. He was definitely Jim's shadow."

"Maybe he could never live up to Jim," Cat suggested. "Maybe he never felt good enough."

"No," the man said. "It wasn't like that with Jim and Larry." He spotted someone across the room and seemed to have grown weary of Cat's line of questioning anyway. "If you'll excuse me..."

"Certainly." Cat suddenly felt self-conscious, standing there by herself. She looked around the room for a familiar face and saw Anita's bright red hair, pulled into a ponytail. When Anita turned, she locked eyes with Cat and smiled. Cat smiled back.

Cat didn't want to push her luck with this crowd any longer, and besides, it skewed much older than the age she was pretending to be, and that made her feel doubly conspicuous. She decided to see who else was still around from the Teen Scripture Squad.

Back in the dorm, she found Tina packing a bag; she was headed to stay with her parents for a couple of days. Cat had met them in the refreshment lounge, and it was easy to see the resemblance, as her mother looked like a fortysomething Barbie, and her father reminded Cat of John F. Kennedy. The other girls were out shopping at the mall, Tina said.

Cat plopped down on her bunk bed to chat. Instead of the thong underwear commonly worn by most college-aged girls, Cat noted, Tina had a stack of neatly folded white briefs in front of her on the bed. Cat couldn't help herself. She picked one up, unfurled it, and waved it.

"Seriously, Tina? These look like surrender flags."

Tina grabbed it out of her hand. "And I suppose you wear a G-string every day," she snorted.

"Not every day. Only when she's stripping," quipped Wendy, who'd come into the room just then.

"I thought you were at the mall," Cat said. She'd been hoping to get to talk to Tina alone. Her parents were close to church leadership, she'd noticed. They might know more and could have said something in front of Tina.

"Nope, not today," said Wendy. "The mall is depressing when you can't buy anything. I'm broke, and the fosters aren't forthcoming."

She always referred to her foster parents as "the fosters," which Cat had quickly realized was a put-on, the girl obviously trying to affect an emotional distance from them.

"Am I interrupting girl time?" Wendy lilted, her voice dripping with sarcasm.

"Wendy, that's not very nice, and it's Sunday, even," scolded Hope.

"Well, I don't know why you're acting so sanctimonious with me. When I walked into the room, the two of you were discussing G-strings."

"Cat was making fun of my lady briefs," Tina said.

"Oh, those," Wendy shrugged. "Big deal. We all wear them. I mean, mine don't quite offer the same, ah, coverage as Tina's," she pulled down the edge of her skirt to reveal a pair of modest hip huggers, "but then I'm not as hot as Tina, either, so I don't need a chastity belt to keep 'em away."

Tina blushed, laughing. Wendy and Cat laughed, too.

Just then there was a knock at the door. It was Tina's parents, who whisked her away after a few niceties, leaving Cat alone with Wendy.

"So what kind of underwear did you bring?" Wendy asked, bounding up and heading toward Cat's chest of drawers. They hadn't dressed in front of each other, as the practice was to dress in modesty in curtained changing rooms, or she wouldn't have had to ask, as the bunk beds were in such close quarters otherwise. She flung Cat's top drawer open and picked up a pair of white lace bikini bottoms.

"These are sweet," she said. "I haven't seen anything but cotton in a really long time. Not since the last time I was with my mom..." Wendy's facial expression clouded.

"Where is she?" Cat asked, taking the bikini out of Wendy's hand and stowing it back in her drawer.

Wendy shrugged. "I don't know. Hanging out at Diamond Dick's, probably." It was a strip club with a shady reputation that had been busted for drug trafficking and prostitution in the past.

"Oh," Cat said. "I'm sorry."

"Yeah, Mom's a real winner," Wendy said. "She used to be a stripper, but she's too old for that now. She just hangs out there for the drugs."

Cat sat down on Tina's bunk, facing Wendy, who was perched on the edge of hers.

"What's *your* mom like?" Wendy asked Cat. "Wait. Let me guess. You have like seven siblings, 'cause you're Catholic, so she doesn't use birth control. That's why you're here. It's not that the Catholic Church wasn't your bag, it's that you never got enough attention."

Cat smiled. "I wish that were true. Actually, I'm an only child. But my parents wanted to have more. They just can't."

"Well, doesn't that suck?" Wendy said. "I've never understood it. My mom shouldn't have had any kids at all, and yours should have had, like, twenty. There's no justice in that."

"Wouldn't Anita say it's all part of God's plan?" Cat asked.

Wendy snorted. "Yeah, she would. I get it. I do. It's just the hardest thing for me to deal with here. I mean, it's not fair. It's not fair I had my childhood, and Tina had hers."

Cat let the silence between them linger for a few beats. Then Wendy spoke up again. "So how are you liking it here, anyway?"

"It's so nice," Cat gushed. "Everyone's really welcoming, more than I thought they'd be. But I guess..." She paused. "I guess the suicide thing is freaking me out."

Wendy's face clouded again. "Yeah. It's more than freaky. It's positively unexplainable."

"What do you mean?" Cat asked. "Nobody saw it coming?"

"Nope. Larry Price? He was awesome. He taught me to box. I had a... lot of anger issues when I first came to this church. So the fosters enrolled me in his boxing class. He taught me how to take out my anger on the punching bag, and how to defend myself. And he was just a great guy, always happy and positive. I can't see him blowing his head off."

"Is *that* how he did it?"

"Yeah. Brains and blood splattered all over the wall behind him," Wendy said. "He lived here, you know. His office and living quarters are behind the main hall. It's all closed up now, though." Cat saw tears in her eyes.

They were silent again for a minute.

Then Wendy spoke. "Anita says you're going to college."

"That's the plan."

"Where?"

"Seattle. My grandmother lives there."

"Oh."

"What about you?"

"I was liberated last month," said Wendy.

"Congratulations!" said Cat. "Is that like being confirmed?"

Wendy looked at her quizzically and then laughed. "What? Oh, no. Liberated from the foster care system. When I turned eighteen."

Cat suddenly understood why Wendy would want to distance herself from "the fosters."

"Are your foster parents still in touch with you?"

"Oh, yeah," Wendy replied. "But they're pretty busy with their new projects. Justin and Jennifer, aged eleven and fourteen. Brother and sister, been in the foster-care system for five years. Justin's special needs."

Cat already knew the answer to her question, but the investigator in her made her ask it anyway. "Are they sending you to college?"

Wendy flinched, but then smiled. "They gave me a dorm fridge, the one Foster Dad had out in the garage. The rest is all on me."

"Why don't they—"

Wendy interrupted Cat. "Don't even go there. You don't understand. It's not like they're made of money. Foster Mom is stay-at-home, so there's no paycheck coming from her. Foster Dad sells insurance. They're very nice people who've devoted themselves to the Lord's work. They saved my life, and that's enough. Besides, I don't need a free ride. Wendy Lewis makes her own way in the world."

Cat smiled. "Wendy, you're all right."

"Catholic girl, you're not so bad yourself. But you better get rid of the stripper undies. I hear Auntie Briggs has a weak heart, and when she sees those on laundry day, she'll think it's the Rapture."

Chapter 10

P.J. Simms stood on the pitcher's mound waiting for the next batter to take his place. He glanced up into the stands for Cat as if he knew she'd be there. She was close enough to catch his eye, plus she was wearing the wide-brimmed white hat she told him she'd be wearing. P.J. tipped his cap to her and smiled, then turned back to wind up his next pitch.

He struck the batter out, and Cat knew that one was for her. P.J. would be waiting for her after the game. She felt her heart grow warm at the thought.

P.J. played beautifully, making her feel proud. Hardly a batter got a hit off him in the first three innings, and in the next two, he got several outs when runners tried to steal bases. By the top of the seventh inning, the Cardinals led the Braves 5-0. During the seventh-inning stretch, one of the ushers brought her a red rose. "It's from P.J.," he said with a wink. There was a note wound around the stem. She carefully unfolded it. *My darling Hope,* it said, *I'm yours in Christ. Love, P.J.*

Or at least that's what Hope's mind told her it said, Cat realized, as the words on the page were unintelligible scribbles, as in all dreams. The part of the brain that processes the alphabet and written language isn't accessed during dreaming, she knew, so any writing that actually appears in a dream is illegible.

Hope touched the golden cross around her neck, a perfect match to the one she knew P.J. wore underneath his uniform. Cat felt for the edges of Hope's mind, which was full of sentimental daydreams about a man she'd never meet in person, and pried her own mind away from Hope's. It worked. Cat finally had the technique down. Out of Hope's head, Cat sat back in a seat to watch the game. She was curious to see what would happen when Hope met P.J. The girl was always prim and proper; of all the girls in the precollege program, Hope toed the party line the best. But her interest in P.J. Simms bordered on, well, bona fide obsession, so maybe she cut loose in the safety of her own mind.

The Cardinals won, of course, as Hope was calling the shots in this dream world. Cat followed Hope down to the dugout.

At the entrance to the dugout, the security guards simply nodded to let Hope through, and Cat followed unseen. There was the door to the locker room. Hope went to the door, put her hand on it. Cat expected her to push through, but she stayed there, with one palm

91

touching the door. Cat wanted to know what she was thinking and feeling, but being out of Hope's body meant she was separated from Hope's mind, too. Hmm... Could she go back in? Cat walked up behind Hope and tried reversing what she'd done to remove herself from the girl's mind. She listened very carefully for Hope's thoughts. She listened to the sounds of running water, metal locker doors banging shut. She stepped closer so that her invisible self was inside Hope's form. Nothing happened.

She remembered Granny Grace's description of how to pull herself out of someone, by meditating on the areas where the two consciousnesses parted. To reconnect, she must have to meditate on the place where she and Hope were essentially the same. Cat thought back to her own high school crush, the singer of a rock band. Cat knew everything about him, his favorite food, what he liked to sing in the shower, the fact that he wore his hair parted on the right when touring on the East Coast and on the left when touring on the West Coast. Cat had had fantasies about following him, living on the tour bus with him, waiting for him in hotels. How he'd look past the throngs of screaming girls and only have eyes for her...

And then it happened. She felt Hope's feelings again. Longing. She felt an intense longing, in both her heart and... between her legs.

But she would not open that locker-room door. She kept her hand on it, as much to steel herself from opening the door as to feel a connection to the man she knew was on the other side. With her free hand, she fingered the gold cross. She was saving herself for P.J., for their wedding night. Once God had joined them together in spirit, they would join their bodies together. Hope was strong; she could wait for this. It would be the most beautiful night of her life. It would be worth the wait. She quelled the fire between her legs, forced herself to think of that wedding night and all that it meant.

Cat pulled herself out of Hope's consciousness again, gasping. The longing was so intense that she could barely stand it. Thankfully, Hope awakened at that moment, groaning the way a lover might groan. Cat stifled her own groan and realized she was fully aroused. Her nipples were hard, her heart was on fire, and between her legs, she was wet. Hope's bunk was across the aisle from Cat's; she could see the girl roll onto her side, her breathing calm. It hit Cat suddenly that their dormitory-style sleeping arrangements definitely curtailed privacy, and probably by design. With no expense spared in other areas of the campus, it seemed odd that the girls were packed in here like sardines. But it did have the intended result of discouraging any activities a girl might want to engage in privately, such as the one Cat felt an urge to engage in now. It *had* been a couple weeks already since she'd seen Lee.

She'd had no contact with him since the exchange of text messages the morning of the dream, and he still didn't know she was in St. Louis. He'd be returning to Seattle soon, but they hadn't made specific plans to see each other.

Thinking of Lee was not helping her calm down her arousal response and fall back to sleep. She glanced at the clock. It was 5 a.m. She had another hour before she was expected to rise and shower. She might as well put it to good use.

She got up and splashed cold water on her face but didn't bother to change out of her pajamas. She felt in her pocket for her talisman, which she'd taken to carrying with her at all times: the glittery pink barrette left behind in the condo building the night Cat lost Ruth and her mother.

In her careful wanderings about the campus, Cat had found Larry Price's office, which wasn't even locked. The Plantation ministry didn't believe in locked doors. A person could wander about the place freely. It seemed they had nothing to hide.

She padded on bare feet to Price's office. She'd opened his door before, been surprised to find it unlocked, but hadn't had the chance to explore. This time, she stepped inside.

The place was spotless. If there had been blood splatter on the walls here, it had been thoroughly scrubbed out of existence. The office smelled of pine-scented cleaner and bleach. A seating area to the right was arranged around a gas fireplace, the mantelpiece adorned with carefully placed pictures in silver frames. There was one of Jim, Anita, and what appeared to be a past incarnation of the Teen Scripture Squad. There was another of Jim, Larry, and some of the other men in the ministry's leadership; Cat recognized Rev. Chambers, as well as Tina's handsome father. Above the fireplace was a large counted cross-stitch bearing this Bible verse:

Guard what God has entrusted to you.
Avoid godless, foolish discussions with those who oppose you
with their so-called knowledge.
(1 Timothy 6:20)

Cat read through the quote a few times. It was certainly a clarion call to ignore opposition, and for a church with such a strong, conservative position, it wasn't surprising that a church leader would choose to foreground it.

There was a door at the back of the office that she realized must lead to Larry's private rooms, but this door was bolted shut. There was no way for her to open it. She searched for a key but didn't find one.

His desk was in an alcove off to the side, his chair facing the window, which was a ceiling-to-floor glass wall overlooking the ministry garden. Instinctively, Cat sat down at the desk. From there she could see a fountain in the center of the garden. Aesthetically, the fountain seemed out of place in the conservative grandeur of the ministry overall, with its clean white lines and glowing metal surfaces. In contrast, the fountain resembled a rock formation that seemed vaguely familiar to her, but she couldn't quite place it. It was comprised of several tiers of silver boulders, hollowed out in the middle and tipped forward so that water would cascade from one to the next. Partially covered with a tarp and unfinished, the sculpture was nonetheless clearly intended to be a fountain. She could see that water would rush from the center of the topmost boulder and whirl through the bowls of the other rocks before splashing to the base and disappearing.

Her bare foot kicked over a wastebasket under the heavy oak desk. Peering beneath it, Cat saw a mishmash of crumpled receipts, gum wrappers, and staples that had been pulled out of a document with a staple remover. She dropped down on all fours and went through the papers. She sniffed the gum wrapper: cinnamon. There was a receipt for gas that included a car wash, several slips from the same coffee shop listing a latte with a shot of caramel syrup. And there it was: a receipt for drinks at a bar. It bore a double-D logo but no bar name. Perhaps that was meant to preserve discretion for the clientele, but Cat recognized the logo from the garish pink-and-silver billboards advertising across southern Illinois and Missouri. It was Diamond Dick's, the strip club. There had been several rounds of drinks for several drinkers, as the order came to $77.

"Why are you going through Larry's trash?" The voice was incredulous and accusatory. The voice was Rev. Chambers'.

Cat froze. She looked up through the legs of the desk and saw the man's reflection in the glass. She palmed the Diamond Dick's receipt in her left hand and picked at the pulled-out staples with her right. They were stuck into the carpet.

"This must look pretty weird, huh?" Cat said. She sat up on her knees and twisted around to look at him, a staple between her fingers. "I'm prying used staples off the ground." With her other hand, she stuffed the receipt in the pocket of her pajamas, next to Ruth's barrette.

"Pardon me, miss?" His suspicion was a bit disarmed, but he tapped his cane on the floor for emphasis, and that unnerved her.

"I know I shouldn't have come in here, but the girls said this is where that guy killed himself. I guess I couldn't help my curiosity. I wanted to see where it happened. I sat down here at the desk and kicked over the trashcan. It was full of staples. Used ones. They're impossibly stuck into the carpeting."

His face softened some, but Cat could see he was still on guard.

"Didn't anyone ever tell you that curiosity killed the cat?" he said rhetorically.

Cat allowed herself to chuckle.

"Young lady, death—whether it's the death of the man who once occupied this office or the death of an overly curious feline—is most assuredly no laughing matter."

"It is if your name is Cat," she said boldly.

"Cat, you say? Well, what kind of name is that? I'd say it's a common noun, not a proper one."

"It's short for Cathedral," she said, sitting back on her haunches on the floor. "My mother got religion in her thirties, when she had me. I'm sort of the commemorative Catholic baby."

"And a papist at that. In Larry's office. Such a thing shouldn't be condoned." He stepped over to one of the sofa chairs and sat down with grace, his hands balancing on the gleaming eagle atop his cane. He watched Cat pick up staples as if the sight pleased him immensely.

"You seem a bit, ah, older than the other girls," he said, setting Cat's alarm bells off in more than one way. First of all, she felt like her cover was being blown. Second of all, was he flirting with her? She suddenly felt self-conscious of her body, kneeling there before him in her pajamas. She wasn't even wearing a bra.

There was an awkward silence as Cat tried to think of something appropriate to say. "I'm sorry," she finally muttered. "I shouldn't have come in here."

"No," said Rev. Chambers. "You shouldn't have."

"Who did the cross-stitch?" Cat asked, pointing to the one above the fireplace and trying to sound upbeat. "It's very nice."

"You know something about cross-stitch?" he asked, looking dubious. "Most high-school girls think it's too old-fashioned. There's little appreciation for the domestic arts nowadays, a woman's rightful work in the home."

"My mother taught me," Cat said. "I've never done one that big, though. It looks like whoever stitched it didn't use a pattern."

He smiled appreciatively. "Oh, I'm sure ol' Anita marked out the pattern herself. She'd make a good wife for the right man, if she weren't married to the church."

"She sounds like a nun," Cat said, standing up. She threw the staples into the trashcan.

"We don't keep brides of Christ here," he said, using his cane to stand up. "And we don't tolerate nosy little girls who are too big for their britches. And I mean that in more than one sense." As he said that last part, his eyes appraised Cat up and down.

She had no choice but to gulp back her natural inclination to tell him to go fuck himself. Instead, she cast her eyes downward, muttered "Yes, sir," and left the office.

That afternoon, she was still burning with anger toward Rev. Chambers as she sat in the back of the ministry classroom, listening to Anita.

"College will be a very exciting time in your lives. You'll learn so much about the world and about yourselves. But you will also be met with the greatest temptations of your lives, especially those of you who aren't planning to attend bible colleges." Anita paused and cast a glance at Cat, as well as at a few of the other girls in the back of the room. "One of the goals of our precollege teen program is to adequately prepare you to meet these challenges with all the blessings of Christ in your hearts."

Cat glanced around the room. The girls were all nodding in agreement with Anita. She thought about her own four years at college, at a Catholic Jesuit university. Had she encountered the greatest temptations of her life? She supposed that was true in some sense, yes. There had been marijuana and other recreational drugs if she wanted them, and one-night stands if she wanted those, too. Alcohol was easy to come by. And of course there was the temptation of the education itself, which could have led her to atheism. But it hadn't. Her religious studies teachers encouraged her to question her faith, but they had all been priests who believed that questioning one's faith only strengthened it. As for the other temptations, well, Cat came out of her four years in college with a degree and full honors, and she was neither drug- nor sex-addicted, and she still believed in God.

But she would have to quell these thoughts if she didn't want to blow her cover. Anita was staring at her just then, so she put an open, beatific smile on her face.

"Today's Bible lesson is about love and marriage," Anita announced. "It's about walking the path with Christ in your hearts. It's about being pure, body and soul." Anita passed out a piece of paper on which were listed several Bible verses. On the back was a Purity Pledge.

"I know you're all eager to pledge your purity," she said. "But this is Bible study, so let's start with the lesson."

Anita asked Hope to read a passage from 1 Corinthians: "Every sin that a man doeth is without the body; but he that committeth fornication sinneth against his own body. What? Know ye not that your body is the temple of the Holy Ghost which is in you, which ye have of God, and ye are not your own? For ye are bought with a price: therefore glorify God in your body, and in your spirit, which are God's."

Hope read in a clear, measured inflection. Cat couldn't help but flash back to her dream, the sexual arousal it produced.

"What does this passage mean?" Anita asked. Several hands shot up.

But Hope still had the floor. "Fornication is a sin," she declared.

"That's part of it, yes," Anita said. "Anyone else?"

Several hands were still in the air, but Anita was looking at Cat. It was clearly her moment to step up.

"All the other sins don't have an effect on the sinner's body," Cat observed. "But fornication does. It's like committing a crime against your own body."

Anita's face broke into a wide, surprised smile. "Yes," she beamed. "Exactly. Well done, Cat."

After a few more rounds interpreting various Bible verses dealing with the subjects of purity, lust, and setting an example for others, it was time for the Purity Pledge. There were several provisions to the pledge, ranging from "I will always dress in a manner that honors the sanctity of my body and shields me from tempting others" to "I will only commit to a man who shares my commitment to God."

Just to show Anita that she was undergoing an authentically challenging transition, Cat took issue with that last one, asking if she would ever be allowed to marry a Catholic man. "If he's raised in a faith, it shouldn't matter which one," she pointed out. The room went silent. It was Wendy who took her on.

"How will you worship together if you're going to different churches?" she asked. "You can't build a life together in Christ if you're not practicing together. You'll be talking about Jesus, and he'll be talking about *Mary*. You know how the Catholics obsess over Mary."

The girls all giggled at that one. Hope spoke up next. "If you met someone you loved, you could spend some time at each other's churches, talk about how you want to build your Christian lives, and then decide how you'll do that."

"That's great advice for Cat," Anita said. "Thank you, Hope. Now let's all sign the pledge."

Cat signed it, no more questions asked. At the end of class, Anita announced there would be a Purity Ball, a father-daughter ball, which would give the girls in the precollege program a chance to honor their fathers for "warring on behalf of their purity." Cat sighed inwardly. Oh, her father was going to love this one.

They were all treated to ice cream after signing the pledge, as a reward, Cat supposed. They took their cones out to the garden to watch the setting sun. Wendy was at a bench by herself trying to tame a rapidly melting chocolate cone, and Cat sat down next to her. "I noticed something today," Cat said. "The Purity Pledge. It didn't mention being a virgin."

"Yeah, that's Anita for you," said Wendy between licks, her signature glittery orange nail polish getting covered in chocolate drips. "She's pretty smart. By the time you're getting ready for college, there's a good chance you're no longer a virgin. She figures it's better to focus on purity. Then it's not a lost cause if you've already stepped over that line. I mean, look at me. I'm not a virgin, but I'm pure as the driven snow these days." She grinned, a bit of chocolate ice cream in the corners of her mouth.

Cat offered her a napkin. Everyone else had wandered off to watch a group of guys from the boys' dorm playing volleyball on the lawn. Cat lowered her voice anyway, leaning in toward Wendy. "Are the church fathers pure? What I mean is, would any of them hang out at Diamond Dick's?"

Wendy looked at her hard. "Of course not," she whispered.

Cat reached into her pocket where she'd stowed the receipt she found in Larry's wastebasket waiting for just this moment with Wendy. It was a risk to confide in Wendy, even just this little bit, but it was a calculated one. "I knocked over Larry's trashcan on accident this morning. This fell out."

Wendy's face registered shock and disappointment the moment she saw the Diamond Dick's logo, which she would of course recognize because of her mother. "No," she said. "She can't be right. No." She shook her head. "Damn it," she hissed, tossing the receipt into Cat's lap.

"Who can't be right? What's the matter, Wendy?"

Wendy got up, stalked over to a trashcan and tossed her half-eaten ice cream cone inside. "Thanks for ruining my appetite," she said, and walked away.

Cat ran after her, falling in step as Wendy kept walking. "Wait. I'm sorry. I shouldn't have shown you that. After you told me your mom—"

"—is a liar," Wendy cut her off and kept walking. "Who says things just to hurt me. It's like a hobby for her."

"I'm sorry," said Cat.

Wendy stopped walking and turned to Cat. "Well, your receipt says my mom was right. I thought she was just jealous... of how much I love this church. She hates the fosters, never says anything good about them, and talks down the Plantation Church every chance she gets. One day she... Oh, it's awful the way she did it. 'You think those guys at that Jesus freak show are any different?' she said. 'Well, they're not. Those good ol' boys hang out at Diamond Dick's all the time. They're some of the best customers, if you know what I mean.'"

Tears were running down Wendy's face. Her hands were clenched into fists. "I thought she just said it to hurt me," she sobbed. "I thought she made it up."

Cat felt terrible. She was getting the information she needed, but she'd had to hurt Wendy in the process. She hugged Wendy, not sure whether or not Wendy would welcome the gesture. The girl was hesitant at first and then let go in Cat's arms. She wept, and Cat figured there was more that was coming out than just this one slight. It seemed as if years of frustration and heartache were bottled up inside Wendy.

"I'm sorry," Cat repeated. "I'm so sorry."

When Wendy had calmed down, Cat gave her another napkin to use to wipe her face. "It's just a receipt for drinks," Cat said softly. "He could have gone there for any number of reasons."

"Men only go to Diamond Dick's for one reason," Wendy retorted. "But it's okay. I get it. Larry was a guy. And he wasn't married. Whatever. So he went to a strip club. Big deal. He was just a hypocrite, that's all. So maybe I'm glad he killed himself. Maybe that was God's way of punishing him."

"Maybe he went there for other reasons," Cat offered. "And just because he was at the club doesn't mean he paid for sex. Some guys just go for the strip show, right? It's not such a bad thing."

"I guess," Wendy said.

Cat hesitated, unsure whether or not she could push Wendy any further. "Would it help to find out?" she asked hesitantly. "We could talk to your mom."

Chapter 11

"It's Wendy-the-Pooh! It's Wendy-the-Pooh!" A woman with bleached-out streaks in her hair and frosty green eye shadow had Cat by the hands and was dancing around with her. Cat felt a mix of emotions: she was glad to see her happy for a change, but she also felt a little frightened of her as well. Her breath smelled of alcohol, and her eyes were red and puffy.

"It's Wendy-the-Pooh!" she kept yelling over and over again. Cat couldn't get free of the woman's grip. She realized this must be Wendy's mother.

Over and over the woman kept saying the line, dancing in circles. Cat felt dizzy. Then they were on a merry-go-round, spinning at an incredible speed. Cat was so woozy that she couldn't concentrate on the place where her and Wendy's consciousnesses separated. All she could do was hang on for the ride.

Cat felt something she'd never felt before. Wendy was struggling, trying to bridge the space between her own consciousness and the power her mother had over her in the dream. Wendy was struggling to get out of the dream somehow, to make it all stop.

Wendy's words broke into the dream half-formed, as if Wendy were struggling to speak for the first time. "S-s-stop. Stop! STOP IT!"

Cat was kicked forcefully out of the dream, awakened, and she heard Wendy in the bunk next to her. She had actually yelled, "Stop it!"

"Wendy?" a voice asked. It was Hope. "Are you okay?"

Feeling overwhelming dizziness, Cat sat up and looked at Wendy, who was trying to catch her breath.

"It's okay," Hope said. "You just had a bad dream."

"A nightmare," Wendy said. "My mother. Oh, God. Not these again. I thought I'd kicked them." She plopped back onto her pillow and curled up into a fetal position.

"Do you need anything?" Hope asked.

Cat dropped down off her bunk and padded over to Wendy, placing her hand on her shoulder. "You were yelling 'stop it.' You got out of the dream that way. I mean, I think. That's what it looked like."

"Did I really yell?" Wendy sat up and looked at Hope.

"Yes," Hope nodded.

"Sorry to wake you guys up," Wendy said.

"No worries," Hope said in unison with Cat's, "Don't worry about it."

They all went back to sleep, but at breakfast that morning, Cat took Wendy aside and apologized. "I didn't mean to give you nightmares," she explained. "I'm so sorry I showed you the receipt."

The nightmare had given Cat a crisis of confidence. She hadn't been able to get back to sleep and wondered desperately what Granny Grace would think of what she was doing. She didn't like hurting Wendy, however inadvertently.

"It's okay," Wendy said. She sighed. "I think you're right, anyway. We should go talk to my mom. I want to know the truth. Like it says in the Book of John, 'Sanctify them in your truth; your word is truth.' And I can tell her she was right, if she was right after all."

"Are you sure?" Cat asked.

"Yeah. You know the only reason I've had anything to do with her for the past five years is because I'm trying to save her, Cat. I'm trying to bring my mother to Jesus. Trust me, it's been a little like trying to save the whore of Babylon. That woman does not wish to be saved. But it's like Anita said: she's the only mother I've got. If I can't share God's love with her, who can I share it with? Maybe if I go to her and say she was right, and listen to her, I'll get closer to saving her."

Cat had not been prepared for this, and she chided herself for not seeing it. Of course. Wendy didn't *have* to see her mother. She was taken from her and put into the foster system years ago, and it sounded like her mother had made no changes in her life nor fought to get Wendy back. At eighteen, it would be Wendy's choice to see her mother or not anyway. Why would she, except to save her? Cat's heart went out to Wendy. She had reason to resent her mother, and here she was trying to share with her the one thing that had made a difference in Wendy's life.

"Okay," Cat agreed. "If you're sure."

"I'm sure, Cat. And we've got the day off anyway," she said. The precollege program gave the girls Mondays off for free time or to visit their families. "Let's spread some light into that den of iniquity."

Diamond Dick's was in a small town on the Illinois side of the Mississippi River that had only two businesses: a copper smelter and Diamond Dick's. The copper smelter had poisoned the small river running through it to the point where local dogs suffered burns just from wading in it. It was generally believed by the god-fearing set that Diamond Dick's polluted folks' minds as bad as the smelter polluted the river.

Wendy had called her mother and arranged to meet her at the strip club. It was Monday, and the place was getting ready for the noon business. Wendy wasn't technically allowed in the bar, and Cat wasn't either since she was pretending to be under twenty-one, but ironically, they could both strip since they were over eighteen. Wendy's mother ushered them in through the back door without a problem.

She brought them into the dressing room, where several strippers were changing out of their street clothes and putting on scant costumes for the noon show. One pulled herself into a red unitard with a hole cut out of the butt that revealed more than the garment covered. A similar hole in the front showed off cleavage that made Cat envious. Another wore garters and a pink teddy with heels and stood in front of the mirror, loading her cheeks with blush. A third was sitting in a director's chair and wearing a robe, a pair of red patent-leather heels peeking out the bottom. She wore glasses and was reading out of a very thick textbook, a highlighter pen in one hand.

"Hey, Chi Chi, Ms. Thing, Mitzi," Wendy's mom announced, calling out the girls' stage names. "My kid's here for a visit. Say hi to Wendy."

The girl at the director's chair looked up long enough to nod, but then bent back over her book. The other two glanced over, smiled, and waved.

"So you said you wanted to apologize," her mother said, waving her hands as she spoke. They were done up in an overly elaborate French manicure, with the nails of both index fingers sporting dangling heart-shaped charms. She wore the same green frosty eye shadow that Cat had seen in the dream, and she could see that it did bring out the woman's green eyes. She'd been a gorgeous girl at one point, Cat thought. But life had clearly been hard on her body and looks. She had deep, dark circles under her eyes, her teeth were stained grey, and her skin was like the leather on an old football.

"I can't imagine what you'd want to apologize to me for, Wendy," she said. "You're always telling me how sorry I should be for fucking up your life. And for being such a sinner. I'm going straight to hell when I die, ain't I?" She tossed her dyed-red hair over her shoulder and laughed for the benefit of the strippers, who were busy ignoring the whole scene.

"Mom, listen," Wendy said. "I want to apologize for not believing you. For calling you a liar. You told me once that the men from Plantation were regulars here. And you were right."

All three strippers stared at them now. The bookworm had even looked up from her text.

Cat produced the receipt she'd found in Larry's wastebasket. "We found this in the assistant director's office. Maybe you know him? Larry Price. He committed suicide recently."

Chi Chi, the one in the red unitard, let out a gasp and ran over, sort of stilt-walking in her stilettos. "Not Larry!" she cried, peering at the receipt. "Yeah, that's his signature," she said. "He's one of my regulars. Or was, anyway. I wondered why I hadn't seen him in a while." She looked genuinely crestfallen.

Cat watched Wendy's face as Larry's strip club attendance was confirmed. Her jaw was set with a hard edge. "One of your regulars?" Wendy asked.

"Yeah, he and that other one, the one who always seemed like he was the ringleader, in charge," she said. "They sometimes come in here together, with a group of other men."

"You mean Jim Plantation?" Cat asked Chi Chi.

"Yeah," she replied. "The guy from that cable show? The one who wants to get us all into heaven." She rolled her eyes.

The girl in the pink teddy, presumably Ms. Thing, spoke up. "The one with the cane tips me outrageously," she added. "I'm like his favorite."

"Is he an older dude?" Cat asked.

"Yeah," she said. "White beard, very old-fashioned, the way he acts."

A self-satisfied smile was plastered over Wendy's mother's face. "You see? Your old lady doesn't make this shit up. You should listen to me."

"Yes, Mom," Wendy said. "I should." She reached out and took her mother's hand. Cat thought of the dream, the spinning, how she wouldn't let go of Wendy.

"Maybe you two should sit down and have a nice, long talk," Cat suggested, motioning to a table in the back. She wanted to talk with the strippers some more without distraction.

Wendy and her mother took her cue and sat in the back, out of earshot of the rest of the room. Cat turned to Chi Chi, who was at the mirror again, brushing her hair. "What kind of customer was Larry?" Cat asked her.

Chi Chi smiled. "Very gentlemanly. Never tried to touch me against the rules. Sometimes I'd go out and sit with his group, and Larry and I talked about boxing. He's a big fan, and my brother's a fighter."

"And Jim?" she inquired.

Ms. Thing chimed in. "Not as nice as Larry, but he never tried anything. Those guys from the church are great customers. Always well behaved. Generous, too."

Cat wanted to ask something but wasn't sure how to go about it. "Did either of them ever request... um... private services?"

Someone snorted in disgust. It was Mitzi, the one with her nose in a book, who had yet to speak. She laughed incredulously. "Is that what you think we are?" she scoffed. "Hookers?"

Chi Chi and Ms. Thing were frowning. Cat felt her face grow warm with shame. She didn't know what to say.

"Listen, Susie Sunday," Mitzi snapped, standing up and placing a hand on her hip, "just because we dance around on stage in our undies doesn't mean we're prostitutes. There's a difference. A rather big difference."

"I'm sorry," Cat apologized.

"Besides which," Mitzi continued, "boy, are you barking up the wrong tree. Larry Price wouldn't have actual sex with any of us. I'm quite certain he only came here for the dancing and the outfits. Now if you'll excuse me, I have studying to do. You see, I might have time to blow a few johns on the side if I weren't prepping for the bar exam."

Cat walked over toward Mitzi. "Are you telling me that Larry Price was gay?"

Mitzi looked Cat square in the eyes. "I'm just saying that guy was a pretty good actor, but I've got an even better gaydar. And around Larry, it was always in the red zone."

Cat looked at Chi Chi and Ms. Thing. They nodded and sort of shrugged agreement. Chi Chi ran her hands down the sides of her body and said, "You'd have to be gay to not want to get with this."

Ms. Thing smacked her with a towel. "Go on, girl. Isn't it time to get your bad self up on stage?"

Chi Chi left. But Cat had more questions. "What about Jim?" she asked.

"Ah..." Mitzi poised one finger in the air and then acted as if checking off a box as she pronounced, "Gay."

"And the others. The guy with the cane?"

"Those guys, they're not gay," Mitzi declared. "Who do you think Jim was putting on the show for? It wasn't for us. It was for the other men."

"Are you kidding me?" Cat said. "Jim Plantation is the most antigay leader in the bistate area."

"Yeah, well, methinks the lady doth protest too much," Mitzi said.

"He's married," Cat stated, knowing her voice sounded unconvincing.

Mitzi shot a meaningful look at Ms. Thing but directed her words toward Cat. "Yeah, and you'll never guess who he married."

"Don't tell her," Ms. Thing cautioned. "C'mon, Mitz. After all her attempts to start a new life."

"Why not? Don't you want the church girl here to know who Jim married? It's not a reflection on Sherrie. I'm proud of what I do, and it's too bad Sherrie wasn't. It's too bad she married that self-righteous hypocrite who turned her away from all her friends."

"Sherrie wouldn't want it..."

"He didn't—" Cat said.

"Don't," said Ms. Thing.

"Jim married a stripper," announced Mitzi. "Sherrie is her name. She used to work here. She used to be our friend."

"Damn, Mitz," sighed Ms. Thing. "You always have such a big mouth."

"I told you I don't believe in keeping other people's secrets," Mitzi replied.

Cat's head was swimming. Larry had been gay, and so was Jim. Yet Jim had married a stripper from Diamond Dick's, and that was the woman she'd met in Seattle in the abandoned condo building. Sherrie.

Wendy and her mother got up from their table in the back just then, breaking up the conversation. They walked arm and arm together, and then Wendy turned to her mother to say good-bye.

"Think about the rehab program, okay?" she said, squeezing her mother's arm as she let go. Cat knew Wendy was trying to talk her mother into the ministry's antidrug program. So apparently her faith in the Plantation Church hadn't been shaken by the revelation that Jim and his cadre weren't exactly living what they preached.

They bid good-bye to Ms. Thing and Mitzi, who called after them, "Feel free to come back here for a reality check any time."

Once they were headed back to the church, Cat turned to Wendy and asked, "So, how are you doing? Did knowing that Jim, Larry, and those guys were regulars at Diamond Dick's change your mind about the church?"

Wendy was driving and kept focusing straight ahead. "At first, yes," she said solemnly. "But then, I'm not exactly a perfect little angel, and the fosters accepted me, and so has the church. I thought of Jim and Larry as gods, and that was on me. They're not gods. They're of the flesh, just like me and you. I'm not excusing what they did, what they all continue to do. But I'm not going to be the one to cast the first stone, either."

Cat wondered who would cast the first stone, if anyone. But she couldn't let herself get wrapped up in this internal church drama. She needed to focus on her investigation, which had taken more than one unexpected turn.

What in the world should she do next? From her years as a student in Midtown, she knew where all the gay bars were in St. Louis. She could hit the obvious spots that Jim and Larry most likely went to. She'd also been trying to figure out a way to get into Jim's private residence. He had an office at the church, but Anita's front desk was adjacent to it, her door always open between the two. After the run-in with Rev. Chambers in Larry's office, she hadn't tried to find a way into Larry's private apartment there on church grounds, either, but it was on her list.

With the rest of her day off, Cat decided to head to St. Louis, swinging by to visit her parents first.

She called to let them know she'd be by, and her father had set out snacks and drinks on their patio, with a festive sun umbrella to block the glare. The weather had cooled off a bit for St. Louis in early August; an uncharacteristically balmy breeze blew through her parents' small city backyard. The garden was in full bloom, her mother's prized hydrangeas putting on a stately show and her yellow daylilies looking dependably jaunty.

Her father had set out a shrimp ring and dipping cocktail as well as a bowl of chips. The food from the Plantation Church kitchen had skewed heavily toward the healthy and wholesome side. While certainly not vegetarian, the dishes were well balanced and decidedly plain, with the Saturday ice cream social the only moment of decadence in the week. Cat scarfed down the shrimp and chips as if she were starving.

"So how goes the undercover work?" her father asked. Her parents knew she was in the precollege program at Plantation because she'd needed to feign getting their "permission" to enroll her. Even though she was playing the role of a legal eighteen-year-old, the church believed in good relationships between parents and their children, and they did everything they could to get the parents' support of their kid's participation in the program.

"They've already sent us a request for a donation," her mother interjected, rolling her eyes. "That was rather fast."

"They probably figure they'd get us while we're feeling grateful to them for taking our college-bound kid off our hands a few months early," he joked. "Y'all are antsy and tough to be around that last summer."

"That must be why you shipped me off to Granny Grace's," Cat said.

Her father winked, and her mother just smiled. They were all sipping white wine, and since she hadn't had a drop to drink in weeks, Cat felt it warm her cheeks immediately.

"I rather like this feeling of getting to start over," Cat teased. "Maybe I'll move back home and re-enroll at St. Louis U. I could always get a second degree."

"Sure," her father said. "While you're at it, pick me up a degree. I never even got a first degree, let alone a second. Unless you're talking burns, of course." He rolled up his arm to show off the scars he got from an electrical fire on one of his construction projects. "Got plenty of those."

Cat and her mother giggled. "Joe, put your arm away," her mother scolded. "No one wants to see that. We're eating shrimp, for God's sake."

"We're eating shrimp for God's sake? Well, why didn't you say so? I better eat more, in that case."

After the teasing died down, Cat began to talk about what it was like to be undercover. She couldn't tell them details about the case, but she told them about the church teachings. Her father became animated when she came to the Purity Pledge.

"I can see where this is going, Cathedral Spire, and I'm not having it," he cautioned, waving a shrimp in her face. "Under no circumstances will I be escorting my grown daughter to something as ridiculous, insulting, and patriarchally presumptive as a Purity Ball."

Cat couldn't help busting up at the sight of her father wiggling a shrimp in her face. Affecting a high Southern-belle tone, she replied, "You mean to tell me you're unwilling to wage a spiritual war in honor of my chastity? Daddy, I'm deeply disappointed, and so is my chastity. Lately it has been feeling quite threatened."

The three of them were laughing now, and Cat was surprised to find she felt a stab of guilt at having fun at the expense of those she knew in the Plantation Church.

"I'm afraid I've made them sound like idiots," she said regretfully. "But they're not. They want the same things anyone wants. And I find their passion to be admirable."

Her mother looked a bit pained and worried. "They're getting to you, aren't they, Cat?"

"What? No," she said defensively. "At least I don't think so. Not the way you fear. It's just..." She stopped. "There's this girl at the church, Wendy. Her mom's a real piece of work. Wendy's been with a foster family all through high school—that's how she joined the church—and her mother's sort of this lost cause. But Wendy keeps trying to reach out to her."

"That's lovely," her mother said. "You obviously care about your friend very much. But Jim's teachings are very divisive. They actively support the most reactionary Republican candidates. And I bet there's not a black face to be seen in that ministry."

"All true," Cat conceded. "But Mom, look what the archbishop is saying these days about homosexuality."

Her mother was silent. "Well, that's different."

"Is it?" Cat said quietly. She felt her temperature rise but didn't want to fight with her mother. Not today, not over this.

Her mother got up from the table. "I'll leave you two to chat. I've got to get my things together for the sewing circle."

Cat and her father sat in silence for a minute before her father sighed. "Well, that didn't last long," he observed.

"I'm sorry," Cat said.

"It's not just your fault," her father said. He reached over and squeezed her arm. "My ladies... Ugh. What's a man to do?" He stood up and began clearing the table. Cat checked her phone for the time. She had better start canvassing the bars if she wanted to hit all of them tonight.

"Stay for dinner?" her father asked, but Cat demurred, noticing she had a voice mail message from Granny Grace.

"Mind if I go upstairs to make a phone call?" she asked.

"Knock yourself out," her father said, taking the wine glasses out of her hand. "I'll take care of this." He had taken responsibility for the kitchen when he retired, saying Cat's mother had handled it for the last thirty years, and he was effectively relieving her from duty.

Cat closed the door to the guest bedroom and sat down on the bed. The macramé owl was in her eye line again as she tapped "Granny Grace" in her cell phone listing.

"Hi, Gran," Cat said. "How are you?"

"Oh, I'm fine," Granny Grace answered. "But I miss you. How's the case? Have you tracked down Jim? I've been worried about you."

"Yes, well, I'm sorry I haven't been in touch," Cat said. "I'm undercover in Jim's church."

"You're what?!" Granny Grace exclaimed. "Wow. Now that takes guts! Good for you, Cat."

Cat quickly filled her grandmother in on the details, relieved that she could finally unburden herself. However, her grandmother was even less charitable than her mother had been about Cat bonding with others in the church. "Be careful, Cat. It's like *Invasion of the Body Snatchers* in places like that. You won't even know what hit you. Suddenly, you're just one of them."

"Thanks. I should think you'd have more faith in me than that."

"Oh, don't take it personally. It's not a reflection on you. It's just how those cults are. I should know. I went undercover in a so-called satanic cult once."

"What?!" Cat gasped. "You never told me that."

"It's not as exciting as it sounds. There wasn't anything supernatural going on at all—not even anyone with our sort of ability. Just a lot of wayward girls and boys following this guy who ended up basically using them as prostitutes and drug runners. He used the 'satanism' as a way to control them."

"Jeez, Granny Grace," said Cat. "That's really sad."

"Yeah, I know. But at least I sent him to prison."

"Is there anything you haven't done?" Cat asked.

"Well, I've never spoken in tongues, but it sounds like you might," said Granny Grace, laughing.

"Let's hope it doesn't come to that," Cat replied. Then: "How are things in Seattle?"

"Oh, same-old, same-old. But I am working on a little side project for the mayor. Just a simple little case. Not as exciting as yours."

"Well, tell me about it."

"His son scored very high on his ACT test. The problem was, so did another kid in the same testing pool, and both their tests were flagged for being too similar, as if one had copied many of his answers from the other."

"Oh, no," said Cat. "Isn't there a way to see who was cheating off whom?"

"They run all these checks to try to catch any anomalies or similarities between the tests in every batch," explained Granny Grace. "They also look for significant jumps between one test and another, if the student has taken it more than once. But they don't call it 'cheating' outright. They 'withhold' them and do an audit."

"What are you going to do?"

"The mayor's son—Felix is his name—he's taken the test before, and his score was a good deal lower the first time. This only adds to the suspicion. The mayor is very worried. If he doesn't clear his son's name, the test will be sent on to colleges with the flag attached, which isn't the same as being called a cheater, but it might as well be. Felix is really hoping for a scholarship to Yale, his father's alma mater."

"Sounds impossible," said Cat, shaking her head.

"The other student has also taken the test before," said Granny Grace. "And his was even lower the first time. But Felix has been through an extensive—and expensive, I might add—round of tutoring courses in order to improve his score. The other student has not."

"That's a start, but there's probably not enough evidence to clear Felix," said Cat.

"You're right," agreed Granny Grace. "But I've got some other ideas. I'll let you know how it all pans out. Oh, and before I forget, I saw Lee's parents again the other night. They asked about you."

"That reminds me, Gran. Have you ever slipped into the dream of someone who is hundreds of miles away at the time?"

"Mmm... No, I haven't. But my grandmother told me a story once. She swore she continued to slip into the dreams of her childhood best friend, Carmen, even after Carmen and her family had long since gone back to Spain."

"Really?"

"Yeah," Granny Grace said. "The two of them had a preternatural connection, though. My grandmother talked about Carmen on her deathbed. It did raise certain questions... Why do you ask?"

Cat suddenly felt too self-conscious to talk about Lee over the phone, and to her grandmother. "Oh, no reason," she said. "It's just something I wondered."

"Yeah, right. Have you been having Lee's dreams out there, Cat?"

Cat was silent for a few beats. "Maybe. I'm not sure. I'll have to talk to him to find out."

"Well, isn't that something!" Granny Grace said. "How many miles?"

"Eight hundred," Cat said. She felt her face flush. "Listen, I have to go. I'm canvassing the bars around here tonight for anyone who's seen Jim and Larry."

"Well, good luck," Granny Grace told her, adding, "Don't go home with anyone whose dreams you wouldn't want to see."

Cat laughed. Her grandmother had just hit upon the main reason that, unlike for many of her college friends, the one-night stand had never really worked for Cat.

They said good-bye, and Cat ran downstairs. Her mother had gone already to her sewing circle meeting. Her father was at the dining room table, wearing reading glasses and working on a model of a '71 Corvette painted yellow.

She pecked her father on the forehead. "Tell Mom I love her," she said.

"Cathedral Candle, that's something she probably needs to hear from you," he replied.

Cat sighed. "You're right, Dad. I'll be back."

He smiled. "Remain pure and chaste, my good daughter."

Cat curtsied. "As you command, dear father."

It took Cat a few tries before she found a bar where anyone recognized Larry or Jim, but she finally found what she was searching for in Oasis.

It was a new bar in a revitalized section of downtown that Cat remembered fondly from her early college days, before the money

111

moved in and took over. Back then, she'd frequented a hipster bar called Tangerine, which had a bubble machine out front and a slide show featuring old eighties TV shows inside. Martinis were cheap, and they always gave you the remainder in the mixing glass along with your stem, so it was like getting two or even three drinks for the price of one.

In stark contrast was Oasis. If it were trying to convey its namesake in any way at all, it would be as an oasis of old-world maleness in a sea of sports bars. Oasis was dark wood and red walls. The bar itself was leather. The lighting was low but somehow still cold. The clientele in Oasis was almost entirely male, and all were well-dressed. There wasn't a T-shirt in the place, and there were no TVs.

She found a seat at the bar and had to put up with a couple of snobby waiters, who studiously ignored her, till a young newbie waiter took pity on her and lent her his ear. She showed him photos of Jim and Larry.

"I've never seen that guy," he said, pointing to Larry. "But I remember this one really well," he said about Jim. "It was my first night here, and he totally hit on me. Saddest sack I've ever seen. Drank straight whiskey, shot after shot, and cried in his glass for hours. Then he was all over me, asking me to take him home."

Cat looked at him inquisitively.

"No, I didn't," he retorted, miffed. "Do I look that desperate?"

"What night did you start working here?" Cat asked.

"Oh, it was June 12," he said.

Cat knew the date. The night of Larry's death. "Can you get me someone who can ID this other man? Someone who's worked here longer."

It took some convincing, but an uptight waiter came over to Cat's end of the bar and looked at her photographs.

"They're two of my regulars," he said. "A couple. Eyes only for each other."

Cat was taken aback. "What? Your newbie said this one hit on him." She pointed to Jim's photo.

"Not likely..." he said, "unless something's changed. I haven't seen them all summer."

"You know who this one is, don't you?" Cat asked. "The Christian leader. Jim Plantation."

"Of course I know," the waiter sniffed. "Am I supposed to be shocked?"

"He campaigns against homosexuality."

The waiter laughed. "I know that, too," he said, putting his free hand on his hip. "It's the best cover in the world, if you ask me." He paused. "Look," he said. "One night our two love birds in the photo

112

were in here, and in strolled another couple, also regulars, but they'd never been in here before at the same time. All undercover gays, you know what I mean? Well, as soon as the two camps spotted each other, they collectively began to, ah, repent."

"What?!"

"Yeah, right here in the bar. Really killed the atmosphere that night, let me tell you. All four guys started praying together right here. I had to ask them to leave, which they did, together."

The waiter paused to let that sink in, and then with a sniff he announced, "Now if you'll excuse me, I have real customers to serve."

Cat could tell she'd exhausted her avenue of information at Oasis, and she was herself exhausted, so she drove back across the river and plopped into her bunk bed, mulling over the behavior of the men in the church. When caught out on their homosexuality, they help each other sort of get back on track. What a tremendous amount of effort to deny a natural inclination in the name of an ideology, she thought, feeling the futility of it all.

It actually felt good to be "home," and that she could feel hominess at the Plantation Church startled her. If she weren't so exhausted, it was the kind of thing that could keep her up at night.

Chapter 12

C at turned over in bed and saw her lover lying there on her side, the curve of her hip a perfect sloping arch. She traced it with her fingertips. Her lover stirred. Cat let her fingertips press harder into the woman's flesh, tracing up and down the curve of her hip and then over to the small of her back and to the cleft in her bottom. Her lover moaned and turned to face her. It was Cat. She was staring at herself.

She looked at her hands. A man's hands. She recognized the calluses on the knuckles. They were Lee's.

Okay, making love to herself the old-fashioned way was one thing, but this was just too weird. She was fused with Lee's consciousness, and she felt an overwhelming desire to fuck herself, which just felt... wrong? She needed to pop out of this now. But then... She was captivated by the lost look in her own eyes. Cat's eyes—the Cat in the dream, anyway. She realized that Lee's version of her had no cellulite, no stretch marks from when she hit puberty and her hips grew too fast, no ugly moles that should probably be removed by a dermatologist. He seemed to think her nose was the cutest nose ever created. Her broad shoulders that often made her feel like a linebacker for the Seahawks he apparently found sexy. As Lee turned his attention to her chest, she held her breath for a second but was relieved to find that Lee's dream fantasy version of her had the same small breasts the real Cat had.

Now she was kissing them, and that was just unbearable. She concentrated on the silvery outline between Lee's mind and hers, pried the two apart, and there she was, sitting on the edge of the bed, watching Lee make love to her. It was oddly arousing, watching him caress and adore her this way. He was also very commanding, taking and moving her this way and that, and the dream Cat responded to his motions with spasms of excitement. Cat was surprised by how lusty and wanton she looked, coaxing and begging him, directing him when he needed to be. The two of them responded to each other as if sex itself were a form of Holy Communion.

She hadn't had a lot of time to think about her night with Lee, what with the events of the past few weeks and her trip to St. Louis. Seeing them together like this—herself and Lee was... oddly moving.

Cat heard a shot suddenly zing across the bed, and Lee disengaged from dream Cat, rolled the two of them onto the floor, and pushed her under it. The shot had come from the stairwell of his loft bedroom. The sniper—Cat recognized him from the grocery store dream—was standing on the spiral staircase, pointing a gun at them.

Cat backed away instinctively even though she knew it didn't matter; neither of them could see her. Her dream self was under the bed. Lee lunged for his closet, where he grabbed his own gun, spun around, and shot the sniper, who fell to the bottom of the staircase. Lee sat breathing hard for a few minutes, poised with his gun in case there were more of them. But it was quiet until Cat under the bed called out, "Lee?"

He rolled under the bed with her. Cat wanted to be a part of their embrace instead of an invisible entity in the room, so she fused with Lee again. Then Cat woke up; the dream had ended. She lay in bed a long time, the feel of her arms around herself as Lee seeming more real to her than her present surroundings. Then she fell back to sleep and dreamed her own dream this time.

Anita morphed into her mother and scolded her about coming back to St. Louis too soon. "You're not a very good Catholic," she said, "so you might as well sign the Purity Pledge."

Cat woke up in her bunk at Plantation just as the macramé owl on the wall in her dream flew out the window of her parents' guest bedroom, squawking like a parrot as it went. "Adam and Steve," it called. "Adam and Steve."

She spent the day helping Wendy draft a Bible lesson plan for the rehab program. Since Wendy's mother was planning to attend, Wendy wanted it to be good. They decided to use the story of Mary Magdalene to show God's loving mercy for all.

Wendy had been preoccupied with her mother when Mitzi revealed the true back-story of Jim's wife. Cat was curious to know if Wendy's mother had ever mentioned that, if she even knew, and what the official story was on Jim and his wife.

"So how did Sherrie and Jim meet?" Cat asked.

"Sherrie? Jim's wife? Hmm..." Wendy had to think about it for a minute. "I don't remember. A church camp, I think?"

"So she wasn't part of this congregation."

"Not till Jim married her. There were plenty of women who wanted to be Mrs. Plantation, that's for sure. But he brought someone in from outside."

"Your mother never... mentioned her?"

"No. Why would she?"

"Oh, I don't know. She seemed to pick up on all the Plantation Church gossip." The two of them giggled and rolled their eyes at that one. So if Wendy's mother knew how Jim had met Sherrie, she had kept the secret that Mitzi'd let out of the bag, most likely for Wendy's sake, but maybe for Sherrie's, too.

"Plantation Church gossip? The biggest news these days is you two." It was Tina, who'd walked into the meeting room in time to pick up on the tail end of their conversation. News of their strip club Christian intervention had already spread like wildfire through the Plantation community, and the two girls were being heralded as heroes. The story had grown a bit in proportion, and some versions included an altercation with a bouncer and a quick getaway in Wendy's Buick.

"I can't believe you guys spent your only day off bringing a wayward woman to Christ," Tina said. She put her hand on Wendy's shoulder, closed her eyes as if breathing in the Holy Spirit itself, and then sighed. "I'm so, so proud of you," she said. Then her eyes flew open, and she came over to Cat's side of the table. "Both. I'm so proud of both of you. Cat, you've been such a beacon of righteous action in our church!" Tina's arms flew around Cat. There were tears in her eyes. Cat didn't know what to say.

"It all—it all just... happened," she sputtered, then recovered. "Really, it was Wendy," she said. "She reached out to her mother, and her mother responded."

"I can feel Jesus' love coursing through both of you," said Tina.

Wendy's face was red. "Tina, please."

Anita walked in. "It's wonderful, isn't it?" she gushed. "Oh, what the Lord can do when his flock comes together."

"Amen," said Tina. "Hey, aren't you hungry? I'm famished."

"Me, too. Should be almost time for dinner, and if we get there early, we get seconds," said Wendy. She stood up, Tina linked arms with her, and they walked out the door. They'd come to the end of the lesson planning anyway. Cat gathered up her things.

"The only thing I can't figure out," Anita said as if wondering aloud, "is why the two of you were at that... fleshpot to begin with. Did you go there with the express purpose of talking to Wendy's mother? Or was there another reason?"

Cat felt put on the defensive, and playing the role of high schooler was wearing on her. Anger about the church's hypocrisy flashed through her. Maybe it was time anyway to show Anita a little authenticity.

"No," Cat said. "Her mother said she had evidence that Larry had been to Diamond Dick's. She had one of his signed receipts."

Anita gasped, clutching the gold cross around her neck. "It's a lie," she hissed.

"Well, the card ran in his name, Larry Price. And I don't think her mother would lie. About that, anyway. At first Wendy thought she was just trying to ruin something Wendy loved, but she realized her mother was telling the truth. There were some dancers there who said he was a regular."

Anita sighed. "I suppose Larry had his weaknesses."

"What's all this stuff with the Purity Pledge and everything if your church leadership is hanging out in strip clubs? Does the fight for chastity not apply to those women? Some of them aren't much older than we are."

"Don't get judgmental on me," Anita warned, her steely blue eyes boring into Cat's. "I'm not entirely sure about you. You ask a lot of questions for someone who's trying to find her path."

"Let's just say I have high standards," Cat sniffed. "I've been looking for a church whose leaders practice what they preach. I thought this was it."

"Larry was the weak link," Anita said, spitting out her words as if they were distasteful. "That should be evident by his suicide. Now he's gone. The dead wood has been eliminated. We're a strong, healthy forest now." Her eyes beamed.

Cat waited a beat, looking Anita straight in the eyes. "But what about Jim? You don't think he ever went to those clubs, too?"

"No!" she shot back. "That man is pure. Pure!"

"I hope he is," Cat said. "I hope he is."

Between conversations at dinner and after Bible study in the evening, when the girls convened to watch Christian-friendly movies, she surreptitiously gathered more details about Sherrie Plantation. The official cover story seemed to be that she and Jim had met at a convention of Christian leaders, which she had continued to serve after her first husband died. She was a widow with a young child and all alone when the Lord brought them together. She was from California. She married Jim and moved to Illinois, where she and her new husband could continue to serve the Lord together.

She also found out that Jim and Sherrie didn't clean their own house. That task was completed by a cleaning service run by Tina's parents, in the true church fashion of supporting each other's business— as well as spiritual—enterprises. Tina sometimes helped her parents out at work, and Cat volunteered to help Tina the next day; her parents were looking after the Plantation house in the family's absence. Tina was treating Cat like a celebrity for Christ because of her role in Wendy's mother's salvation and seemed eager to be her new best friend.

It was 10 p.m. and lights out in the girls' dorm. Cat lay in her bunk running through the events of the day. She hoped her measure of honest indignation had worked on Anita. She wanted to be as authentic with that woman as possible, especially the closer she got to the truth. It was hard not to feel as if she were headed toward a dead end, despite the juiciness of the facts she'd found out. If Larry and Jim had been lovers, then Larry's death could simply be a heartbreak suicide. Maybe he couldn't keep living the lie. But that didn't explain why Sherrie would bolt, with the kid in tow. What could have happened that would make her run off to Canada? Maybe she hadn't left her strip club past in the past. Something might have caught up with her, something so bad she had to run to get away from it. It seemed crazy to Cat that Jim had married her. Why marry a woman you don't love, whose past you have to cover up?

Then Cat remembered Jim's dream that night by the condo site, the vicious anger he felt, how crazy protective he was of their sexuality. Rescuing Sherrie could be a way for him to rescue his "Auntie" from his childhood, the imperfect angel. But would he hurt her or Ruth? Could he have killed Larry?

Cat realized her days in St. Louis were numbered. Despite the generosity of the Plantation Church, about which she felt some guilt, she couldn't live on the money from Dave and Simon forever... Oh, no. Dave and Simon! Cat hadn't had any contact with them since she got to St. Louis, and she was technically on their dime, pursuing their case. She must positively be the worst PI in the world not to have filed a single report with her own clients. And what was she doing here, anyway? This case stopped being about their condo building the minute she lost Ruthie and her mother in Seattle. Where were they now? She'd never track them down. So she had the mysterious disappearance of a midwestern religious celebrity and his family, and she had a church congregation that soldiered on for the Lord amidst an ever-growing pack of lies. No real crime had been committed here, at least not that she'd uncovered so far. Ruthie's dream hadn't led her to any molestation suspects. Her mother could be fleeing for reasons unrelated to Jim's faux lifestyle.

But it couldn't be a coincidence: Larry's death, Sherrie and Ruthie's escape, Diamond Dick's, Larry and Jim's peccadilloes. What was she missing?

Just then her cell phone buzzed. She kept it on her nightstand at night with the cord attached for the recharge. It was a text from Lee: *You could have told me you went back to St. Louis. Nice knowing you, Kitty Cat.*

She got up, unplugged her cell, and slipped outside. It was a full moon night, and the day had been so hot that the sidewalk was still warm under her bare feet. Cat remembered Granny Grace saying she'd run into Lee's parents. Ah, they must have mentioned to Lee that she'd gone back to St. Louis. He was back in Seattle now, and he'd jumped to the conclusion that she'd left for good.

Cat dialed his number. He answered.

"How's life in the river city?" he asked.

"It's okay," she said. "You know, I'm just visiting. I didn't move back."

There was a long pause. She heard Lee suck in his breath and let it out. Then he laughed. "My parents..." he said, laughing. "Shit."

Cat laughed, too. "I wouldn't do that to you, Sergeant Stone," she said. "I wouldn't move back here and not tell you. We're... friends."

"Friends," Lee said. "Is that what we are?"

Cat didn't know what to say, and the silence was palpable.

"I want you, Kitty Cat," he finally said. She winced at the longing in his voice. "Why the hell are you in St. Louis? Because I will fly out there right now and drag you back here for a fuck."

"Are you drinking?"

"Yes, I am. Alone. Because the woman I wanted to be with tonight isn't back here where I left her. She's a couple thousand miles away, and she still hasn't explained why."

"I'm investigating."

"You're on a case? Really. I thought you moved to Seattle to be a PI."

"I know. It's weird. I'm undercover."

"What?! You're undercover. In St. Louis."

"Well, Illinois, to be precise. At a church."

"A church! Which one?"

Cat figured it wouldn't hurt to have one more person besides Granny Grace know where she was. "Plantation Revival. Jim Plantation's church."

"I've seen that guy on the news. He's rabidly antigay. Women don't fair too well, either."

"Yeah, but there are some good people in here."

"I'm not worried about the good ones."

Just then, Cat heard someone clear her throat behind her. She spun around to find Wendy, with a look on her face that showed she'd heard Cat say she was undercover.

"Wendy," she said.

Lee on the other line laughed. "Hey, is that a new pet name?"

"You're a big fat liar," accused Wendy, her fists clenched at her sides. "You were never really my friend at all, were you? You're just using me. You're using us all."

"Wendy, you don't understand," Cat pleaded.

Lee, hearing the exchange, said, "Cat? Are you okay?"

"My cover's just been blown," Cat said. "I gotta go."

She hung up on Lee mid-protest.

"I can't believe I fell for your act," Wendy said. With that, she turned around and went back inside the dorms.

Cat sat outside for a while, thinking over what to do. She wasn't sure whether Wendy would tell the others or not. They were supposed to lead the rehab program's Bible study the next evening, with Wendy's mother due to attend. And she couldn't miss the chance to help Tina clean the Plantation house in the morning. She was so close... She had to chance it. She crept back inside and crawled into her bunk. If Wendy's door slam had awakened any of their bunkmates, they'd gone back to sleep already. The look on Wendy's face haunted her, though, and she slept fitfully, dreaming only her own dreams, which weren't pleasant.

Tina woke her early, at 5 a.m., and the two of them hit the road to make the cleaning rounds.

Cat was no stranger to cleaning, but the equipment that Tina gave her was intimidating: a vacuum cleaner that strapped to her back and an arsenal of cleaning products most likely laden with noxious chemicals of which Granny Grace would not approve.

The first house was a behemoth two-story near a golf course. The subdivision as well as the golf course, she realized, were owned by Rev. Chambers, a.k.a. Reynolds Chambers of Reynolds Chambers Homes. The development was called "Duck Harbor," a ridiculously ironic name for a group of homes that were landlocked. The only water to be seen was the glimmer of a water trap on the tenth hole.

Cat thought she was in good shape, but vacuuming the carpeted stairwell with that thing strapped to her back nearly killed her. There were five bedrooms, three and a half bathrooms, a gargantuan kitchen, a great room, and a pool, which, thankfully, fell under another company's jurisdiction to clean. The family was expressively Christian; the stairwell was decorated with framed biblical quotes rendered in flawless needlepoint, and Cat counted a Bible next to every bedside, plus one on the coffee table in the great room.

Three houses later, Cat was wiped out, but Tina, who was used to the work, was still as cheerful as ever. She was still singing the same hymn she'd started the day with, "Let the Children Come to Me." She had a high, clear soprano voice that Cat could barely hear over the whine of the vacuum cleaner. The fourth house was the Plantation house, and Cat hoped that in her exhausted state she wouldn't miss anything.

She'd got Tina into a rhythm in which the two of them were always cleaning in different rooms, in preparation for when they'd get to this house. Luckily, the place was wall-to-wall carpeting, so she'd need to clean in every room except the kitchen and bathrooms. She left the vacuum cleaner running and searched the chest of drawers and closets in the master bedroom. Their clothing collection was modest but comprised of well-made name brands, all organized neatly, the ties hanging evenly, the shoes on racks with the toes pointed outward.

But she couldn't find anything that would constitute a clue. No shoebox full of love letters, no porn stash, no secret box of drugs. They seemed like a "normal" family. If anything, they were too normal. Even Sherrie's chest of drawers held nothing that could be traced back to her former life as a stripper. Her underwear drawer was filled with white cotton bikini underwear. Good grief, Cat thought. At least they weren't oversized granny panties. Not that oversized briefs should be automatically associated with grannies. Her own granny, she had observed when they'd done laundry together, wore bikinis, with an occasional thong thrown into the mix. Yes, at her age. Sherrie's bras were equally utilitarian, the only adornment a pink flower stitched into the heart of one and a bit of lace trimming the edge of another.

She'd just closed Sherrie's underwear drawer when Tina appeared in the doorway with her hands on her hips. "You're taking longer," she said, glancing over at the vacuum cleaner Cat had left running and had ditched by the side of the bed.

Cat ran over and shut off the vacuum and then stood up and stretched her back. "Sorry," she said. "I guess I'm not used to this grueling manual labor."

Tina giggled. "I caught you looking at yourself in the mirror, didn't I?" she motioned toward the large mirror poised above Sherrie's chest of drawers.

Cat tried to look sheepish. "Yeah."

"Oh, it's okay," Tina said. "I do that sometimes, too. It's not vanity. I like to look to see what other people see when they look at me. It's odd, isn't it? Other people know your appearance better than you do."

"Yes, it is," Cat agreed. "I guess I'm done in this room anyway. What's left?"

"Well, there's the kid's room and Jim's study up here. I'm going to hit the half-bath downstairs."

"Okay." Cat strapped the vacuum cleaner back on and made her way to Jim's study. Her hopeful searching turned up nothing, however; that man was just too careful.

The only thing of any interest to Cat was a photograph on his wall, taken at Johnson's Shut-Ins, a state park in southern Missouri. The river rocks there, due to a special geological formation, had been carved out to create bowls you could sit in. In the summer people flocked there for bathing, as the bowls were like sitting in a cool, jetted spa tub. She'd been there a few times herself. In the picture, Jim posed with Larry Price, their arms flung around each other. They were really, really young but looked happy, wide smiles on both their faces. It made her want to like Jim, despite the fact that in this case, he was her suspect.

Ruthie's room was obscenely tidy for a child's room and done up in excessive amounts of pink. Cat didn't think she'd find anything here, but it didn't hurt to look. And she was glad she did. At the back of Ruthie's closet, too high for the girl herself to reach, Cat found a tiny chest. It was locked, and there was no key nearby, but Cat had seen a tiny key in Sherrie's sock drawer. She'd assumed at the time it was a stray spare, as it was mixed in with a bunch of other loose keys.

With the vacuum cleaner still strapped to her back, Cat lumbered to the master bedroom, retrieved the key, and went to open the chest.

She found a graduation tassel, the fringe in dark blue and light blue, and a gold "98" dangling from the rim. If Sherrie graduated in 1998, Cat realized, she'd be thirty-two now. That seemed right, and not at all atypical that Jim would marry a much younger woman. Underneath the tassel was a prom picture, a high-school-aged Sherrie in a strapless black dress, her hair permed curly, standing next to a tall, skinny boy in a black tuxedo. On the back of the photo, someone had scrawled, "Sherrie and Dave, True Love Forever." Next, Cat found a tightly folded nest of papers. She carefully unfolded them and smoothed them out. It was a divorce decree, and the husband's name was David Morro. "True love forever" turned out to be a lie, she thought.

She didn't have time to read through it now, so she folded it back up and stuck it in her pocket. She rifled through the rest of the chest but didn't find anything else too revealing: A pair of unused chopsticks, still sheathed in their paper wrapper. A men's class ring wound with enough string so it would presumably fit Sherrie's smaller finger. Ticket stubs from a Shania Twain concert in 1999.

At the bottom was a piece of paper that must have come with the chest. It was from Olson's Furniture in Belleville, Illinois, and explained that the chest was a gift to all of the girls in the graduating class of Belleville East High School, who could bring the coupon in and get fifteen percent off a regular-sized hope chest. Cat's mother had a hope chest; it was a large redwood chest that sat in the entryway of her parents' house. Her mother kept Cat's baby book there, along with other keepsakes—drawings Cat had made as a child, her first communion dress. It seemed sad that Sherrie had never traded in the coupon for a real hope chest, and now her entire history was relegated to this tiny box.

Cat closed the chest and put it back on the shelf. The whir of the vacuum cleaner was at this point giving her a headache. The house wasn't that dirty, so she figured she'd skimp on the floor downstairs. But as she turned to leave Ruthie's room forever, her eye fell on a small photo album, clearly the girl's own, on the nightstand. It was as pink as the room, and the cover had been decorated with glitter, which came off in Cat's hand. She flipped through the book. There were Sherrie and Ruthie at a birthday party, followed by Jim and Ruthie smiling happily. And then her eye caught the Space Needle. Underneath it were Sherrie, Ruthie, Jim, and someone else, someone she instantly recognized. She took a step back, dropping the photo album. It couldn't be. She picked it up again and flipped till the Space Needle came into view. Yes, it definitely was.

It was Mr. M&O, from the security firm. She fished the photo out of its sleeve to look at the back. "Visiting Uncle Greg in Seattle" was written there. Greg Swenson—that was Mr. M&O's real name, she remembered.

Cat suddenly felt the same way she felt when she'd returned to the condo building in Seattle to find the mother and girl gone without a trace. Greg had been lying to her all that time, and then he fired her. But where were Sherrie and Ruthie now? Had Greg been able to rescue them from Jim? Cat kept turning it over in her mind. Maybe Jim was after Sherrie because she killed Larry. Larry Price was dead, and maybe it wasn't a suicide. Maybe someone murdered him. She needed to treat Sherrie Plantation as a suspect. Sherrie was the only person to have fled the scene. There was also the possibility that Sherrie had seen something, that she was on the run from Jim because she knew too much. And Cat couldn't rule out the other church leaders—Anita and Rev. Chambers. There was something rotten at the core of this church, that was for sure.

Cat was exhausted and sore from the day's work but had much more to do now on the case. After she and Tina returned to the dorms for showers, she drove to a public park so she could make a few phone calls without the risk of anyone eavesdropping. She'd left her phone in the dorms all morning, as Tina said they weren't allowed to have them with them when they were cleaning. As soon as she turned it on, a whole string of text messages from Lee popped up:

R U OK?

Kitty Cat, talk to me. I'm worried.

OK, Grace hasn't heard from you either. You're scaring me.

Those church freaks better not have hurt you.

He'd also left several voice mail messages most likely saying the same thing. She felt bad that she hadn't gotten in contact with him that morning, but she hadn't had time. She dialed his number but got his voice mail, so she left him a message saying she was all right and that he shouldn't worry about her.

Then she called Granny Grace. "Well, hello, my darling," her grandmother's voice rang out, and Cat felt a surprising pang of homesickness for her life in Seattle. Cat filled her in on the case.

"Granny, you were right," she said. "Remember the first dream I had on the plane ride to Seattle? The one where the devil drove his pitchfork into the girl's crotch? You said it could be someone making her feel ashamed about her sexual curiosities. You were right. I haven't found anything to suggest Jim's a child molester."

"Well, that's a relief," Granny Grace said. "I hate those cases. I try to stay away from them. Unfortunately, there's an awful lot of them."

"Listen, there's more. Jim's gay, and his dead assistant director was his lover. I think someone might actually have murdered him, though it was an apparent suicide."

Cat ran down the suspects. "Oh, I see," Grace said. "Yes, that's how I'd approach the case as well." She paused. "It's a shame about Jim being gay and demonizing gays," she remarked.

"Yeah, a classic case of reaction formation," Cat said with disgust. "'You can tell how gay I am by how loudly I say I hate gays.' But here's the reason I'm calling. Sherrie has a brother. And guess where he lives."

"Seattle. But then why were they hiding out in the condo?"

"Because Sherrie's brother is my old pal at the security firm," Cat revealed.

"Mr. M&O," Granny said.

"The same."

"I'll see what I can turn up out here, Cat. You keep working there until you're ready to come back."

"Thanks, Gran. His name is Greg Swenson. It might be good to look into the background on him and a Sherrie Swenson from Belleville. She graduated from Belleville East in '98. When you look that up, throw the word 'Township' in there—I think the whole name of the school is Belleville Township High School East. It's a mouthful, for sure, and pretty old-fashioned. One more thing: I haven't filed any reports with Dave and Simon, but I'll do that now."

She laughed. "Forgot who paid your bills, did you? Oh, it's okay. I gave them some information to tide them over, and reassured them that you weren't off in St. Louis vacationing on their dime."

"Thanks, Gran. It's nice to know you've got my back."

"Oh, and your doughboy's mighty worried about you, Cat. He called over here when he overheard your cover was blown. By the way, I find it interesting that you let him in on what you were up to."

"I figured it wouldn't hurt if one more person knew where I was. You know, for security reasons."

"Right," Granny Grace said. "Security."

After they hung up, Cat dialed the Fletcher-Bander residence and had a good conversation with Dave. He was doubly intrigued that the case involved two closeted homosexuals.

"You might want to consider something else, Cat," he said sadly. "You might want to consider that Jim killed Larry himself. If his love for Larry was something he could no longer contain, he might have killed him out of desperation, just as he's fighting homosexuality out in the public sphere. In a strange way, he might have thought killing Larry would kill the gay man inside himself."

"Good point," granted Cat. This case was getting more complicated by the day, she thought. After they said good-bye, Cat hit "end call" on her phone and sat for a minute, staring at a flock of crows chasing a robin, thinking about what Dave said. She needed to get a look at that police report on Larry's death. Bearing with the tiny screen on her phone, she looked up the current roster of the St. Clair County Sheriff's Department. The Plantation Church compound was located in an unincorporated part of the county, so Larry's death would have fallen under their jurisdiction. She wanted to see if anyone she'd gone to school with was now on the force, which was possible, since it was one of the main law enforcement employers in the bistate area. Granny Grace had taught her to work her connections, or any connection she could possibly forge in the absence of a real one. One name jumped out at her, but it wasn't too promising: it was Tim Schlein, a guy she'd once turned down at a dance. He hadn't taken her rebuff very well.

But a visit there would have to wait. She was due back at the church for the Bible study lesson she and Wendy were giving for the rehab program. She'd already missed dinner, so she pulled into a Taco Bell for a quick meal first. When she got back to the church, she had just enough time to grab her materials and meet Wendy in the study room. Wendy barely acknowledged her existence, but other than that, everyone welcomed her warmly, so it was clear Wendy hadn't outed her. Maybe the authenticity of their bond had outweighed Wendy's feelings of betrayal.

The rehab participants slowly arrived: A mother of three who'd lost her job as a receptionist, couldn't find other work, recently relapsed into alcoholism, but was trying to stay clean. A teenager whose parents were clearly making her attend. Several men of varying ages, one bald and carrying a cane who said he'd been addicted to cough medicine. They waited while a few others drifted in, but not Wendy's mother. At ten past the time they were supposed to start, they went ahead with the lesson on Mary Magdalene, which had been designed with Wendy's mother in mind. It seemed a bit off-topic for this audience otherwise, but they pushed on. Cat noticed Wendy watching the clock and glancing at the door, still hopeful that her mother would arrive.

But she never did, and the lesson was soon over. They broke for tea and biscuits, which Anita brought in on a cart. Once the participants had left, Wendy, Cat, and Anita cleaned up the room in silence. Anita looked at Cat, her look urging her to talk with her friend. Of course Anita hadn't picked up on the rift between the two girls. Cat had no choice, and she was genuinely worried about Wendy anyway.

"Wendy," she said. "I'm sorry your mother didn't come. But some people are harder to reach. You just have to keep trying." She put her hand on Wendy's shoulder.

Wendy shrugged her off. "What do you know about it? You're an impostor! You're probably just playacting right now. I can't believe a word you say."

Anita had been bent over the table, polishing it. She stopped and stood up. "Wendy? What do you mean by that? How is Cat an imposter?"

Cat held her breath.

"She's a reporter just here for a story," Wendy said bitterly. "I heard her tell someone on the phone that she's undercover."

Cat let out her breath, relieved almost to the point of amusement. She wished she'd thought to mock up some press credentials ahead of time.

Anita's eyes blazed. "Excuse me? Cat, tell me this isn't true."

Cat looked down and nodded, thankful to Wendy's imagination for the new ruse. "It's true," she said. "I'm sorry for not being honest." She looked up at Anita, trying to make herself sound as genuine as possible. "That's how it started out, anyway, but I found myself being called to stay."

"You're lying," said Anita. Her hands clenched a towel so hard her knuckles turned white.

"You're just a fake," Wendy accused, glaring at her with her arms crossed over her chest. "And I thought you were my friend."

Cat felt as if she'd been slapped. She couldn't think of anything to say to defend herself. She was surprised by how painful their rejection felt.

Anita cleared her throat. "I've never turned a soul away from this ministry, but I'm going to do that now. Cat," she ordered, raising her chin in defiance, "pack up your things and leave us, please."

"You're throwing me out?" Cat sputtered, trying to control her own emotions from taking this so personally. Her mind latched onto Wendy's story. "But why? It's just an article. And it will be favorable. Don't you want the publicity? It's for the good of the church."

Anita responded to none of Cat's pleas. She turned and left, followed by Wendy, leaving Cat alone in the study room. There were quotes from Proverbs on the wall opposite, and one in particular seemed to mock her: "A man of many companions may come to ruin, but there is a friend who sticks closer than a brother."

There was no way to rectify this situation. Cat went to the dorms and packed her things, alone. Wendy and the other girls were watching a movie in the lounge. She knew that Anita wouldn't want a scene, that Cat was to go quietly.

Chapter 13

C at was in the driver's seat of a big red plastic car. It was a model '66 GTO, but it was either life-sized, or she was Barbie-doll-sized. Either way, she was driving it. She realized other cars were racing past her, G.I. Joe figurines behind the wheels. She stepped on the gas, and the GTO lurched forward. She caught up to and passed a helmeted Joe in a Dodge Charger and another in a Barracuda. Must be a muscle-car race, she thought with glee, realizing by this point that she was clearly in her father's dream. Rather than separating herself from his consciousness, however, she hung on for the ride. She and her father swerved to avoid hitting a Chevelle and overtook a Mustang. They were first across the finish line, where a battered Joe waved a black-and-white checkered flag.

Cat woke exhilarated, waving her arms above her head in victory. She stretched, winked at the owl on the wall. She felt liberated, somehow, the responsibility of pretending to be someone that she wasn't now gone from her shoulders. She hadn't realized how much it had been wearing on her. She was relieved to have been evicted from the church.

Which is not to say that she wouldn't miss the people she met there. She felt a ton of guilt when it came to Wendy, whom she really had thought of as a friend. The others had charmed her as well, but even though she held God in her heart in her own way, she had never felt as if she truly belonged at the Plantation Church. Maybe she'd been too focused on the investigation, but she hadn't heard God there, either. Maybe she wasn't listening, but she'd heard His voice at other times in her life, so she knew it was possible. She didn't doubt that others had found God in that church, but her spiritual path evidently had only been passing through.

She lay in bed a while, luxuriating in the fact that she didn't have to get up at the crack of dawn and endure communal showers, breakfast with the same set of girls every morning, the constant presence of scripture and Jesus talk.

Then she heard the sound of laughter filtering up from downstairs. She could make out her mother, apparently in a rare mood, as she was giggling. But the other laugher wasn't her father's. This was a younger man's laugh, one she'd heard recently.

Lee. It sounded like Lee.

Panicked excitement shot through her. What the...? Could Lee be here? She flashed on his texts, and realized she still hadn't listened to his voice mail messages.

She threw on some clothes, glanced in the mirror, frowned at her harried appearance, and ran downstairs.

There was Lee, in the living room, chatting up her mother, who was positively sparkling at his attention.

"There's our slug-a-bed," she said, beaming.

"What the hell are you doing here?" Cat demanded.

"Cat, that's no way to greet a guest," her mother reproached her. "And that's quite a mouth you've got for someone who's recently returned from the evangelical fold."

Lee, who had risen to his feet, defended her. "Now, Cat's reaction is understandable. The last time we spoke, I was back in Washington State."

He turned to Cat. "Sorry, Kitty Cat. After you hung up on me and refused to return my calls, I got worried. There was a transport flight out of JBLM last night to Fort Leonard Wood, so I took it."

"So that got you to Kansas City. And then you drove five hours to get here?"

"This morning. I got a good night's rest in KC first."

Well, you must have, thought Cat, realizing that the only dream she'd slipped into that night had been her father's.

Joe walked into the room just then and shook Lee's hand. "It's good to see you, Sergeant," he said. Her parents had met Lee before, on one of their vacations in Seattle, which they would take either at the beginning of the summer to drop her off at Granny Grace's or at the end, to pick her up.

Cat was reeling a bit from the implications of Lee's sudden appearance in her hometown. She sat down in the living room and observed him, wearing everyday fatigues and sitting in her father's favorite armchair with his hand on his hat, which was in his lap. The three of them discussed the weather, the Cardinals, and the ins and outs of military life while Cat let her breathing calm down, her heart slow to a normal beat.

Then it was decided that they should all go out to breakfast in celebration of her release from the church.

They went to Cat's favorite diner, where the walls were lined with vintage record albums. They sat in Cat's booth, under Stevie Wonder's *Talking Book*. They ordered eggs Benedict all around. Her mother was in good spirits, undoubtedly relieved to have her daughter back from the Christian fundamentalist stronghold safe and sound, but also charmed by a good-looking man in uniform.

"So what did you do to get yourself thrown out?" her mother asked, her eyes dancing with delight.

Cat blushed. "Lee called me, and I mentioned to him I was undercover. One of my dorm mates overheard."

"That's my girl," her father said, reaching over to pinch her chin. "Undone by a man."

"Not just any man, either," her mother teased. "One who jumps on a plane and flies halfway across the country at a moment's notice to try to save you."

Cat felt heat flush her face. She didn't know what to say. She and Lee had only just reconnected. There was nothing at all decided between them because it was still beginning. There were no words to explain all of this to her parents over brunch.

Lee shot Cat an "I'm sorry" glance.

Then he cleared his throat. "I probably just overreacted," he said. "But it's not like I bought a ticket or anything. I just hopped a transport."

Cat went from feeling as if he were moving too quickly and smothering her to suddenly feeling as if she were a side trip for him. She glared at Lee, her mother looked at Lee with an arched eyebrow, and he began to sputter an apology.

Her father, thankfully, intervened. "Oh, leave the soldier alone," he said. "Clearly he's fond of Cat here, and maybe he's got more than his share of white knight instincts, and that fusses with his otherwise Ranger-trained judgment. The important thing is, Cat's out of that zoo of zealots, we're all here together, and these eggs aren't going to eat themselves."

Cat smiled shyly at Lee, who winked at her, and the three of them commenced eating.

After breakfast, Cat had a bit of a problem on her hands. Lee was there, expecting her attention, but she needed to follow up on her leads.

"I'll tag along," he offered, pulling her close. They were standing in the living room; her parents had left them alone.

"Okay, but you can't interfere," she warned, letting her arms wrap around his shoulders. "You might have to stay in the car."

"Baby, I'm not a dog you can crack a window for," he said. "But I won't get in your way."

She sighed and let herself fall into him.

Their first stop was the county sheriff's office, where Cat asked to see Sgt. Schlein. Tim came out right away. "Cat," he said, hugging her. "It's so good to see you." She was taken aback by his friendliness, and he cast a suspicious glance toward Lee.

"This is a friend of mine," Cat said. "Sgt. Lee Stone." The two men shook hands stiffly. Then the three of them walked around the corner to a coffee shop.

As soon as they were seated with their to-go cups in hand, Tim smiled at Cat. "I heard you moved to Seattle," he said, pointedly ignoring Lee.

"I have," she nodded. "But I'm here now, investigating a case."

"Really? So you're a detective now?"

"A PI. I'm taking over my grandmother's firm."

He leaned over and patted her on the back. "Congratulations, Cat. That's awesome!"

"That's actually why I'm here, Tim."

He frowned. "Well, I didn't think you were here just to see me, but a guy can dream."

Lee cleared his throat as if to speak up, and Cat kicked him under the table. She gave him a look that said, "Be quiet."

Cat examined Tim. It wasn't that he wasn't attractive. He was a good-looking blonde with chiseled features and bright blue eyes. As a cop on the county force, he looked to be in even better shape than he'd been in college. He was smart, he'd done well in school, and he was sweet. But she felt no chemistry for him. Zilch.

She took a deep breath and plunged in. "I've been undercover at the Plantation Church, and I don't think Larry Price killed himself. I think he was murdered."

Tim's reaction was delayed. "Do you have any suspects?" he asked.

"A few. Jim's wife is trying to flee the country. That could spell guilt... or fear."

"Maybe she just wants out of the marriage," said Tim.

"Then why not just file for divorce? She might have killed Larry. Crime of passion."

"Crime of passion?"

"Larry and Jim were lovers, and they had been for years."

"You're joking."

"No," Cat said. "I'm not."

"So you want me to look at the incident report," Tim said.

"Please," Cat said. "I know you can't share it with me, but look for something. Blood splatter, anything. How was it ruled a suicide? Was there a note? Did they do a thorough investigation?"

Tim sighed. "You know I'm swamped, Cat. Budget cuts. We're understaffed as it is, and we can barely keep up with the meth problem we've got here. That case isn't active anymore. It was never even a case.

Besides, I think the sheriff is pretty chummy with those Plantation guys."

"Please, Tim," she begged. "If I'm right, this could be huge. It could make your career..."

He looked at her, smiled, and nodded. "You know, Cat, you were always really smart in school, but I wasn't sure you'd make it in the real world. Now I see I was wrong."

"Well, thanks, Tim, but the verdict's still out. I haven't made it yet."

He laughed and said he'd call her if something turned up.

When the three of them said good-bye, Tim reached over and gave Cat a hug. He shook Lee's hand mechanically.

As they walked back to her car, she could tell Lee was seething. Once she pulled away from the police station, he let loose. "I don't know whether to commend you or bend you over my knee for a spanking."

"Be careful," she said. She shot him a sideways glance. "I'm working here, so don't read anything into my actions."

"That was torture for me," he fumed. "I wanted to shove that coffee cup of his where the sun don't shine."

She laughed, but she could tell the intensity of the experience hadn't left Lee, who was still giving off an angry vibe.

"Wanna take a little road trip?" she asked him.

"Sure," he said, letting out a breath.

Soon they were barreling down the highway in the direction of Johnson's Shut-Ins. Logically, it was a long shot. But she kept seeing in her mind's eye the picture of Larry and Jim she'd found in Jim's home office. They looked innocent, fresh-faced, unafraid. She needed to see that place for herself, see if it gave her any insights or clues.

On the ride down, they stopped once for a quick lunch, and Lee regaled Cat with stories about his advanced training in Virginia with an old drill sergeant type who still thought Vietnam could have been won.

"He kept telling us the Iraqis just needed to 'pull up their socks,'" said Lee. "It was all I could do not to let him know that the Iraqis don't wear socks; they wear sandals."

Cat laughed. "And not socks *with* sandals, as they do in Seattle," she added, making Lee laugh as well.

It was a weekday, so Johnson's Shut-Ins was deserted and the parking lot empty. She hadn't been in years, and the place caught her by surprise with its lush solitude. She felt her tired, achy muscles relax. She took a deep breath, listening to the soothing rush of the river over the hollowed-out boulders. She'd come here with the soccer player once, and they'd jumped all the way across the river. Just as agile, if not moreso, Lee made it across and back without soaking a foot, but Cat came down once in a bowl, her tennis shoe sloshy. It had turned into a lovely day, despite her one wet foot. The sun came out, and they sat down on a dry rock above the river. They took their time, soaking up the rays.

"This is quite a place," Lee said, admiring the mounds of granite boulders smoothly sculpted by the rush of the Black River. Over time, the river had carved bowls into the rocks, some of them big enough to sit in, like a natural Jacuzzi. "C'mon, Cat," he beckoned. "It's hot out here. I could use a swim."

She hesitated, wishing for a guilty split second that he weren't there, so she could be alone with her thoughts. "I can't," she demurred. "Believe it or not, I'm here for an investigation."

"And I thought this was a date," he laughed, shaking his head.

"Sorry," she said. "I think my church leader came here with his lover."

Lee took Cat into his arms then, his hands at the small of her back, pulling her into him. "If we pretend to be them, maybe you'll discover something."

She felt thrown off balance, though she realized she should have been expecting this. He definitely had an effect on her. Her heart quickened, and then her hands were fingering the back of his head, and the two of them locked in a long, long kiss.

As soon as they came up for air, a thought occurred to her.

"You're right, Lee," she said. "We should take a dip. I mean, that's exactly what Jim and Larry would have done." She imagined herself as young Larry Price, with Jim on some lazy summer weekday when they had the place to themselves just like this.

She and Lee looked for a bowl that would be big enough to fit two men. There were a few.

"Here," Lee said, but Cat pointed out that it could be seen from the path to the parking lot. They kept hopping until they came across a grand bowl that could easily fit two men and offered total seclusion from the riverbank.

She crouched down near the lip of the bowl, and then she saw it: an inscription carved deeply into the lip, *One in spirit, 1 Sam. 18:1.*

"What does it mean?" Lee asked.

"I think it's biblical," Cat replied. "From the Book of Samuel."

She took out her camera and shot several pictures of it. Then she went back to the car, grabbed her backpack, and fished around for a paper and pencil. She took a rubbing of the inscription.

As soon as she had finished and stowed her camera, paper, and pencil in the backpack, Lee took it out of her hands. He placed it on a dry rock above them and pulled her close.

"I can't stop thinking about our night together," he said. He kissed her forehead, her nose, and then her lips. He traced his finger across each spot after he'd kissed it. Then he let his finger slide down her neck to her chest, where he began to unbutton her shirt.

"I didn't bring a swimsuit," she whispered.

"That's why they invented skinny-dipping," he whispered back, continuing to unbutton her shirt.

She looked around. They'd been there for about an hour and had yet to see a soul. It was early afternoon on a Tuesday. Should she dare?

Her heart, with a little help from her libido, made the decision for her. She slid her shirt off, and then unbuttoned her jeans and slid them off. It was hot out, and the heat of the sun's rays soon hit her back, making the cool water whirling through the bowl look delicious to her. Nude, she stepped into the bowl and watched Lee disrobe, a satisfying sight indeed.

The two of them whiled away the afternoon there.

Later, as they drove home, Cat thought to herself that it was enough of a risk for her and Lee to have made love *au naturel* as they had. Two men would have been taking a much greater risk, perhaps even risking their lives, especially back then, had they been discovered by rabidly antigay country boys. Then again, someone else might have taken that photo, unless either Larry or Jim snapped it. Back then the equivalent of a "selfie" would have meant propping a camera on a rock and setting the timer.

Once they got back to her parents' house, Lee announced he had to return to Kansas City.

"As soon as you get back to Seattle, call me," he told her.

"I will," she said. "But this case—"

"I know," Lee said. He grabbed the collar of her blazer and pulled their foreheads to touch. "I... damn, Kitty Cat. You're a hard one to leave."

"You're a hard one to let leave," she replied. And then he was gone.

In the wake of his departure, Cat went upstairs to look up the verse inscribed on the boulder. First she checked her family's Catholic bible, and then she looked online to get a few other interpretations. It was from 1 Samuel 18. The full passage was this:

"After David had finished talking with Saul, Jonathan became one in spirit with David, and he loved him as himself. From that day

135

Saul kept David with him and did not let him return to his father's house. And Jonathan made a covenant with David because he loved him as himself. Jonathan took off the robe he was wearing and gave it to David, along with his tunic, and even his sword, his bow and his belt."

As far as Bible verse went, it was pretty saucy, Cat thought, the way it described a deep affection between two men, such that they became "one in spirit" with each other. The part about Jonathan giving David his clothing could be taken to mean giving someone the clothes off your back. Or maybe it was just metaphorical: Jonathan took off his clothes to be open and vulnerable to David.

But Cat found it hard to deny the literal interpretation. Jonathan took off all his clothes and gave them to David, appearing naked before the other man. There was an offering there, of both the clothes *and* the naked body. There was definitely a romantic, homoerotic theme in this case, as something Larry and David might carve into that rock all those years ago.

"Doing research?" Her mother appeared in the doorway.

"Yes, Mom," she said. "My case has taken a turn toward the homosexual."

"What?! Not Jim Plantation?"

"Yep."

"Well, a man like that will go to great lengths to keep it quiet."

Cat put her laptop down and turned toward her mother, who sat next to her on the edge of the bed. "But would he kill the man he loved most in the world?" Cat asked.

"He might," her mother said, sighing, patting her daughter's hand. "If something else is more important to him."

"But he wasn't that careful about it. He and his assistant director went to gay bars together."

Her mother bit her lip and looked across the room. "I've seen these religious men make justifications all the time. Denial is a powerful force; if you feed it just a little, it takes over. Say someone sees them at that gay bar. Well, what are *any* of them doing in a gay bar? They might say they gave in to curiosity or temptation and then help each other repent and get back on track. They support each other's denial. And the gay community, they know most of their members are still in the closet. There's a code. No one would out Jim, even if he is a hypocrite."

"That's why I'm not convinced Jim killed Larry Price. He would have gone out of his way to reform him. I think that's what they were trying to do—Jim married Sherrie. She was his angel, his Jezebel turned into Mary. He was trying to help her and himself at the same time. Or maybe Jim and Larry continued to carry on their secret love affair all these years under everyone's noses."

"Where is Jim now?"

"In Seattle, probably trying to hunt down his wife and daughter."

"Then why are you here?" Her mother smiled. "Don't get me wrong, Cat. We love to have you around. But I wonder if you're not avoiding your new life out there in some way by being here. And maybe that man of yours who just left, too."

Her mother's words struck a chord in her, and she didn't care for the sound of it. She stood up. "But I haven't solved the case, Mom. I can't go back till I do."

Her mother stood up and put her hands on Cat's shoulders. "I love you," she said. It had been a very long time since Cat heard her mother say that. Cat broke down in tears, and her mother wrapped her arms around her.

Cat pulled away. "Mom, please don't think I idolize Granny Grace," she said. "I know she's not perfect, and that you didn't always get what you needed as her daughter."

Her mother sighed. "I'm sorry I've taken some of that out on you."

Cat nodded, accepting the apology. "I love you, too, Mom," she said, hugging her.

After dark that night, Cat was dressed all in black and heading to the Plantation Church. There was more evidence there; she could feel it. She'd never had a chance to explore Larry Price's private living quarters. She turned her lights off before she pulled into the parking lot and drove very slowly.

She walked through the grounds, circling the main building, which housed Larry's rooms. Calculating the layout from memory, she located the windows that would correspond to his private rooms. They were of course dark, and they were on the third floor. There were no fire escapes, no other ways of accessing the rooms from the outside. All of the external doors were locked, and she knew from having lived there that despite the church's "open door" policy inside, there was good security after hours to keep outsiders at bay. She didn't know how she was going to get inside, and she felt pretty foolish about her plan. Maybe her mother was right. Maybe there was nothing else she could do here in St. Louis.

She sat down on a brick wall to think. What would Granny Grace do?

If there were people milling around, she could follow them inside surreptitiously. But dressed all in black, she was probably *more* conspicuous, not less. And the place was deathly quiet anyway. It was a week night, and late. It was already lights out in the dorms. She could come back during church services, but then Anita would recognize her. She could come back during church services in disguise... But she had the sense that time was running out. Jim could track down Sherrie and Ruthie, or they could flee to Canada under new names, and she'd never find them again.

She took a deep breath and got very quiet.

A breeze blew up out of nowhere, and Cat heard the sound of creaking metal. She turned. It was the scaffolding around the new fountain sculpture. Maybe she could use it to climb up to Larry's rooms. She walked over to the sculpture to inspect the scaffolding. It was enormous and might get her up to the third floor, or at least close. Each of the wheels on the scaffolding had a caster brake that was set. She tried to free them, but they were stuck fast, and they required a tool of some sort to loosen. She tried budging the scaffolding, but it weighed a ton; there was no way she could move it. Frustrated, she kicked the caster, which made more noise than she'd intended, causing a ricochet of creaking that ran through the length of scaffolding. She sat back on her heels, biting her lip in frustration.

And then she saw it. The sculpture. It was Johnson's Shut-Ins.

The first time she'd seen it, through Larry's office window, she thought it looked familiar, but it was half-finished and partially covered in tarp. It was almost done now, and the distinct salt-and-pepper colored boulders were visible. She thought back to the spot where she'd found the inscription. This was it. She knew Larry had been in charge of the fountain project; it was his baby, and no one else had really been involved, even to the point where Anita once complained about having to pick up where he left off, with very few records to go by. Would he have...? Cat had to find out. She climbed up the boulders till she got to one that was big enough for two men to sit inside. What she saw there brought tears to her eyes.

It was the inscription, 1 Sam 18:1, etched into the stone like the one at Johnson's Shut-Ins, only much larger and on a raised lip of stone, where it would be seen by viewers below. It was being wired for lights so that when the sculpture was revealed over the coming weekend, this inscription would be lit for the entire world to see. But now from the ground, you couldn't see the words at all.

Larry had wanted everyone to know about his love for Jim. He hadn't been willing to keep it under wraps. Cat's mind spun. It had to be that no one knew about this except the artist himself, Larry, and now Cat. But the truth would come out as soon as the sculpture was unveiled.

She climbed down from the sculpture, and as she set foot on the pavement, a voice behind her said, "Just what do you think you're doing?"

Cat turned around, and there was Anita, shining a flashlight at her.

"Checking out the view," Cat replied.

"I'm calling the police," Anita said, pulling her cell phone out of her pocket.

"Don't bother," Cat announced. "I'm leaving."

"What is it you're looking for here?" Anita asked, putting her phone back in her pocket. "You had me convinced, you know. I thought you were really listening for God. I thought He brought you here."

Cat took a step toward Anita and softened her voice. "Maybe He did, Anita. Just not in the way you anticipated."

"What are you going to write about us, Cat?" Anita demanded.

"I haven't decided yet," Cat said. "I'm still trying to get to the truth."

"And you think you can get there by trespassing."

"Only because you threw me out."

"I had to. You betrayed us."

"I'm sorry, Anita," Cat said. "I really am."

"That's fine," Anita said. "But I still need to know what you're doing out here this late at night."

Cat feigned giving in with a sigh. "Okay, I was trying to see if I could use this scaffolding to climb into a window upstairs. You never let me see Larry's rooms. I want to see his rooms."

"You have a morbid curiosity about a dead man."

"It's for my story. A prominent church leader commits suicide. Why? I can't just write about the church and not ask that question. No one here seems to be able to explain it. Who was he? Why did he do it? His rooms might help tell the story."

"Show me your press credentials," Anita ordered.

"I don't have them with me," Cat said.

"Who's your employer?"

"I'm a freelancer."

"Who commissioned the story?"

"No one. I'm writing it on my own and plan to shop it around when it's done."

"You're lying, Cat." Anita's voice took on a sinister tone. "Tell me why you're really here."

"I have," Cat said, backing away.

"You are of your father the devil," Anita said in a deep, raised voice.

Cat turned around and began to walk away, toward the parking lot.

"You are of your father the devil," Anita screamed at Cat's departing back, "and there is no truth within you!!!" Her voice echoed across the empty campus.

Cat couldn't get out of the parking lot fast enough. She kept glancing in her rear-view mirror, half-expecting to see Anita following behind her.

Chapter 14

C at was working behind the scenes with a news crew covering a strange, futuristic Olympic sport that looked like underwater bumper boat racing. She was on a submerged set, a large glass bubble overlooking the racecourse near the ocean floor.

Cat wasn't anyone important on the job, just a part of the crew helping to set up the underwater cameras and attend to the racers, who were dressed in elaborate superhero costumes. Apparently measuring tape was a really important tool in underwater bumper boat racing, and the racers were unduly impressed that Cat not only had one, but knew how to use it. They made a big deal about it, and one of the cameramen saw the interaction and decided to film it for a little behind-the-scenes vignette. So Cat began to ham it up for the camera, taking her measuring tape out and acting as if she were measuring the body of one of the racers: his pectoral muscles, his arm, and lower down, where other measurements were of chief consideration to men.

The viewers apparently loved it, with the online forums and chats lighting up immediately. Cat was a relative peon at her job, but she possessed an irrepressible competence. She laughed to herself, thinking that the racers really *didn't* measure up, and her laughter woke her up.

Cat awakened to hear the woman behind her laughing. Then the woman yawned audibly and stretched, knocking the back of Cat's seat. She must have picked up her handheld gaming device, which beeped once before the woman either shifted it to headphone mode or muted it. Cat had heard her playing games when they were sitting on the tarmac in St. Louis before the plane took off.

Was this a good dream? Cat woke feeling amused, but she also felt more than that in the residue of the woman's psyche. The woman had seen herself in a subservient role at work but knew she was much more. It seemed as if even in their recognition of her, her male coworkers were sort of treating her as an amusing source of entertainment. Yet the woman had a lighthearted outlook on it: she knew who she was, the woman who could whip out her measuring tape and see that these guys, despite their schlocky attempts to be superheroes, just didn't measure up.

Cat sat quietly in thought for a while, marveling at the insights into human nature her dreamslipping gave her. Granny Grace was right, she realized for the first time. It was a gift.

Once the plane landed in Seattle, she turned on her phone to see that Granny Grace and Tim Schlein had both left her messages. After she exited the plane and got to the terminal, she ducked into an alcove and called Tim Schlein first.

"What did you find?" she asked him.

"They didn't really investigate Larry's death," he told her. "There wasn't a full forensics sweep, either. And what was done looks fishy to me. The blood splatter isn't consistent with a self-inflicted gunshot wound."

"Let me guess," Cat said. "It suggests Larry was shot from behind, as he sat at his desk."

"Bingo," Tim replied. "Listen—this, combined with your information about Jim being gone all summer and the wife and kid on the run... I think I can get this case reopened."

"Thanks, Tim," smiled Cat. "I owe you one."

"Watch out," he said, "I might try to collect."

She said good-bye and listened to her grandmother's message. Cat had hopped a plane so fast that they hadn't had a chance to talk yet. Granny Grace said she couldn't pick her up from the airport and that Cat should come directly to Simon and Dave's place. There was also a text from Lee: *I already miss you.* That one made her feel a bit of heat. But she couldn't get distracted right now.

Cat put away her cell phone and headed for ground transportation.

It was already rainy and cold in Seattle, but it felt good to be back. She enjoyed the sloshy sound of wet shoes on linoleum in the airport and inhaled the smells of coffee and then the sea air when she stepped outside and hailed a cab.

Dropped off at the Fletcher-Bander home, she rang the doorbell (an antique from a nineteenth-century schoolhouse), and Granny Grace answered. Her grandmother threw her arms around her and squeezed the breath out of her. "You're home, Cat!" she cried. "It's so good to see you!" Granny Grace was as stunning as always in a grey knit sweater and a long strand of pearls that clanged against her belt buckle.

Cat made to walk further into the house to greet Dave and Simon, but Granny Grace stopped her. "Now, Cat, we've got Greg Swenson here, and he won't talk to any of us. He's a bit testy, too. We're hoping you can work some magic on him."

At that point, Cat heard a familiar voice in the living room, a booming male voice, unmistakable. Instinctively, she hung back. "You brought him to Dave and Simon's? What if his sister killed Larry?"

Granny Grace gave her a hard look. "My instincts tell me he's a good guy, Cat."

"Oh, balls," Cat snorted. "That's the jerk who fired me."

"Yes, Cat," Granny Grace said. "He fired you that day. But why? You weren't so much in the wrong, really. I mean, you broke the rules, but the rules were pretty silly to begin with, and you were just concerned about someone hiding in the condo. That's hardly a firing offense, and didn't Greg seem like an okay guy up till that point?"

Suddenly, Cat saw what Granny Grace was aiming at. "He's the one who took them away that night. To safety. It wasn't Jim at all."

Granny Grace made a fist and lightly chucked Cat on the chin. "You got it, kid," she said. "Now, go get him to spill his guts."

Greg was sitting on the crescent-shaped couch, about mid-crescent. He was still in his M&O gear, which on him was a lot more intimidating than Cat's uniform had looked on her. Simon greeted Cat with a hug, and Dave followed close behind.

"Grace told us what you did out there in St. Louis, Cat," said Dave. "That took cojones."

"Oh, I just drew on some acting classes, is all," Cat replied.

"I'm glad you're all right," said Simon. "Now maybe you can talk some sense into this one. He's tight-lipped with us. It was all we could do to get him here. He says he'll only talk to you."

Cat turned to Greg, sitting down on the couch so she could face him. "Sherrie Plantation is your sister," she said.

Greg was looking at Cat as if he couldn't believe she was there, that this was all actually happening. He ran a hand through his thick black hair, which fell across his temple again in defiance. He seemed to be struggling to make up his mind.

"Yes," he finally acknowledged. "Did you really fly to St. Louis so you could try to save her and Ruthie from Jim?"

"Yes," said Cat.

Greg chuckled, this time bitterly. "After I fired you."

Cat smiled. "You did me a favor. I learned a lot in St. Louis."

Greg looked at her, his eyes narrowing, but he didn't say anything.

"Did Sherrie do it?" Cat asked. "Is that why you were hiding her?"

Greg bolted to his feet. "That's it. I'm out of here."

"Wait," Cat said, standing up to face him. She placed her hand on his arm. "If she's not the one who killed Larry Price, we need to find out who did."

Greg shrugged off her touch. "Now why should I trust you? I don't even know you people."

"Then why'd you come here, Greg?" Cat countered. "You could have said no. I mean, Granny Grace is persuasive, but you're a big guy.

With a firearm." She gestured to the weapon in his holster. "Why, Greg? Tell me why you're here."

Greg sat down. "I'm having trouble getting them set up in Canada," he admitted. "I thought I could do it—little brother saves the day. But I'm just a glorified security guard. I had some friends who said they'd help her get a work visa, but... it's not happening. She'd have to stay there as a tourist, but who's got that kind of money?"

Cat sat down next to him, putting her hand on his shoulder. "You've been in this all alone, haven't you?" she asked. "Sherrie came to you, her brother—she's got no one else—and you hid her where you thought Jim would never look. You couldn't have them at your place. You knew he'd check the hotels. The condo was perfect, or so you thought."

Just then, Granny Grace, who'd been standing in the doorway, spoke up. "How did Jim find them at the condo?"

Greg sighed. "It was her cell phone. I thought she'd got rid of it, but she still had it. Ruthie has this game she likes to play, something with ladybugs the kid's crazy for, and she turned Sherrie's phone on while her mom was sleeping."

"And Jim triangulated the signal," Cat guessed.

"Not even that sophisticated, Nancy Drew," Greg said. "He has one of those security plans for his family that shows the location of any phone. Jim's a paranoid control freak. He handled all that stuff, and Sherrie probably doesn't even know the half of it."

Greg continued. "I found the software app on Sherrie's phone after the fact. I should have thought to look for it when she first got to Seattle." He paused, then looked at Cat, his eyes softening. "We owe you a big thanks, Cat. You saved Sherrie's life. If you hadn't tipped me off that he was out there..."

"That's my girl," Granny Grace beamed.

"So it was you," Cat said. "You got Sherrie and Ruthie out of there that morning. You made me think Jim took them."

Greg looked apologetic. "I didn't know if I could trust you. When Sherrie told me that you said Jim was out there, I just reacted. I had to get them out of there as soon as I could, and I needed you to stay away. I had no idea you'd go to St. Louis."

He snorted. "I had no idea you were a budding PI. Boy, Tony didn't know what he was getting when he hired you."

Then he shook his head. "But I'm sorry you got so involved. I'm glad no one at that freak show of a church hurt you."

"There are some good people there, Greg," Cat said, but she elicited no response from him on that point. She turned to the matter at hand. "Listen, we think Larry was murdered. That was no suicide."

"Of course it wasn't," Greg agreed. "But Sherrie didn't do it. She has evidence—it was Jim."

"I knew it," said Dave, who'd come into the room behind Granny Grace. Simon put his hand on Dave's shoulder, both to comfort him and hold him back from interfering.

"What evidence?" Cat asked.

"An e-mail. Larry was planning to blow the cover on their love affair. Jim killed him to shut him up."

"Where's Sherrie now? I'd like to see this e-mail."

"She's staying with an old buddy of mine in Tacoma," Greg said. "Someone I trust. We were on the force together down there. He's retired now."

"I think it's time for them to stop running, Greg," said Cat.

Cat and Granny Grace drove with Greg to Tacoma, about forty-five minutes south of Seattle. On the drive down, Cat briefed him on everything she'd found out during her stay in the church and let him know that the case would most likely be reopened. "It might be enough for them to take Jim into custody," Cat speculated. "That, along with this e-mail Sherrie has."

"All the e-mail does is provide motive," Greg said. "It's not an admission of guilt. You've seen how thick those church leaders are. And Sherrie..." He paused as if considering whether or not to say it, and then pressed on. "Her record's not exactly clean. Jim's threatened to take Ruthie away from her before."

"She has a few drug convictions," pointed out Granny Grace, who'd done her research well, Cat observed. That must be why Greg's having trouble getting Sherrie a work visa, thought Cat, and why Canadian citizenship would be a problem. Cat knew from studying for the PI exam that Sherrie would have to wait four years for her record to clear before she'd be eligible. It would be awfully hard for someone like Sherrie to start over that way.

Cat checked her cell phone for messages from Tim Schlein. Nothing. She called and left him a message that there was an e-mail somewhere that could show that Jim had a motive for killing Larry. She hoped Tim would be able to scrub the server and find the digital version, since for legal reasons, all e-mail is automatically saved on most organizations' networks.

While Greg drove, Cat took the opportunity to text Lee. She felt a surge of fear as she typed in the message, but she took the plunge anyway: *I miss you, too.*

But then she self-analyzed her statement. She didn't actually miss Lee at that moment; she'd only tapped out the message because that seemed like the proper response. Right now Cat felt caught up in her case, and satisfyingly so. She felt as if she were finally using her dreamslipping ability—as well as her training in other skills—to help someone.

When can I see you? came the reply.

Don't know, she responded. *Things happening on the case. Can't talk now.*

It was always a longer drive down to Tacoma than one would think, looking at the city's proximity to Seattle. Lee's place was another thirty-minute drive further. She thought about how she and Lee would make it work with a ninety-minute drive each way between them. It suddenly felt like an insurmountable distance. Then there were their different paths in life. She knew Lee wanted children, and probably soon. He'd always talked about it. It was also likely that he'd return to Iraq for another tour or get stationed somewhere else. It was tough for military wives to maintain careers, with the constant need to move and start over at the whim of the military, regardless of where they were in their current position... Well, let's not get ahead of ourselves, she thought.

When they arrived at the Tacoma house, a squat little brick bungalow with an immaculate yard, the front door was wide open, and no one was there.

Cat and Granny Grace ran through the house but found it empty. There were no signs of struggle, either—just an empty house sitting with the door wide open.

Greg immediately tried to reach his buddy by phone, who picked up, saying he was out running errands. "You were just here, and they were fine?" Greg asked, incredulous. Cat felt him trying to control the panic in his voice.

His buddy was relaying more information as Greg listened intently, nodding. "Okay," he said. "We'll try there, but with the front door left wide open, this doesn't look good."

Greg shoved his cell phone back into his pocket and said, "There's a park around the block that Sherrie's been taking Ruthie to. I told them not to ever leave the house, but the kid was restless. It's been weeks."

Greg, Cat, and Granny Grace began to run down the street. As they turned the corner toward the park, Cat saw movement out of the corner of her eye first, and then a car with its doors standing open. There was Jim, with Ruthie under one arm. He was dragging Sherrie by the wrist with his other hand. Ruthie's stuffed bear dangled from Jim's embrace. Sherrie was putting up a really good fight trying to wrest herself away from Jim.

Greg ran faster, with Cat behind him and Granny Grace following. They had to catch them before Jim loaded them into the car. Sherrie saw the three runners coming her way, and then so did Jim, who must have loosened his grip at the sight. Sherrie broke free long enough to pull Ruthie away from Jim.

"Run, Ruthie!" she screamed, shoving her daughter in their direction. "It's Uncle Greg, Ruthie! Run to him!" The girl did as Sherrie said, while Sherrie whirled on Jim and kicked him in the groin. Jim pushed Sherrie into the back seat of his car just as Greg swooped in and grabbed Ruthie.

By the time the three runners caught up with the car, Jim was behind the wheel and gunning the engine. He took off as fast as he could.

Greg knelt down and inspected Ruthie, who began to cry. "Mommy!" she screamed. "I want Mommy!"

She was otherwise all right, not so much as a bruise or scrape. Greg looked at Granny Grace. "Can you take her? I've got to go after Sherrie."

"I'm coming with you," said Cat, and Granny Grace nodded. She took Ruthie's hand and began walking her back to the house.

Cat and Greg ran to his car and took off in the direction they saw Jim go.

But there was no sign of the maroon sedan he'd been driving, a different car than the one Cat had seen Jim driving that morning at the condo site. They didn't have a license plate number.

They drove mainly in silence for a while, only swapping short phrases—"Try that hotel parking lot," or "Over there, the supermarket." There was no sign of them.

"He might have hopped on the freeway," suggested Cat. Tacoma was situated on a promontory near the water with a major interstate highway hugging its midsection like a belt. Secondary highways headed across the Tacoma Narrows Bridge into the Olympic Peninsula in one direction, down south toward Portland in another, and then back up to Seattle. They could have gone anywhere in a matter of minutes.

She didn't have to say any of this, because she knew Greg was thinking it. He kept driving, this time taking the exit for Highway 16 and heading across the Tacoma Narrows Bridge. It was an impressive expanse, newly rebuilt, tall and commanding, with water churning around its legs. A low fog filled the Narrows. She could see the lights of a few boats in the distance, winking like fireflies.

He drove to Gig Harbor and cruised the little dockside town slowly, pausing to look at every maroon sedan. They finally found one right by the marina, in the parking lot of a motel, the Driftwood Inn.

He and Cat walked into the manager's office together. Cat let Greg take the lead.

Greg held up his wallet to the man at the desk. "Have you seen this woman?" He showed him a picture of Sherrie, Jim, and Ruthie together. It was a family photo with a Christmas tree in the background and a gold cross stamped into the bottom-left corner.

The man looked startled and instantly on guard. "Just who are you?"

Cat intervened. "I'm Cat McCormick, a private investigator," she said, holding out her hand. The man shook it. "We're looking for this woman, who was abducted by him this afternoon," she said, pointing to the man in the photo.

"Wouldn't that be her husband?"

"Yes," Cat said. "But they're estranged. And he's dangerous."

"I haven't seen them," the man said. He looked to be telling the truth.

"Whose car is that?" Greg asked, pointing out the window at the maroon rental car.

"An elderly couple's," the man said. "They come here every year to fish, but the old guy's slowing down. Now they just put a couple of crab pots out and call it a day."

Greg looked immediately deflated. "Are you sure?" he asked. "What room are they in? I want to see for myself."

"I can't let you disturb my guests," the man insisted.

"Just a quick check," Cat pleaded. "It won't take long."

The man sighed, stuffed his hands in the pocket of his flannel shirt, and nodded. "All right," he said. He led them outside and to a door that had once been painted bright green but had obviously faded to its present sea green, the paint peeling in jagged slices.

An elderly woman answered, her skin weathered but tan, as if she'd just come up from a less sun-deprived part of the country. Her bright blue eyes sparkled with intrigue as she gazed at her unexpected visitors.

"Why, hello!" she greeted them, and to the manager's apologies she said, "No trouble at all. Please, come in."

It was a small, old-school motel room with a tiny kitchenette in the back and a single table under a lamp near the window, two chairs flanking it. Greg stood back, shrugging off her invitation to sit down.

"We can't stay long," he said. "Sorry to trouble you. Is that your maroon rental car outside?"

She looked disappointed, but maintained her polite demeanor. "Yes, it is."

"Who wants to know?" said a voice behind her. It was clearly her husband, who was carrying a bucket of crabs.

The manager spoke up. "They're investigating some joker with a car like yours," he explained.

Cat and Greg made their apologies to all three people and got back into Greg's car. Once seated, he pulled out his keys and then slumped over the steering wheel.

"I can't believe I lost her," he said.

"We'll get her back," Cat promised, putting her hand on his. As she did this, she felt a current of electricity there. He looked into her eyes, and she could see the pain.

"I'm sorry," she said.

"Let's get back to Ruthie," he said, turning from her and starting the car.

They went back to Greg's buddy's house. The man—Boyd was his name—had returned long ago but was still visibly angry with himself that Jim had gotten to Sherrie and Ruthie on his watch.

"It's not your fault," Greg told him, collapsing in an armchair. "It's mine."

Boyd was an ex-cop whose formal uniform shots lined the walls in the foyer. He kept shaking his head and looking at Ruthie, who sat quietly in Granny Grace's arms on the couch.

"I should never have left them," he reproached himself, clenching a fist. There was a picture of him with a wife and kids on the TV set. Both the TV and the photo Cat could date back to the 1980s, judging by the design of the set and the clothing and hairstyles in the photo.

"This your family?" Cat inquired.

He nodded. "Rita died a few years back. Breast cancer. The kids are grown, with families of their own now."

"You must miss them," she said.

"It's been nice having Sherrie and Ruthie here," he said, the worried frown breaking for a moment. "Made this old place feel like a home again."

He showed Greg the front door, which showed some damage where it locked into the frame.

"Jim must have broken in and then left the door open," Boyd said. "He saw there was no car in the driveway, so he figured they were alone. He didn't find them there, but then he found them at the park."

Cat saw an old hulking PC sitting on a desk in the living room. It was on and open to Facebook. "Are you two connected on this site?" she asked, looking at Greg and Boyd.

"Yeah," Boyd said.

"Greg, you were probably connected to Jim through here at one point, right?"

"I unfriended that crackpot years ago," he said.

"Yeah," Cat said. "But Sherrie's account—he's still connected to that, even though she's not using it. And you can bet Jim has access to it. He used her account to discover who Greg's friends are."

"Don't tell me..." said Boyd.

"He probably just used process of elimination," Cat reasoned. "How many people is Greg connected to in Seattle? He knew Greg wouldn't hide them too close to home, and he'd have to have someone who'd be able to handle the situation. And there you were, Boyd, a guy who served on the force with Greg, and lived just the right distance away."

"She's right," said Granny Grace, settling a sleeping Ruthie onto Boyd's couch. "It didn't use to be so easy to get that kind of information, but now everyone's posting it for all the world to see, for free."

"I guess that makes me the idiot here," Greg muttered, picking up his keys. "C'mon," he said. "I'm going to the police. We need help finding Sherrie."

The whole troupe of them went to the Tacoma Police Department and filed a report against Jim. With their credibility, they were able to get officers looking for her and Jim right away.

After a long night of questioning and paperwork, Boyd went home, and Greg took the rest of them back to Granny Grace's house. Cat carried Ruthie into the Perfectly Pink Parlor and tucked her in. She'd been awake again at the police station and then had fallen asleep on the drive home. Cat hoped she didn't have any bad dreams after all she'd been through.

Cat walked Greg to the door. "You should go home and get some rest," she said.

"Yeah," he said. "Like that's going to happen."

Just before he walked down the steps, he squeezed her arm. "Thanks for trying so hard to help them," he said.

Cat nodded and watched him go.

Chapter 15

C at was standing in the doorway of Larry Price's office. There was that fiery devil again, but this time his attention was turned toward Larry Price sitting at his desk, working. The devil raised his pitchfork up and sunk it into the man's head, over and over again. Each time the devil sunk the pitchfork in, a shower of sparks flew out of the wound, and Larry kept slumping forward and getting smaller and smaller with each blow.

Cat looked down at her feet, which were bare and small, like a little girl's. In her hand was a teddy bear with a red bow around its neck, which had come undone. She must have slipped into Ruthie's dream.

The devil kept striking Larry Price, and he grew smaller and smaller, until finally he disappeared in a puff of smoke. At that, the devil turned his attention to Ruthie.

"You're next!" he yelled and came for her with his pitchfork.

"Snap out of her," said a voice behind Cat. Granny Grace. She turned to see her grandmother had slipped into Ruthie's dream, too.

As Cat tried to separate herself from Ruthie's subconscious, the girl turned, dropped the bear, and ran, the devil chasing behind. Cat was still focused on grounding herself, making herself stay put, and it was almost as if Ruthie physically tore away from Cat.

"Nice work," said Granny Grace, smiling. Then the two of them chased after Ruthie and the devil.

The hallway turned at a right angle and dead-ended. Ruthie was trapped.

Cat looked at Granny Grace for help. "You can make Ruthie see you, Cat," she whispered. "Think about how she looks right now in the real world. She's lying in the Perfectly Pink Parlor, all alone. See her there?"

"Yes," said Cat.

"Good," said Granny Grace. "Now here she is, awake and all alone, with the devil himself stalking her. Reach down and grab her hand, but think about touching Ruthie's hand in the real world, where she's sleeping."

Cat did as she was told, reaching for Ruthie's hand and picturing her asleep on the chaise lounge in that rosy pink room in Granny Grace's house.

When Cat touched the girl's hand, it felt electrifying, their hands crackling together as if charged. Ruthie looked up, and Cat saw herself materializing in Ruthie's view of the dream. She was in the flannel pajamas she fell asleep in, but that would have to do. Ruthie's frightened demeanor relaxed at the sight of Cat.

The devil stalked down the hallway, breathing audibly, his pitchfork raised.

Cat looked to Granny Grace for further assistance, thinking her grandmother would have some method in mind for stopping the devil.

But Granny Grace shook her head. "You're not here to stop this thing from playing out," she explained. "You're just here to comfort Ruthie. Remember—it's just a dream."

As the devil reached Cat and Ruthie, he folded his wings up over his face once, and when he lifted them again, it was Anita Briggs standing there instead. Ruthie screamed, and the dream ended.

Cat woke up, too, and she could hear the little girl crying in the Perfectly Pink Parlor. She got up and wandered down the hall, where Granny Grace joined her. They shared a knowing look, and then Cat said, "The woman in the dream was Anita Briggs, Jim's right hand."

"Do you think she—"

"Killed Larry Price? Yes, I think she may have."

They walked into the room to find a very upset little girl. "The devil's after me!" she yelled. "She's going to kill me!"

Granny Grace knelt down beside the fainting couch and petted Ruthie's head. "There, there," she said. "Now look around this room. Do you see any nasty little devils in here?"

Ruthie stopped crying and looked around the room. She shook her head.

"You want to know why?"

Ruthie looked up at her and nodded. Granny Grace walked over to one of Great-Uncle Mick's paintings, which served as the focal point in the room. It was a glorious, white-haired fantasy angel, done up in purple and pink. He'd painted it for his best friend Charlotte, who'd decorated her house with angels during her struggle with cancer, which finally took her in 2004. Cat often wondered if the painting had been inspired by a dreamslipping experience. Perhaps the angel had come from one of Charlotte's own dreams.

Granny Grace continued with Ruthie. "I'll tell you why. Because Mickey Angel won't let any devils in here," she said. "She protects you from them all."

"Mickey Angel?" asked Ruthie.

"Yeah, she's the queen of the angels."

"The queen?"

"That's right," Granny Grace affirmed. "The queen."

Cat took Ruthie's hand, the same way she had in the dream, this time without any electricity but plenty of warmth. The girl looked at her with newfound recognition. "I dreamed about you," she said, and Cat squeezed her hand.

"It's always nice to dream about people you know," Cat said. "Unless they're bad people." Ruthie nodded.

They all migrated to the kitchen, and Cat gave Ruthie a sheet of paper and crayons to occupy herself with. Cat sat down across from Ruthie and tried to find out more about the dream.

"Ruthie," Cat said. "Do you know Anita Briggs?"

"She's the lady at church." Ruthie was drawing the devil from her dreams, and a pretty good replica, too, down to the pitchfork.

"Is she a nice lady?"

"She has red hair," Ruthie stated. She put down her red crayon and picked up purple. She began the outlines of what could only be Mickey Angel.

"That's right," Cat said. "She does have red hair. Do you like her?"

"No."

"Why don't you like her?"

"She yelled at Daddy Jim."

"When did Anita yell at your Daddy Jim?" Cat asked.

"A long time ago. Before we went on the plane." She put down the purple crayon and reached into the box for silver. She began drawing a sword in Mickey Angel's hand.

Cat kept going. "Were they talking about Larry Price?"

"Yeah. I think Anita did something bad to him. She had Daddy's gun, the one from the safe I'm never supposed to touch."

Cat leaned in, pointing at the devil in Ruthie's drawing. "Is this Anita?"

"Yeah."

Cat and Granny Grace stood up and left Ruthie at the table, stepping into the hallway outside the kitchen. "I'm going to call Tim again," said Cat.

"I think that's wise," agreed Granny Grace. "Anita's the one who kicked you out of the church, isn't she?"

"Yes," said Cat. "And if she's the killer, Jim helped her cover up the crime. So he's guilty, too."

"And Sherrie's got that e-mail in her possession."

Cat ducked into Granny's office and called Tim Schlein immediately. "I have some new information in the Plantation case," she announced.

153

"I got your message about the e-mail," said Tim. "It certainly gives Jim a motive. We'll scrub the Plantation network for the digital."

"Have you talked to Anita Briggs? She's Jim's assistant," Cat said. "We have reason to believe she's the one who killed Larry Price."

"What's that? Not Jim?"

"He was most likely involved."

"Anita Briggs was pretty rattled when we showed up at the church," remarked Tim. "She turned everything over to this guy named Reynolds Chambers. We haven't questioned her yet."

"You definitely want to track her down," urged Cat. "Sherrie's daughter overheard her and Jim talking, and Anita had Jim's gun."

"Okay, Cat," said Tim. "We'll bring her in."

She thanked Tim, got off the phone, and conferred with Granny Grace. "We need to find Jim and Sherrie," Cat said. "If he's innocent of Larry's murder, maybe we can convince him to come forward. We have Ruthie. He knows he can't do what he originally came out here to do, and that's bring them back to the fold. He has to know this thing's over. There's no going back now."

The doorbell rang, and Cat went to answer it. It was Greg, looking disheveled, as if he hadn't slept at all.

"You drove around all night, didn't you?" Cat said, ushering him into the front room, the Daring Damask Den. "I'll get you some coffee."

"I can't believe I let that man take my sister," he said angrily.

Granny Grace came in, sat down on one of the damask chairs, and addressed Greg directly. "Jim's desperate," she acknowledged, "but I don't believe he'll hurt Sherrie."

"Maybe we can get Jim to come here," Cat added. "He'll want to see Ruthie."

Greg stared at them silently, considering.

"Jim might let Sherrie and Ruthie go on his own," said Cat. "Plus, he's the one person who can convict Anita. If he knows it's all coming out anyway, he might talk."

"If that guy comes anywhere near here, he's a dead man," snarled Greg, reaching for his sidearm.

"Jim won't hurt them," Cat insisted, gently touching his arm. A spark ran through her hand as she did so, and for a moment, she looked deeply into his dark eyes and saw the worry and warmth in them. She pulled away, startled by the connection.

Just then Greg's cell phone rang, and he scrambled to answer it.

"Sherrie," Greg said. "Are you all right? Where are you?"

He listened for a few moments, and then he said, "I don't believe Jim's innocent." He looked deeply into Cat's eyes, and she stared back at him with a pleading look and nodded. He continued. "But I'm with Grace and Cat, at their house on Queen Anne Hill. Bring him here. I'll tell you where to go."

When he got off the phone, he shot Cat a look. "I'm trusting you on this one."

"It'll be fine," said Cat.

Not fifteen minutes later, Greg's phone rang again. Cat watched his face, which contorted with pain and concern. He went to the picture window facing the street and looked out.

Cat followed his cue and went to the front door with its beveled glass, where she could scan the street. There was Sherrie, a cell phone at her ear, and Jim's hand at her back. His posture suggested he had a gun in that hand. Cat opened the door and walked toward them. Greg came up behind Cat. "Careful," he warned. "Jim's got a gun."

"I know," said Cat. "And so do you."

Sherrie and Jim walked up to the house, slowly. Cat squinted in the early morning glare. Sherrie looked surprisingly calm. "Are you okay, Sherrie?" Cat asked her.

"I'm just fine," Sherrie said. "Jim wouldn't kill me. He hasn't killed anybody. It was Anita who did the killing. Isn't that right, Jim?"

"I just want to see my daughter," said Jim. "To make sure she's all right."

"Give me the gun, Jim," ordered Cat. "Then you can see Ruthie. But you're not setting foot in that house like this."

Jim looked at Cat for a very long minute. "You're that security guard," he finally said. "The one who came up to me on the street."

"That's right," said Cat. "I've been all the way to St. Louie and back trying to keep up with you. First I thought you were a child molester. Then I thought you were a murderer. Turns out you're just narrow-minded."

"I want to see my daughter," Jim demanded.

Greg butted in. "You can see Ruthie, Jim, but only if you give Cat your gun."

"You're some brother," Jim sneered. "Keeping a man away from his wife."

Greg scoffed. "I think you'd prefer to have a *husband*."

Jim shrugged. "I may have committed sins of the flesh, but that's between me and the Lord."

Greg opened his jacket, revealing his gun. "Give Cat your gun, Jim."

"I'd never hurt them," Jim said angrily. "They're my family. I'm their protector."

"That's right," Sherrie said. "You don't need the gun, Jim. Now give it to Cat."

Cat held her hand out, and Jim slowly placed the gun into it. Sherrie slumped into Greg's arms with relief.

Slowly, the four of them went inside, and Cat walked Jim back to the parlor to see his stepdaughter. Ruthie yelled "Daddy Jim!" and huddled into his arms.

"You're okay?" he inspected Ruthie frantically for signs of injury, touching her head, her arms, her legs, all with care and reverence.

Greg hovered in the doorway, wary. Sherrie sank down across from Jim and Ruthie. Cat went over to her.

"So Jim told you about Anita," Cat said. "And you believed him?"

"Yes," she said, wringing her hands. "I should never have suspected him in the first place. It's just that... I thought Larry's e-mail pushed Jim over the edge. That night, Larry called. He and Jim argued on the phone. I heard Jim say, 'You have no right. That's my secret. I'll kill you before I let you ruin everything we've built.' Then Jim went out and didn't come back till almost morning. Right afterward, I went to his computer. He'd left in such a hurry, it was still on, and there was this e-mail in his inbox. Larry had just sent it."

Sherrie reached into her purse and pulled out a piece of paper. She unfolded it and pushed it across toward Cat, who read it aloud:

"From: Larry Price <LPrice@plantationchurch.org>

Date: June 12, 2012 8:23 PM

To: Jim Plantation <JPlantation@plantationchurch.org>

Subject: Coming clean

To my beloved congregation members:

All our lives, Jim Plantation and I have been living a lie. We built a church dedicated to God's work, and this is good. We are very proud of what we have accomplished with your help. But the one thing we have not been able to cut out of our hearts is the love that he and I feel for each other. It's more than the brotherly love that you all have witnessed and embraced. We love each other the way a man and wife should. Please know that he and I have spent countless hours praying and testifying to Christ that He would stamp this apparent evil out of us. We have been vocal proponents of the church's teachings, which is to fight for marriage between a man and a woman only. We believed in our hearts and our souls that this is the right path, the path of the Lord. But despite all this work, the love between us has grown.

Jim and I are at a loss for what to do about this. He married in the way of the church, and still the love between us resisted all our attempts to kill it. As much as I admire Jim for trying to love a woman the way he should, I could not bring myself to do this. I love one and only one, and my heart cannot betray that love with another. As loving as Jim is with his wife and family, he continues to return my love in spirit, if not in deed.

We wanted you to know the truth because, as it says in John 4:24, 'God is a Spirit: and they that worship him must worship him in spirit and in truth.' So let there be no more lies in this congregation. Jim and I are flawed human beings who have not been able to conquer this evil within us. For this you have our deepest apologies.

Yours in spirit,

Larry Price"

Cat looked up at Sherrie. "This is written as if he were planning to send it to the entire congregation," Cat noted. "But the only recipient is Jim."

"I know," Sherrie said. "I think he sent it to Jim first, hoping that Jim would join him in coming clean with the truth. But Jim wouldn't do it. Maybe Larry was going to send the e-mail anyway, and that's when Anita killed him."

"What else did they say on the phone?" Cat asked.

"I remember," Sherrie said, still wringing her hands. "I think Larry was telling Jim what he was planning to do. He wanted Jim to agree. I thought Jim went over there to stop him..." She broke off, biting her lip.

"Why didn't you go to the police with this evidence? You could have turned Jim in."

Sherrie erupted. "Are you kidding? The county sheriff, he's a member of the congregation. They didn't even investigate Larry's death. And Jim would have taken Ruthie away! That man," she said, tossing her head in Jim's direction. "He fights like hell to keep what's his. He thinks that we belong to him, that he owns us. With my past, all he had to do was say I'm unfit."

Cat looked over at Jim to see him holding onto Ruthie a little too hard and desperately, his tears falling onto her face. Sherrie pulled her delicately from his arms and gave her to Granny Grace, who walked her into the kitchen. Sherrie bent down in front of Jim and took his hands in hers.

"It's time to really come clean, Jim," she said. "Talk to us."

"Sherrie, I—"

Cat stepped in. "It's all over anyway, Jim. The sheriff has reopened Larry's case. They're going to find this e-mail. Everything's coming out."

"It was Anita, wasn't it?" Sherrie said. "She killed Larry. Goddamn Anita. She and Reynolds are the ones who really run that church. You just think you're in charge." She was quiet for a moment, and then it all dawned on her. "Oh, God, Jim. Did you help her cover it up that night? You were gone so long..."

Jim looked painfully at the e-mail message in Cat's hand, and then at Sherrie.

"Yes," he conceded. "I helped her clean it up." It was as if everything in the man broke in that admission. He crumpled into himself. "Larry's suicide. Oh, God, Larry. I'm so sorry. I helped her fake it. It was the only way. It was the only way to save the church. She'd overheard him on the phone with me. She knew and she—"

Cat thought of something then. "Where was Ruthie that night? Was she spending the night at the church? Was she with the Baby Bible Brigade?"

Both Sherrie and Jim looked at her and nodded.

"Ruthie heard you and Anita," Cat said to Jim. "She knows Anita used your gun on Larry."

"She was there?" asked Sherrie, as if pieces of evidence were coming into place together in her mind's eye. "You always took her to Larry's office," she said to Jim. "She would have looked for you... She liked to wander around the church..." She looked at Jim angrily. "How dare you drag her into this... nightmare."

"I'm so sorry, Sherrie," Jim pleaded. "I failed you. I failed the Lord."

After observing him cry a few rounds, Sherrie touched the side of Jim's face. "Honey, it's over. You have to let us go now. Do you understand that? It's over, Jim."

Jim kept nodding as Sherrie spoke. "I'm sorry," he said. "I didn't mean to hurt you or Sherrie. You're my angels. I'm sorry."

"Let us go, Jim. You have to let us go."

He nodded again and cupped his hands around Sherrie's face. "I know," he said. "You have to leave me now. God will take care of you, Sherrie."

Sherrie embraced him and then walked over to her brother Greg, who hugged her tightly. Then they both joined Granny Grace and Ruthie in the kitchen.

Jim collapsed onto the fainting couch, defeated. He looked up at Cat, suddenly aware of her presence.

"Security girl. You went out to St. Louis? You were undercover in my church?"

"Yes, I was, Jim."

He laughed bitterly and swept his hand through his thinning hair. "You really gave ol' Anita a scare. She thought you were going to blow the whole thing wide open. And I guess she was right."

"You've been in contact with Anita? She told you I was there?"

"Yes," Jim said.

Cat walked out of the room, whipped her cell phone out of her pocket, and found Tim Schlein's number in her recent list. "Anita Briggs knows we're onto her," she told him.

"That explains it then," Tim said. "We haven't been able to find her."

Cat thanked him, told him to keep her posted, and hung up. She regarded Jim again, sitting on the fainting couch, his face buried in one hand. "Larry loved you, Jim," Cat said. "How could you do it?"

"I loved Larry," Jim said. "Despite years of trying not to love that man, I loved him. But in the end, it was the church I loved more." He began to sob again.

Cat let him be, joining the others in the kitchen. Something told her he was too beaten down to present a flight risk. He was finally allowing himself the room to grieve Larry's death.

Granny Grace had phoned the police to let them know that Jim was there and that they could call off the search for Sherrie. She also rang Dave and Simon to tell them about the developments in their case. Only five minutes away, they arrived before the police did, and Dave, appalled that it was closing in on dinnertime and no one in the house had eaten yet that day, began making everyone an impromptu meal in the Terra Cotta Cocina.

So everyone except Jim was in the kitchen, like a reunion of misfits. Sherrie sidled over to Cat, offering her a piece of bread. "I'm sorry I couldn't tell you the truth when you first found us," she apologized. She had a pretty, rounded face, but these months on the run had obviously been hard on her, with dark circles smudging the skin under her eyes and tired lines etched into her cheeks.

"I can't say I blame you," Cat said, taking the bread. "You thought Jim killed someone."

"We all thought he was a killer," commented Dave, who was standing at the stove. "I was sure it was a case of gay self-hatred."

Greg was standing at the counter, brushing Ruthie's hair. "I was sure it was all about the church's self-preservation instinct," he said.

"How did you end up with Jim in the first place?" Cat asked Sherrie. "I know about your work for Diamond Dick's."

"I did the rehab program at a church in St. Louis," she explained. "It worked for me, and you know, I really do believe in God. I know this sounds crazy, but I got a sign from Him to go there in the first place. I was walking down the street, looking for the guy I usually bought stuff from. I was like a zombie, numb because I'd lost Ruthie. The courts had taken her away from me, put her in foster care. I needed something, and this woman stepped out in front of me, blocking my path. She had a flyer in her hand.

"It was for this church—not Jim's church, but one in the inner city. Salvation Evangelical. 'God will listen,' was printed across the top. Well, it seemed like I hadn't had anybody to talk to in forever, and I realized that if I got my fix, I'd just need another one after that, and another, and no amount of fixes in the world would stop the pain of losing Ruthie. So I turned around and went to the church instead. Just went in and sat there. I'd been there for hours when someone came and sat down next to me."

"The church took me in, and I did their rehab program. I met Jim when he came for a weeklong workshop, and I guess... I knew he wanted to save me, and I let him. He helped me get Ruthie back. I tried to love him, but it wasn't there. I couldn't do it. I couldn't live that way in his house any longer. I tried. I really did. But it's stifling to be Jim's wife. It was too far to come from where I'd been: a drug addict, a stripper. Jim wouldn't even let me wear makeup."

At that, Cat led Sherrie down the hall to Cat's bedroom where the Raggedy Ann doll was perched on her mantel.

"I have to ask you this," Cat said, picking up the doll. She raised the doll's skirt to show her the scribbles and deep gouges from the pen. "Did Ruthie mark this doll like this?"

When she saw the doll, Sherrie broke down crying, putting her hand over her mouth. She nodded, took the doll from Cat and sat down on the edge of the bed, holding the doll in her embrace as if it were childhood itself.

Cat waited for her to calm down, and then Sherrie explained. "Jim reprimanded Ruthie for every little thing that looked like she was headed down the path of 'whoredom,' like her mother, no doubt. He screamed at her all the time for touching herself. I asked my doctor, and it's totally normal for kids her age to explore their bodies."

"So Ruthie scratched up her doll herself out of shame," Cat said.

Her words set Sherrie off crying again, and all she could do was nod.

"It's not your fault," Cat comforted her. "You tried to give her what you thought was a good home."

Cat reached into her own pocket and touched the pink barrette that she'd found in the empty condo the night Sherrie and Ruthie had disappeared on her. She'd been carrying it with her all this time. She showed it to Sherrie. "Let's give this back to Ruthie," she suggested, and the two of them walked back into the kitchen.

Cat went over to Ruthie, who was still at the counter, with a tray of olives that Dave had set in front of her.

"Do you remember me from a long time ago?" she asked the girl.

Ruthie was playing with the olives and had several stuck to the ends of her fingers. She looked up into Cat's face.

"You're the lady who scared Mommy," she said. "Before Uncle Greg took us away to Boyd's."

"I'm sorry I scared your Mommy. And you," Cat said. "I didn't expect to see you two there in that icky old building."

"It's okay," Ruthie said.

Cat held out her hand with the pink barrette in it. "I think you left this there."

Ruthie snatched it up right away. "My hair glitter!" She ran over to her mother, showing her the barrette. "Mommy, look! My hair glitter. That lady found it."

Ruthie burrowed into her mother's lap.

Jim appeared in the doorway then, to everyone's surprise. He stood in the doorway tentatively, as if unsure he'd be welcome. Granny Grace leapt up and motioned for him to take her seat.

Dave turned from the pot he'd been stirring and looked at Jim quizzically, assessing him. He waited for him to settle in his seat. "I just have one question for you, Mr. Plantation," he said.

Jim startled, as if coming out of a fog. "What's that? A question?"

"Yes. If you didn't go over there to kill Larry that night, why did you go over there?"

Jim stared at Dave for a long time. Simon, who'd been chopping vegetables for a salad, paused mid-chop. Greg and Sherrie watched intently.

"I want to know what you were feeling that night, Jim," continued Dave. "You've got nothing to lose." He waved his hand at the gathering there in the kitchen. "Right now, this is the closest thing to family you've got. And you're staring at a man who's as gay as they come. But I was married to a woman once, too. So here's your chance to really come clean."

Jim paused, looking at every face in the room. All were staring back at him expectantly.

"Larry was in pain," Jim finally said. "He was in pain, and I wanted to... comfort him. He had failed to cleanse himself of sin, and I wanted to... tell him it was okay, that I would take care of him, no matter what."

"And if the truth had come out?"

Jim paused. "Honestly... I would have been... relieved."

"So when Anita killed Larry, she wasn't just killing him to keep it quiet," Dave observed. "She was killing him to end the love between you, once and for all."

Jim hung his head, recognizing the truth in Dave's words. "Yes."

The room was quiet for a long minute. And then, Simon spoke to Jim: "You haven't had much to eat yourself lately, have you?"

Jim raised his head, surprised. "Oh, no. I guess not. I haven't been hungry."

"Here," he said, placing a bowl of olive oil and vinegar and some bread on the table in front of him.

"God bless you," Jim said. And then Jim looked at Sherrie, offering his hand. "Will you say grace with me, one last time?"

Granny Grace grabbed Jim's other hand. "We'll all say grace with you, Jim," she offered, and one by one, everyone around the table joined hands.

Jim led them in grace, saying the lines first alone and then a second time with every voice in the room joining him. "Bless this food, oh Lord," he said. "Let it nourish our bodies that we might be cleansed of our sins. We are not worthy of such gifts, but we give thanks in Jesus' name, all the same."

They ate in silence at first, as if the intake of sustenance had become a hallowed event. But then Greg broke the spell by making a silly face at Ruthie, who laughed. Cat thought the sound of her giggle was like church bells.

As they were cleaning up the kitchen afterward, the police arrived, and Granny Grace startled them by waltzing back to the kitchen, where the suspect they were apprehending was drying wet dishes with a towel. Bewildered, they somewhat reluctantly waited for him to finish his chore before reading him his rights and placing him in handcuffs. Greg distracted Ruthie with a book in the parlor so she wouldn't have to witness her stepfather being arrested.

When the police began to read Jim his rights, instead of remaining silent, he began confessing at once, in an even, measured, resigned tone. "So help me God," he said. "Larry Price was murdered. Anita Briggs killed him. I not only kept her secret, but I helped her cover it up." He said this once, and then he repeated it two more times. As the police led him out to the squad car, he looked up into the sky, now covered in thick, velvety grey clouds, and said, "Lord, have mercy on me."

Dave and Simon left Granny Grace's after congratulating Cat on solving her first case. Granny Grace installed Sherrie and Ruthie in the Perfectly Pink Parlor, where they both fell asleep at once.

Cat walked Greg to the front door, and he lingered there a moment, seeming a bit awkward with her after all they'd been through over the past twenty-four hours.

"I don't know how to thank you," he said. "You saved my sister's life. Twice."

"Oh, I think you get the credit for that," she countered.

"No, Cat. Really. I'll never forget your courage, and your care." He leaned toward her and then wrapped her in a bear hug. His touch made her feel zingy, which again caught her off guard.

When they separated, he stood there for a few seconds, as if mulling something over. "You know," he said. "I'm aware that this could be gratitude, or exhaustion, or any number of other things, but it could also be just what it feels like. So I'm going to assume it is... and ask you out on a date."

"Oh!" Cat exclaimed, surprised, but not completely. She paused. "That could be good," she said, stammering a bit. "I think."

Greg chuckled. "You think, huh? Well, take some time with it, Nancy Drew. There's no hurry. We both need some sleep, and at least one of us needs a shower, and it's not you."

"I'm sort of dating someone," she blurted. Greg looked immediately crestfallen, but then he recovered.

"Well, 'sort of' implies there's some doubt," he said. "So, think it over anyway."

Cat nodded, too tired for further clarification, even to herself. They said good-bye, Greg smiling wistfully as he turned to go.

Then at last, it was just Cat and Granny Grace left awake in the house. They found themselves standing in the den, finally alone.

"Well done, my dear," her grandmother said, turning to her. "Really. I'm quite impressed. So impressed that I'm thinking you should name your agency after yourself instead of me."

"Really, Gran? But I wanted to keep Grace, to honor you by."

"That's very sweet of you, but you'll soon have more name recognition than I do at this point, Miss McCormick. This case will put you on the map. You're going to be very busy from now on. Trust me."

"Thank you," Cat said. "To tell the truth, the whole time I was working this case, I doubted I could pull it off."

"Well, don't ever doubt yourself again."

Granny went over to a side table and poured Cat a brandy. They both collapsed into chairs, their feet up on footstools.

"So whatever happened with the mayor?" Cat asked, her mind filtering down to a question she'd been meaning to ask her grandmother for a week or so. At least it seemed like it had been that long. Time was feeling a bit mushy these days.

"I wrapped that up before you flew home. It was a simple case, really, but he paid me handsomely for it. Enough to wipe out my little debt problems."

Cat sat up. "Granny Grace! Are you serious?"

"I told you the Buddha was right," she said, winking.

"Can you tell me how you solved it?"

"Sure," she said, putting her drink down and sitting up so she could tell the story properly, with hand gestures and all.

"Remember I told you about the two tests, the differing results, and the mayor's son having undergone tutoring?"

"Yes."

"I went and found the proctor for that test and interviewed him. It turns out there'd been a fire drill that day. He assured me that no one could have cheated during the fire drill. Both students had been present and accounted for during the drill."

"So how did the cheater get away with copying the test?"

"Well, I asked the ACT people to do a full comparison, question by question, of each student's first and second tests. They found that the other student got the same types of answers wrong on the second test that he'd answered correctly on the first, and vice versa."

"Good," said Cat. "Was that enough?"

"Almost," said Granny Grace. "But you know how these things are. You need three good pieces of evidence to clear a name. So I had them send me copies of the actual tests myself. I noticed that the other kid's second test was hastily filled in, as if he'd done it in a hurry. Furthermore, it hadn't been filled in by the same hand. His first test was filled in entirely in a left-handed manner. His second test was mostly filled in by someone who is right-handed, which he is not. So he must have had a right-handed accomplice, someone who got both tests during the commotion of the fire drill—maybe the cheater slipped them to his buddy, or maybe his buddy got into the room during the drill. He filled in the tests while our cheater was busy being recorded as present in the parking lot during the drill."

"What do you mean, a 'left-handed manner'?"

"Right-handed people fill in the dots in a clockwise motion," explained Granny Grace. "Left-handers go counterclockwise."

"Crazy," mused Cat. "And you solved the case without any dreamslipping."

"Well, you can't always count on that," said Granny Grace.

"So how much did the mayor pay you, if you don't mind my asking?"

"Half the price of tuition at Yale for a year," smiled Granny Grace, picking up her drink again.

Cat clinked her glass against hers. "Well done, Grandmother Amazeballs."

They sat in silence for a moment, sipping their drinks. Then Cat noticed them: a dozen roses, sitting there on the mantel.

"From one of your admirers?" she asked, gesturing toward them.

"Nope," Granny Grace replied. "One of yours. In the commotion, I forgot to tell you about them. They came while you were away."

Cat got up and pulled down the card. *Welcome home*, it read. It was from Lee.

"Have any more long-distance dreamslips with him?"

Cat hesitated, fingering the card in her hand. "Yes. A recurring one, about the war. And then one about me, which was extraordinarily... intimate, not to mention, um, somehow wrong. There ought to be laws against having sex with yourself."

Granny Grace laughed. "Well, if Jim Plantation had his way, that *would* be illegal."

Cat smiled.

"I think Greg likes you, too," said Granny Grace. "Doesn't he?" She smiled, leaned back in her chair, and closed her eyes. "Lee represents dangerous territory, but Greg is risky new ground. Don't you agree?"

"Yes on both counts," Cat said, feeling immoral for entertaining the idea of going out with Greg when Lee was sending such strong signals. She inhaled the powerful scent of the roses sitting on the table in front of her. "A dozen roses! That's over the top. We only had one date. At least, officially."

"One date, and you're not counting that whole weird St. Louis thing he did. Plus, you've known each other for a decade."

"Yeah. Since we were in junior high."

"You're in trouble, kid," Granny Grace said. "Big trouble."

"I guess I better give Lee a call," said Cat. "Oh, after I fax Larry Price's e-mail to Tim at the county sheriff's office. It'll help them find the digital more quickly."

"Good idea," concurred Granny Grace, who bid her good night and sauntered off to her own room. Cat ducked into Granny Grace's office and faxed to Tim the copy of the e-mail that Sherrie had carried with her all this time, hoping it would help his team work on that end. While waiting for the fax to go through, she sat down on a stool and called up Lee's number on her cell.

"Hi, Cat." He picked up on the first ring.

"Hi." Oh, yeah. She was feeling particularly eloquent tonight.

"Did you get the flowers?"

"Yes."

"Did you like them?"

"Yes."

"I guess if I'm going to get anywhere in this conversation, I better not ask yes-or-no questions. What are you wearing?"

"A parka."

"You're lying."

Cat broke on that line. "Why is everyone accusing me of lying these days?" she asked.

"Because you seem like a perfect angel on the first date, but then it's mighty difficult for a man to get a second, unless he flies half way across the country to save you."

"I don't recall being saved," Cat said. "Not even in the religious sense. And I guess you're saying that road trip we took wasn't a date."

"It's not a date if one of us is working," he replied.

"Fair enough," Cat said. "But you haven't asked me out on a second."

"I'm asking now."

"That doesn't sound like a question."

"Cat McCormick, I'd like to take you to dinner and a movie. How does that sound?"

Cat giggled. "You're still not really asking me on a date. You're asking me how it *sounds*."

"For the love of God, woman," he said. "Will you please go out with me on a second date?"

"Yes, Lee. If you didn't ask me soon, I was going to ask you myself."

She decided to table the question of whether or not she should see Greg. For now, this seemed right.

Chapter 16

She was lying in bed, unable to move. It was as if she were paralyzed.

Cat felt herself sweating with fear. The mattress beneath her was already damp, and the dampness made her feel cold. It was a vicious cycle of sweating, feeling the bed grow damper, and then growing colder, but all the while, she was absolutely unable to move. Whose dream was this? She couldn't tell—at first. Then she looked at her hands and recognized the orange, glittery nail polish at once: Wendy's.

She hadn't thought about her undercover BFF in a while, and doing so now made her flinch with pain. But she was in Wendy's dream now, Wendy's body, Wendy's head. And the terror consuming Wendy was undeniable. Cat felt as if she were going to suffocate from it. She desperately searched along the edges of her mind for where she could pry herself away from Wendy, and then finally she was out.

She stood by the side of Wendy's bed, looking around. It was a utilitarian metal bed, the kind one would expect to see in a military hospital. On the wall was a God's eye made from Popsicle sticks and yarn. There was a battered dresser that someone had tried to spruce up by covering it in a coat of white paint. On the wall above it were pop star posters with creases across the stars' bellies where the posters had been folded and stapled into magazines. A small closet in one corner had no door, and its contents were spilling out into the room.

Wendy herself held in one arm a Winnie-the-Pooh bear and in the other a Snoopy doll. She clutched them to her as if they could protect her from whatever she was afraid of.

The door creaked slowly open then, emitting a sliver of light from a hallway. Cat stood and waited, and at first she didn't think anything had caused the door to open, as she didn't see a soul. But then something moved in her peripheral vision, and she realized there was a very large snake slithering across the floor, right toward Wendy's bed.

It slid up the leg of the bed and under Wendy's covers. Cat wanted to do something to help her friend. She thought of her grandmother's telescoping umbrella that pulled her out of the waters of Puget Sound in her own dream. But she found herself paralyzed again, standing there, even though she was no longer stuck to Wendy's consciousness. She could only stand by and watch her friend in terror.

Cat could see the snake move under the covers, between Wendy's legs. It kept going till it reached her crotch. Then it reared up once and struck her there, between her legs, and held on. Wendy screamed but couldn't move to disengage the snake, which had sunk its fangs in deep. Then Wendy must have awakened, as Cat was let out of the dream.

Cat woke in her own bed in the Grand Green Griffin, sweaty and breathing hard. What had just happened? Wendy was a couple thousand miles away, and they hadn't spoken since Anita kicked Cat out of the church. Could it be possible? Was this another long-distance dreamslipping experience?

She looked at the clock. It was 4:30 a.m. Since St. Louis was two hours ahead, it was already 6:30 there, which Cat reasoned wouldn't be too unacceptably early to contact someone, especially if you suspected she was awake anyway. Cat pulled out her phone and began typing Wendy a text message: *Hey there, Wendy. I apologize for not being honest with you about who I was. But I hope you know I did what I had to do. I really admire your strength.*

She got a reply at once, which startled her: *You're lucky I'm awake this early. Stupid nightmare. What are you doing up? Your guilt about not telling me the truth keeping you awake?*

Cat replied, *Yeah, Wendy. You were on my mind. You okay?*

I'm okay, Catholic girl. Or was that part a lie, too?

LOL. Yeah, I'm really Catholic, Cat wrote. *Can I call you later?*

I guess, Wendy wrote back. *Did you get Jim arrested?*

Cat hesitated. *Let's talk later,* she said.

Fine, Wendy said.

Cat went back to sleep.

Later that morning, Cat got a call from Tim Schlein, who told her that the Seattle Police Department and St. Clair County Sheriff's Office were working together on the Plantation case, and that Jim was being flown back to St. Louis. Police had been unable to find Anita.

Sherrie and Ruthie had already been questioned by Seattle police and had given full reports. Granny Grace told them they could stay at her place as long as they needed to, as Greg's apartment was pretty small. But Sherrie was eager to start her new life in Seattle, so Granny Grace had taken her to a career center to talk to a counselor there. Ruthie would be spending the afternoon with her Uncle Greg as soon as he picked her up.

After Cat got off the phone with Tim, she sat in the Perfectly Pink Parlor with Ruthie, playing with a couple of Barbie dolls that Dave and Simon had brought over for her.

Cat was passing time till her date with Lee.

Greg was already late picking up Ruthie due to a Tony-related crisis at work, and Lee was due any minute. So Cat was facing the awkward possibility that her two would-be suitors might cross paths.

When the doorbell rang, Cat was still sitting on the floor playing with Ruthie. Greg had not yet arrived, and it was time for her date with Lee.

When she saw Lee through the plate-glass window on the front door, Cat simultaneously felt her heart leap and cringe at the sight of him. She opened the door and let herself be swept up into his arms. It was like coming home. He smelled of musky soap and cologne, and he'd dressed up for their date in a pair of dark trousers and a starched white shirt.

"Baby," he said. "I've missed you."

"I've missed you, too," she said, enjoying the embrace for a moment but then disengaging herself before she really wanted to. "But I can't leave yet. I'm sort of babysitting."

"Babysitting? I thought you were a PI."

"Yeah, well, it's apparently part of the job description," she smirked. "C'mon in. You'll love Ruthie—she's a doll."

Lee moved to come in, but a voice behind him pierced the air with its shrillness, stopping the two of them dead in their tracks.

"You Jezebel!"

Cat looked up to see none other than Anita Briggs, pointing a gun at her. As soon as Cat saw the woman, she felt the inevitability of the moment. It was as if the last time she'd seen Anita, she'd had a premonition of this exact event. Deep down, she'd known she and Anita would meet again.

"You're an agent of Satan!" Anita yelled. "You tricked me!" And then the gun went off with a loud bursting sound. Lee jumped in front of Cat, taking the bullet meant for her.

Cat instinctively tried to catch him, but he was too heavy and tumbled through her arms to the floor. In sickening slow motion, Cat saw him slumped there on his side, red liquid leaking out of his head and covering the entryway floor like spilled paint. She knelt down and put her hand on his head to stop it. Oh, to make it stop! She needed to make it stop.

Cat couldn't hear anything but the sound of her own screaming. "Lee, no!" she kept yelling. "No, Lee! Not you! No!"

But then she was aware of Anita standing there, and then another loud shot, the sound ricocheting through the neighborhood, and Anita crumpling to the ground.

Behind Anita stood Greg, his gun still in his hand. He put it away and pulled out his cell phone. Cat could hear him talking to 911, but it seemed to her as if he were on the other side of a long tunnel.

Cat cradled Lee in her arms. He opened his eyes. "He's getting away!" he cried, trying to get up.

Cat held him. "No, he's not getting away," she said, making Lee look at her. "It's me, Lee. We got him. He's dead."

"I think I shot the kid," Lee said. "His shield." Lee's eyes began to close. She was losing him.

"Listen to me, Lee," she said, shaking him. "The kid's okay. We got him. You're okay. Stay with me. The medic's coming."

"The kid," repeated Lee. He reached for the left side of his head. "My ear?"

"You've been hit," Cat told him, feeling herself break into a cry.

Greg knelt down, putting his hand on Cat's shoulder. He'd grabbed a blanket from the parlor and was holding it on Lee's head wound.

When the ambulance arrived, they took Anita Briggs away on a stretcher, her face covered by a white sheet. She was already dead.

They tried but couldn't stabilize Lee at the scene. He was taken to Swedish Hospital, where they worked for hours to save him. Cat stayed at the hospital waiting to hear, Granny Grace with her as much as she could be. By morning he was stable but still unconscious, and they were worried that he wasn't going to wake up. He was effectively in a coma.

Granny Grace brought Cat a blue cornmeal muffin from home and placed a vase of purple tulips next to Lee's bed. Cat was sitting with him, holding his hand.

"I keep thinking he's safer in a war zone than he is with me," Cat said wryly, and Granny Grace squeezed her shoulder.

"It's not your fault, Cat. Anita would have shot anyone. Maybe you."

"She would have shot me next if Greg hadn't shown up."

"I'm so grateful he was there," Granny Grace said. "That was really something."

"Lee saved me," Cat said, her voice broken by a sob.

They stood in silence for a moment, watching the blips on Lee's monitors. Tears streamed down Cat's face. Granny Grace held her hand.

"He doesn't deserve this," Cat finally said. "Not after all he's done."

"I know, Cat," she replied. "I know."

Cat hadn't told Granny Grace about what Lee said when he was shot, about shooting the kid. Could that have been the truth? She didn't believe so, not Lee. If something like that had happened, he'd be the first to convict himself, even if it was an accident. Lee didn't believe in human beings as collateral damage. It had to be lingering guilt, some manifestation of the trauma of what he'd been involved with over there.

Cat looked at his monitors, willing them to change, to register something more than the bland blip signaling he was alive, but not alert. His hand was limp. Every once in a while, his body would jerk a bit, but she couldn't feel him there. It was as if he were in another country, in another time.

While Cat sat in the hospital waiting room aching to hear about Lee, she watched as the Plantation Revival Church dominated news reports, with two top stories making headlines. The first was about Jim Plantation being taken into custody by the Seattle police, in coordination with authorities in southern Illinois, concerning the death of Larry Price. Price's apparent suicide case had been officially reopened as a murder investigation. Anita's attempted murder of Cat, Anita's death, and Lee's critical condition were also splashed across the TV screen. All of this felt horribly surreal to Cat.

Then there was the second reason the Plantation Church was in the news. Before word had been received that Larry Price's murder had been covered up as a suicide, the remaining church leadership had gone forward with the plans to christen the statue in the middle of campus. Before she disappeared, Anita had done a great job setting up media coverage of the event, so the statue's unveiling had been captured by more than one camera. What would have been a small news item covered strictly by ultraconservative and Christian fundamentalist outlets had instead gone viral, the footage playing for the entire world to see.

It was the Reverend Reynolds Chambers who presided over the press conference. Most outlets had cropped his introduction, showing only the moment the sculpture lights came on to reveal the inscription, *One in spirit, 1 Sam 18:1*, pairing it with headlines like "Murders, Gay Love Scandal Rock Plantation Church." But a few aired his introduction, which went like this:

"Our church was led by two men who sacrificed everything for Jesus' love. Today Larry Price isn't here to unveil this sculpture himself, but it is a symbol of how he labored on behalf of the church and on behalf of Christ. No matter what we think of his death, in life, Larry Price was a true prayer warrior, and none of us should ever forget that. Amen."

Cat wondered about Chambers, whose sole crime, it turned out, was a certain leering hypocrisy where women were concerned. How much had he known about all this? Cat thought back to his sermon the day she met him for the first time. It's possible he'd seen what was coming and had already mindfully begun to separate the congregation from Jim. He was a smart man, and it would be up to him now to salvage the church.

Cat also talked to Wendy, who called to see if Cat was all right after the news broke. "I'm praying for your soldier," Wendy said. "He's the one you were talking to that night, right?"

"Yes," Cat said.

"And to think, I assumed you were doing some kind of story on us. But the whole time, you were actually some badass PI. Imagine that."

"I don't feel very badass right now," Cat said.

"Listen, I want to tell you something," Wendy announced. "I don't like being lied to. It's like the worst thing you can do to me, but I forgive you."

"Thanks, Wendy," Cat said. "I don't deserve it, but that means a lot to me."

There was a pause, and then Cat ventured, "You've been through some shit, haven't you?"

She heard Wendy sigh on the other end. "Yeah," she admitted. "Shit that nearly broke me, if you must know. But I survive."

"Well, I wish I were there in St. Louis so we could hang out," Cat said. "But you can call me anytime just to talk. I mean it."

"Likewise, Cat," said Wendy. "And I might just get a wild hair to come out there and visit you, too."

"Well, you have an open invitation," smiled Cat. "Anytime."

Chapter 17

Here it all was again: the rotisserie chicken smell, the glaring fluorescent lights, the two-for-one olives. She was in the grocery store again; she was in Lee's recurring nightmare.

This time, she understood it. The grocery store was like any ordinary grocery store here in the States, but the enemy soldier and Lee were from Iraq. His two worlds, colliding in one dream. But what had really happened that day?

Instead of peeling away from him, she tuned into his thoughts, his feelings. His heart was erratic; she could feel his pulse in her ears.

"You're not really here, Lee. You're dreaming," she heard herself say. Her own voice was so loud in her head that it seemed to reverberate in her skull.

It made him stop. He stood in the frozen food aisle, looking around.

She tried it again. "You're not really here. You're dreaming. You keep having this same dream, Lee. Look at your hands."

He looked. She looked. His hands were muscled, veined, with calluses on the pads of his palms. Then he gazed at the glass door of the ice cream case, as if he expected to see Cat's face reflected there. She couldn't believe it. She could hear his thoughts—he recognized her voice. Amazing.

Of course, only Lee's face stared back at them in the reflection. But somehow, miraculously, she knew *he knew* that she was with him. He smiled into the glass.

She couldn't stifle a giggle, and it seemed as if he heard it. For a moment, it was as if the two of them were playing. He waved his hand.

"This didn't happen in the States," she said. "You were in Iraq. Take us back there. We need to go back and see what happened."

Just then the enemy soldier flashed by at the end of the aisle. She lost Lee's attention as it shifted to his objective. She knew what came next. She peeled herself away from Lee, which was actually painful this time, a separation that felt unnatural. She watched his back turn at the end of the aisle. She followed close behind. She had to see with her own eyes what happened.

There was the girl in the cart, the enemy behind her. But then suddenly, everything shifted. The grocery store aisle became a narrow alley. The girl turned into a young boy, sitting in the back of a wagon. The enemy soldier was behind the boy. He was trailing a wire from the boy, the wire connected to a pack secured around his chest with heavy black tape. The boy was a bomb.

Lee knew logically he should stay back, he knew in his head what this was, but he kept running toward the boy. He wanted to grab the bomb off his chest and fling it away, but it went off too soon, and Lee was knocked back. Cat covered her eyes. It was a sight too horrible to witness.

Then she opened them and ran over to Lee, imagining herself standing next to his hospital bed, holding his hand, the tubes coming out of his nose and veins, the beeping of the monitors. She wanted him to see her, and she wanted to be able to touch him there in the dream world, just as she had with Ruthie in her dream about Anita. She concentrated hard, imagining Lee's physical form in the real world, and in the dream she knelt down beside him. There was blood and a mash of flesh on one side of his face. His eyes were closed. She called to him, "Lee, I'm here."

He opened his eyes. "Kitty Cat," he said, reaching up to touch her. "The kid?" he asked.

"Listen to me, Lee," she said. "It was too late for the kid. You tried to save him, but it was too late. There was nothing you could do. You have to let him go."

Tears began to stream out of Lee's eyes. He moaned and sobbed. She touched him, stroked his forehead, squeezed his hand as he let out all the pain and loss he'd been keeping inside for so long.

Cat leaned over and kissed him and then kept her face close to his, looking deep into his eyes.

"Lee, you saved my life," she told him. "That awful woman appeared out of nowhere and tried to shoot me. She wanted me dead, Lee. But you were there. You jumped in front of the bullet. You saved my life."

"I'd do it again," Lee said, kissing her hand. Then, after a beat, he looked up at her and said, "I've been in love with you since day one, Kitty Cat."

"I love you, too, Lee," she said in return.

He nodded acceptance.

Then he said this: "That's a pretty neat trick you've got there with the dreams."

So he understood about her gift. Cat felt a flush of recognition and acceptance, something she'd been craving her whole life. She smiled, and Lee smiled back.

Suddenly there was the sound of alarms going off in the distance, and then it came closer. A Humvee arrived with a red light on the top, as if it were an ambulance in the States, and paramedics in scrubs jumped out. But then they all disappeared, and Cat and Lee were back in the grocery store, the sound coming from the cash registers, which were going haywire with malfunctions.

"I have to go, Cat," Lee said. "No more dreams."

"No," Cat cried. "Don't leave me!"

"It's time for me to go," Lee said. "Good-bye, dear, sweet Cat."

He closed his eyes, and she tried to hang onto him, but she was knocked out of the dream, awaking at Lee's bedside, where his monitors were beeping and flashing alarms. People in scrubs rushed in and pushed her aside.

They couldn't save him. They worked a long time, and they couldn't save him. Soon his room was filled with a hushed quiet: no beeps, no pumps and hisses, no sounds from Lee. She stood next to his bed and held his hand for a long time, and all she could say was, "I'm sorry," over and over again. Granny Grace found her there and led her to the waiting room so his parents could have some time with him alone.

Cat felt only pain, and through that thick cotton of pain, there was Granny Grace's cool touch. Cat's cell phone kept buzzing in her pocket, so she took it out and shut it off. She and Granny Grace sat in the waiting room outside Lee's room, where they could hear the terrible grieving sounds of his mother and father wailing against the injustice and shock of having to lose a son so young.

And there on the TV screen appeared Jim Plantation himself, announcing that he was filing for divorce, freeing his two perfect angels at last.

Acknowledgements

F irst, foremost, and above all, a tremendous wave of gratitude to the love of my life, Tino. His constant support, encouragement, and space-clearing over far too many weekends and vacations spent writing this book—instead of walking on a beach—deserves the greatest recognition. Thank you for believing in me even when I didn't believe in myself.

Second is his son, Zander, AKA the rapper "Zar," who proved every other weekend and in between that blended families can be whole, and wonderfully so.

Third, thank you to the talented, astute readers who pored through early drafts, championed the project, and kept me on my toes. Anne Harrington, I'm blessed to have your support. Mary K McBride, your spirited feedback sings to me still. Elisa Mader, you pushed me in the best directions, and your editorial care made me feel pampered. Chrysanne Taull, thanks for the dreamslipping.

I'm grateful to my friends and family for lending their support, even when they didn't understand what I was doing or why. Shout-outs to Kathy Samuelson for her friendship and cover art assistance and to Camille Carnahan and Kim Harleaux, who are like family to me. Love to my sister, Amy, my brothers Chris and Jason, and to my mother, Pat, whose own religious path I greatly respect. Also to my dear Grandma Pete, may she rest in peace and beans, and to the whole cantankerous Brunette clan, especially those who lost their boys, like Lee, too soon.

Thanks to Eric O'del, Colette Mercier, and their flock at the Amazing Grace Spiritual Center, which came into my life after I wrote this first draft, as if I'd written my own perfect church into being.

Finally, thanks to my posse at the day job for letting me be one of your game story "experts." It's a tall order, and I doubt I've lived up to it, but I'm glad I get to exercise my plot muscles on your games. Let the mystery be.

About the Author

In some form or another, Lisa Brunette has been earning a living with her words for more than twenty years.

She's the story designer behind hundreds of bestselling computer games published by Big Fish, including the following series: Final Cut, Mystery Case Files, Mystery Trackers, Dark Tales, Myths of the World, and Off the Record. Brunette has also written scripts for games that you can play on the Nintendo Wii and DS, Xbox Kinect, and Sony PlayStation.

Prior to joining the gaming industry, Brunette was a journalist whose work appeared in newspapers and magazines such as the *Seattle Post-Intelligencer, Boston Globe, Seattle Woman, Poets & Writers,* and elsewhere. She's interviewed novelists, a sex expert, homeless women, and the designer of the Batmobile, among others.

Brunette holds a Master of Fine Arts in Creative Writing from University of Miami, where she was a Michener Fellow. Her short stories and poetry have appeared in numerous publications, including *Bellingham Review, The Comstock Review, Icarus International,* and *Spire.* She's also received many honors for her writing, such as a major grant from the Tacoma Arts Commission, the William Stafford Award, and the Associated Writing Programs Intro Journals Project Award.

Brunette also researched and wrote text for the St. Louis Science Center's Cyberville exhibit, when she wasn't helping the Science Center tell its story to donors.

Cat in the Flock is the first in the McCormick Files trilogy.

For updates on upcoming publications, sample chapters, early drafts of *Cat in the Flock,* as well as links to her Twitter profile, Facebook page, Pinterest, Instagram, and numerous other hideouts on the Interwebs, visit the author's site at:

http://lisa-brunette.com

Book Club Discussion Questions

Chapter 1

1. What kind of relationships does Cat have with her mother and grandmother?
2. What is the nature of their "dreamslipping" ability? What are its strengths and limitations?
3. Describe Cat's emotional state at the close of the chapter.

Chapter 2

4. How did Cat violate Granny Grace's rules regarding dreamslipping? Why is this important?
5. Discuss the first two chapters in terms of the economic situation that both Cat and Granny Grace are experiencing.

Chapter 3

6. Who do you think is hiding in the condo building?
7. What real life experience is Cat learning on the job?

Chapter 4

8. What kind of man is Lee Stone? Contrast him with Cat.
9. Compare and contrast the Fletcher-Bander household with Lee Stone's. What does each dwelling reveal about its owners, and about the larger Seattle culture?

Chapter 5

10. What makes Lee's dream different than the other dreams Cat has slipped into? What will be Cat's main challenge in her relationship with Lee?
11. Describe Cat's soul-searching. What does she find helpful in Granny Grace's spiritual instruction, and what's missing for her?

Chapter 6

12. Discuss Cat's decisions in this chapter as she approaches the dreamer in the car, talks to Ruth and her mother, visits the rental car agency, and plans to travel to St. Louis. Do you agree with her? If not, what should she have done differently?

13. What do you think about the coincidence that the mother and girl are the same people Cat saw on the plane? Discuss in terms of the concept of kismet, or fate.

Chapter 7

14. What is the state of Cat's relationship with her mother? Contrast Mercy McCormick and Granny Grace.
15. One of the author's favorite characters is Cat's father, Joe McCormick. What type of man is he? Does he remind you of anyone you know? How would you describe his relationship with Cat?

Chapter 8

16. What challenges does Cat's dreamslipping ability pose in her relationships with her parents?
17. How does your impression of Jim Plantation change after hearing about him through the eyes of the young adult women in the church?
18. Describe Anita Briggs. What kind of woman is she?

Chapter 9

19. At this point in the story, how are Cat's adult relationships developing? Discuss her tie to Lee, as well as her connection with Wendy.
20. How has the Plantation Church reacted to Larry Price's death?
21. Contrast Anita Briggs and Rev. Chambers.

Chapter 10

22. How does Cat maintain her identity while playing along as her undercover persona?
23. What is Cat learning about the church community and church leadership?
24. What are the facts in the case so far?

Chapter 11

25. What do you think about Wendy's campaign to save her mother? Do you think she'll succeed?
26. Discuss the revelation that Jim and Larry are gay.

Chapter 12

27. Try playing PI and, assessing the clues so far, deduct what really happened the night Larry Price died.
28. Were you surprised to find that Greg Swenson is Sherrie's brother? Why do you think he lied to Cat?

29. Do you think the friendship between Cat and Wendy is salvageable?

Chapter 13

30. Discuss Larry's motivation for creating the sculpture and keeping the biblical quote a surprise.
31. Is Anita onto Cat? What do you think she knows about Larry's death?

Chapter 14

32. Did Jim really kill Larry?

Chapter 15

33. Jim says he loved Larry Price but that he "loved the church more." What does that mean?
34. Are you Team Lee or Team Greg? Why?

Chapter 16

35. What might Wendy have actually been through to cause her nightmares?
36. What is your impression of Rev. Chambers? Will he be able to salvage the church?

Chapter 17

37. Discuss Cat's final dreamslipping experience with Lee. How does she help him? What does she get in return?
38. How do you feel about Cat losing Lee?

General Questions

What does the story have to say about one's spiritual path?
Discuss the story in terms of the ideal of family.
How does Cat come of age in this story?
Which character has the greatest impact on Cat?

Read on for an exciting glimpse of the next book in the McCormick Files trilogy:

Pillow Fright

F lames licked across the floor, following a roll of canvas that had been left unfurled. They devoured the canvas hungrily and then leapt to the already stretched canvases stacked against the wall like oversized dominoes, first eating the canvas cloths and then attacking their hardier wooden frames. Now fed, the fire grew in power, the flames leaping and dancing, lighting up the darkness of the studio at night.

In a far corner of the studio, behind a curtain, lay a man sleeping. Smoke flowed over, under, and around the curtain, filling the little cubbyhole where he lay on his back on a futon. On the floor next to him was an open bottle of Bushmill's whiskey, three-quarters of it gone. The man did not stir.

Insatiable flames found fuel in the form of paint thinner, kerosene, oil paint, and other bottles of alcohol meant for drinking. Fire caught the bottom of a curtain that stretched the height of two stories, covering warehouse loft windows. It raged up the length of the curtain, a bright orange cascade, shimmering and giving off intense heat.

The sleeping man dreams of romanesco broccoli, steamed and sitting on the table in a big bowl. He's drawn to its fractal quality, the whorls of the broccoli florets spiraling into infinitely smaller swirls of the same dimension and shape. If he could paint that infinitude, capture that impossibly beautiful 3D patterning on a 2D canvas, then he would feel like he had done something.

But instead he eats it. Swallows the fractal florets whole. Soon he can only watch as they emerge from his belly, spiraling out of the core of his body, rippling in space, turning him inside out so that he is now part of the fractal, too, a vibrating, swirling entity of math and energy. He's part of it; his body has dissolved, but he exists in a larger way, his energy flowing as part of that energy that is all of everything.

If any of our dreamslippers had been there to pick it up, they would have known what a man dreams of as his body dies.

About twenty minutes away, past the neon Art Deco lights and the swishing palm trees and the line of shiny cars ambling between the scene on the street and the dark quiet of the beach at night, a party raged. Amazing Grace held a sweaty gin and tonic in one hand, the napkin under the glass damp. In the corner of her eye she could see her granddaughter Cat, looking painfully awkward and withdrawn from the festivities.

The girl had lost too much weight, Grace thought, her cocktail dress seeming to hang on her, and her face lacked color, her spunk gone. It had been four months since her childhood sweetheart Lee Stone had died. Amazing Grace thought the trip to Miami would knock her out of the Seattle doldrums—the weather in January there hardly helped matters. But Cat had remained sullen, non-communicative, depressed. It was all Grace and her brother Mick could do to get Cat to attend this party tonight. She'd wanted to stay in the hotel, reading statutes and case law.

"You're worried about her, I can see," said a voice at Grace's elbow. She turned to see Ernesto Castillo, an old Miami flame of hers she'd bumped into a few days ago. He'd been hovering around her ever since, trying to get her alone for a bit of that nostalgic tradewind-fueled romance they always enjoyed.

Ernesto was dashing, as usual, his hair perfectly trimmed, his face freshly shaven and giving off a musky aftershave scent. His suit was impeccable, his shoes so shiny, they reflected the light of the crystal chandeliers as if a source of illumination themselves. Grace had to hand it to Miami men. No matter how hot it was outside, they were turned out as if every event were red carpet.

But she knew she'd been too distracted to soak up Ernesto's charms this time. "Yes, I am," she replied, her gaze returning to Cat, who was slumped against a balcony railing, a plump Miami full moon hanging overhead.

"It is simple," stated Ernesto, his speech utterly correct but inflected with Cuban rhythm. "Your granddaughter thinks she is to blame for the man's death. She is killing herself quietly inside."

The truth in Ernesto's statement zinged into Grace's heartstrings. Ernesto took her hand. "But she is young, my Grace," he said, lifting her hand to his lips. "She will survive this. It will pass. In time."

"You're right," she said, turning to him. "But you know it's never been my style to wait around for time to take care of things."

Ernesto laughed, revealing unnaturally white teeth, and just then, the band, which had been on a break, picked up again. "Care to dance?" he asked, and she accepted.

The two of them slow-danced across the room, Ernesto a gentle but firm lead.

Suddenly there was a commotion at the entrance to the ballroom. A group of uniform police appeared, a woman officer and two wingmen. "We're looking for an artist," said the woman, and the crowd chuckled at that.

"Almost everyone in this room is an artist," someone in the crowd informed them. "This is Art Basel. One of the biggest art shows in the world."

"The one we're looking for is Mick Travers," said the officer.

At the sound of her brother's name, Grace felt alarmed. Where was Mick, anyway? She scanned the room for his greying but still red hair. There he was, talking with a group of artists less than half his age, as usual. One of them, a woman with her hair piled on top of her head in an exaggerated beehive, nudged him with her elbow and pointed to the cluster of cops.

Someone in the crowd near the door pointed toward Mick, and the police made their way over to him. Grace caught Cat's eye, and the two of them followed suit.

Once all parties had descended upon Mick, who hung back, waiting for them to come to him, the officer announced, "There's been a fire at your studio, Mr. Travers."

Mick dropped his drink, a tumbler of honey-colored whiskey that shattered to the floor on impact. A white-coated waiter swooped in to take care of it, and Mick and the police moved away from the mess.

"What happened?!" Mick asked, rubbing his chin with worry. And then, as if it had just dawned on him: "Donnie."

"We need to speak to you in private," said the officer, her hands dropping to her belt, which supported a sidearm and nightstick baton.

"Okay," said Mick, letting her lead the way. "Is Donnie all right?"

The officer was silent in response, and she took Mick by the elbow and steered him into a side room. Grace followed, and when the officer held up a hand as if to keep Grace out, Grace put a commanding tone into her voice and said, "I'm Mick's older sister and his appointed private investigator. He'll want me present for this interview."

The officer glanced at Mick, who nodded vigorously. "Yeah, Grace can be there." Then Mick saw Cat, looking confused, pained, and hanging in the background.

Before he could say more, Grace interjected, "This is my partner. She's a PI, too. And she's Mick's niece."

"Well, I suppose we've got ourselves a little family reunion here," the officer complained, rolling her eyes. "Just keep quiet while I talk to Mr. Travers."

Then the officer's gaze settled on Ernesto Castillo, who politely hung back. "Don't tell me you're somebody's third cousin twice removed," she said. "And that you're a PI as well."

Ernesto chuckled good-naturedly. "No, no," he said. "Just a friend. Who's perfectly content to wait out here."

The officer nodded for her wingmen to close the doors to the room and motioned for Mick, Grace, and Cat to sit down.

"Now then," she said, putting a booted foot up on the chair in front of her and leaning on her knee. "How long have you been at this party?"

Mick seemed confused. His eyes had that watery look to them, Grace noticed, which meant he was a little drunk.

"This party?" he asked.

"No, the president's birthday party," the officer scoffed. "Of course, this party."

"I think we left the hotel at..." Mick looked at Cat for assistance.

"It was about 10," Cat said. She looked as if she were slowly coming out of a fog.

"We went out to dinner once the exhibits closed for the day," said Grace, breaking in. "The Blue Pineapple. Mick likes their desserts."

The officer nodded, and one of her wingmen took notes.

"What time was that?" asked the officer.

"The exhibits closed at 7 p.m.," answered Grace, instinct telling her to connect with this officer as best she could, for the officer was clearly trying to establish her brother's whereabouts during the fire. She began to fear the worst about Mick's studio assistant, the boy named Donnie he kept asking about. "Dinner got us to about 8:30," Grace elaborated. "Then we went back to the hotel to change."

"And you, Mr. Travers," said the officer. "Did you go with them, or did you by any chance go back to your studio?"

"I-I haven't been to m-my studio since this morning," Mick stammered.

"We thought it would be easier to use our hotel room as our command center," Grace explained. "Since Cat and I are right here next to the convention center where Art Basel is being held."

"The two of you are from out of town then," said the officer. Her nametag read Alvarez.

"That's correct, Officer Alvarez," said Grace. "We're visiting from Seattle."

Alvarez slowly shook her head. "Such a long way to come for an art show," she said suspiciously. She turned toward Mick. "You always let your sister do the talking, Mr. Artist? Or the cat got your tongue?"

Mick's face turned red. "Say, why don't you tell us what this is all about. Where's Donnie?"

Alvarez sat down. She sighed. "I'm very sorry to inform you of this, Mr. Travers, but Don Harris is dead."

"No," Mick said. "He can't be. He didn't want to go to the party. He hates parties. He wanted to paint. His own stuff, not mine. He said he was onto something big. He was going to be big. Bigger than I am..."

Mick broke down then, covering his face with his hands. Cat went over to him and hugged him. Grace could see tears in Cat's eyes, too, and then they spilled onto Mick's linen jacket, where they soaked into the fabric in jagged little streaks. Grace felt the heaviness of their double losses, and her own futility to take that pain away.

Their grief took the edge off Alvarez's questioning. She waited a few beats for them to resume composure, and when she spoke again, her tone had softened.

"I'm going to need witnesses who can corroborate your timeline for the evening," she said. "And your help contacting Harris' next-of-kin."

"Where is he?" Mick asked, standing up. "I want to see him."

Grace touched her brother's arm. "Mick, wait," she pleaded. "The fire marshal, forensics—they're probably still on the scene." She glanced at Alvarez, who nodded. Grace lowered her voice. "And he might be unrecognizable."

Mick slumped into Grace. "Oh, God," he said.

They went back into the ballroom and watched Alvarez find witnesses who could attest to when the three of them showed up at the party. Grace knew they'd check out the Blue Pineapple next to make sure she, Cat, and Mick had had dinner when they claimed. Meanwhile, Grace brought her brother and Cat back to the hotel room, an adjoining suite. She quizzed a distraught Mick about Don Harris' family origins, and between what he could piece together and what she hunted down on the Internet, they had his parents' information to give to police.

The three of them drove over to Mick's studio in his car, a brown convertible Fiat that he'd received in a trade for several of his paintings. It was a '78 and on its third clutch, which Mick rode hard all the way there. Grace knew the authorities wouldn't be keen to let any of them into the crime scene until investigators were done, which might not be till the next day. By the way they were acting, they must already suspect arson.

But she couldn't keep Mick away, and she owed it to him to find out whatever she could.

They turned the corner onto Coral Way and immediately smelled the smoke. Where his corner studio had been was a mass of charred beams and broken glass. Sooty water pooled and dripped. Rivulets of smoke drifted up out of the sodden, burned mess. A palm tree that had filled the two-story bank of studio windows was nothing but a burned stump, its pot cracked and leaking water and soot.

As Grace, Mick, and Cat got out of the Fiat, a woman in a pink peignoir clapped over to them in her silver mules. Her unnaturally red hair was in curlers, a gauzy yellow scarf tied around them. Grace had met Rose de la Crem the night before; she was one of the artists who had studio space in the same building as Mick. Her prominent brow ridge and masculine feet told Grace she had been born a man. But other than that, the transformation to woman was a convincing one. She'd clearly had work done to shave down her Adam's apple.

"Mick!" she exclaimed. "Oh, Mick." She wrapped her arms around Mick, who was gazing at the burned structure, one whole exterior wall now gone, the remnants of his studio exposed to the full moon's judgment.

"I'm the one who called 911," explained Rose. "I smelled the smoke. I'm so sorry about Donnie. At first the cops thought it was you— but I told them you were at the party. They found Donnie's ID bracelet on him."

Donnie was a diabetic, Grace remembered. He wore a medic alert bracelet, which would have made his identification easy, no matter the condition of the body.

Officer Alvarez was back on the scene already, chatting with the fire marshal. Grace sidled over toward them and stood just within earshot. She heard the word "accelerant" several times. Grace waited for a break in their conversation and moved in to talk with Alvarez when the fire marshal went back into the burnt studio.

"Do you suspect arson?" she asked.

Officer Alvarez regarded her suspiciously. "That's police business," she replied and began to walk away.

Grace followed. "If you do, it won't be a secret for long," she reasoned.

Alvarez turned around. "If we determine this was arson, your brother is our primary suspect."

Grace nodded, finding it interesting that Alvarez should feel the need to point out the obvious. Calmly, she replied, "I believe my brother was the intended victim. If it weren't for our visit, he would have been working in his studio last night. The only reason he went to the party is because I insisted."

Grace motioned toward her granddaughter, who was talking with Mick and Rose de la Crem. "I thought the party would cheer up Cat. She's been depressed."

"That's all very interesting," Officer Alvarez commented.

Just then several officers brought out a stretcher that would be loaded into an ambulance. The stretcher was laden with a body bag.

"Can I see him?" asked Mick.

"You can see him at the morgue, after the autopsy," said Alvarez.

"Here's his parents' contact information," said Mick, handing her a piece of paper. "I'll call them first, though. Please. Give me some time."

Alvarez nodded and took the paper.

Cat stepped in then, speaking to Alvarez in an authoritative voice, the likes of which Grace hadn't heard since Lee's death. "We're going to need to see the evidence reports," Cat demanded. "I imagine it will be tough to puzzle out whether there was an accelerant used in this fire, what with all the paint supplies present at the scene. We'll need to see the lab and autopsy reports, too. We're happy to comply with any further questioning you have for us."

Alvarez surveyed the trio. "Don't any of you leave town," she ordered.